Long Hot Summer

Long Hot Summer

BARBARA ANDERSON

JONATHAN CAPE
LONDON

Published by Jonathan Cape 2000

2 4 6 8 10 9 7 5 3 1

First published in New Zealand in 1999
by Victoria University Press

First published in Great Britain in 2000 by
Jonathan Cape
Random House, 20 Vauxhall Bridge Road,
London SW1V 2SA

Random House Australia (Pty) Limited
20 Alfred Street, Milsons Point, Sydney,
New South Wales 2061, Australia

Random House New Zealand Limited
18 Poland Road, Glenfield,
Auckland 10, New Zealand

Random House South Africa (Pty) Limited
Endulini, 5A Jubilee Road, Parktown 2193, South Africa

The Random House Group Limited Reg. No. 954009
www.randomhouse.co.uk

Chapter 2 of this book appeared in a different form
in *Glorious Things* (Jonathan Cape, 1999)
'Of all the works of man...' is quoted with permission from *Bertolt Brecht Poems*,
Willett and Manheim (eds), Eyre Methuen Ltd, 1976
'The Man from Snowy River' is quoted from *The Man from Snowy River*,
A.B. Banjo Patterson, Angus & Robertson, 1987
The author gratefully acknowledges a grant from Creative NZ
to assist with the writing of this book

A CIP catalogue record for this book is available from the British Library

ISBN 0-224-06065-1

Printed and bound in Great Britain by
Biddles Ltd, Guildford and King's Lynn

To Caroline Dawnay

Ann

Duncan is teaching us how to stop breathing.

'Like this, dopeys.'

He stands in front of Charlie and me, pinches his nose and squeezes his mouth tight. His face gets redder and redder as he times himself till he bursts. 'Phew,' he says, checking his watch. 'Nearly half a minute. That's not bad. That'd get me past easy. Bet you kids can't beat that.'

We'll have to practise, he says. If we don't we won't be able to stop breathing long enough to run past the polio house round the corner and we'll cop it. In the polio house, he says, the young victim lies flat on her back in a darkened room fighting for her life.

'Wow,' says Charlie.

'Yeah,' says Duncan. 'You seen the straw on the road? Six bales. Six bales of Williams and Kettles best thrown all over the road outside. All piled up to make it quiet. Because she's nearly dead, see.'

My sandal has come undone. I do it up quick so's not to miss anything. 'But she's quiet anyway. Nearly dead's quiet.'

'It's for the traffic, stupid. To stop the noise of the traffic while she's dying.'

'What if anyone toots?' says Charlie.

'Who's going to toot when there's straw?'

Charlie doesn't know. He starts practising, his face goes scarlet, his cheeks blow out, even his eyes, then he explodes in a puff of air as Dad comes down the back steps. Charlie's only five, so the puffed air hits his trousers. Dad says this is just as well and we must never puff air into people's faces.

'Why not?' says Duncan, checking his watch.

Dad puts his little office suitcase down on the concrete and tells us we must realise the dangers of droplet infection, especially during an epidemic.

'How droplet?' I say.

'In drops.'

'Little drops?'

'Yes, yes, Annie. Little drops of liquid from nose, throat, anywhere really, which may contain germs.'

'Snot,' says Duncan.

'Any damp fluid which might contain germs. If Charlie had had poliomyelitis and had sneezed in my face . . .'

'Puffed.'

'Sneezed, puffed, in my face, I could have been infected.'

Charlie pats Dad's trouser leg. 'But I haven't got it. Not yet.'

'Never say that. Not even joking. You must realise that Mum and I . . .' Dad sort of trails off, then starts again. 'Droplet infection can also occur during kissing if one of the people has the disease.'

'The Dunns'll cop it then,' says Duncan. 'Their Mum and Dad's always kissing. They all do it, coming, going, all the time. Millions of Dunns lying all over the place kissing. They'll cop it. We won't.'

'Don't worry about the Dunns. There's nothing wrong with kissing in itself,' says Dad. 'It is a sign of affection, of joy. The Dunns love life.'

Dad talks to us a lot. He tells us what to do and what not to do and explains things. Duncan says Mr Dunn never goes on like this and why doesn't Dad keep his hair on. Sometimes when Dad's excited like now the words shoot out of his mouth.

'You're spitting,' says Duncan.

'You'll be going to secondary school next year, Duncan. Just promise me one thing. Don't tell the masters they're spitting, even if they are.'

Duncan grins. 'But you just said. Kissing, spitting, puffing. We'll all get polio like Willy Stead,' he says, pretending to fall about like Willy who can't walk.

'Willy's in the Iron Lung,' says Charlie.

'Course he's in the Iron Lung,' says Duncan, grabbing Charlie's good leg. 'They have a pipe for number two.'

'*Ink, pink, pen and ink, I smell a great big stink*,' they shout at each other.

'Boys, boys,' says Dad, picking up his little case.

'Goodbye darling,' he calls. 'I'll be home about the usual time.'

Mum comes to the door in her frock with sunflowers and her yellow rubber gloves dripping soap suds. 'Don't forget the cauliflower.'

Dad smiles up at her and pats his coat. 'I've made a note. Did I tell you the one about the man handing another man his hat at the front door and saying, "I'm sorry Herbert. Apparently it was turbot my wife asked me to bring home for dinner." Goodbye darling,' he says again, and goes.

'Who's Turbot?' says Charlie.

Mum pushes her hair back with the glove. 'A fish,' she says.

'Duncan,' I say as she closes the door. 'Is there really a tube for number two?'

'I said, didn't I?'

'Yes, but where? And how does it work?'

Diane in standard three had brought a book to school for Morning Talk called *Educational Series 1 Your Body. Female*, and she lent it to me at play time. It was a thin book with stiff covers and the pictures opened to each side like two doors to a verandah. Because of being educational the lady had no clothes on. She was pink and bare on the outside and you went deeper and deeper into her as you turned the pages. There were loops and tubes all coiled up and red lines for Arteries and blue for Veins, and Organs coloured yellow and purple and red. The Organs had long thin arrows pointing to the side saying Stomach, Lungs, Brain. The lobed pink Lungs reminded me of the whoopee cushion owned by

9

Diane's brother which made a loud noise when you sat on it and was very funny. The trouble is most people know to look out for it now and you need surprise for whoopees. It's only funny if the sitter doesn't know.

On the last page beneath everything else was a small pink baby, snug as a bug in a yellow sack in the lady's middle. Everything fitted together very neatly, but there was nothing about number two.

I thought about the Iron Lung. The lady's right lung had been cut open to show its inside, all bubbly like a sponge cut in half but pink. The Iron Lungs would be black, black as the engines huffing and puffing at the railway station in town. And as busy, they would be, when they took over the breathing from Willy's real lungs which had gone phut from kissing.

Usually we swam at the Baths all summer. Everyone liked the Baths, everyone, even the little kids like Charlie who couldn't swim well: the smell and the duckboards and the funny low dunnies in the changing sheds and everyone shouting and bouncing around down the shallow end till their fingers went white and wrinkled from being in so long. All of it was good, everything.

The big kids stayed up the deep end, diving off the boards or sometimes doing belly flops on purpose. Belly flops still hurt a bit even if you do them on purpose, but not so much.

So everyone hated the Baths being closed, but they had to because you can swallow germs as well as breathing them and droplet infection.

Fingernails, Duncan told us, keep growing after you are dead. And hair. 'Some people eat maggots.'

'They do not.'

'Do so.'

'Never.'

Duncan is twelve and skinny and gets ratty when you don't believe him. Usually he plays with big kids like the Dunn twins and Bruce Crutchley and Barry Purdy. They tear round on their bikes and crash them for fun and play Chicken at the crossroads. They pinch Tangee lipsticks from Woolworths for dares and dive off the high board and flick wet towels at the tarts, they call us.

When I was little and they needed a lady to stick in a tepee or something they used to let me play, but not now. Last year Bruce Crutchley stuck a compass in my bottom to get rid of me, he said, but I tripped him up on the concrete and he was knocked out which was nice. He lay there sort of twitching for a minute or two then went home. There was no blood.

Duncan doesn't like being stuck with us, me being eight and Charlie only five and not good at keeping up because of his foot, but this summer he is because all the big kids have gone away to uncles' farms or to visit aunties or gone camping, some of them, up the coast. The Dunns even went to the South Island to see their Nana in Balclutha. Mr Dunn said it had set him back something chronic, but Nana was failing and what could you do.

Charlie had two feet when he was born but one went backwards so he couldn't walk properly before his Op, Mum calls it. They cut it off when he was three.

'Tell us about the Op, Charlie, what was it like?' I say, but Charlie shakes his head and his hair falls across his eyes. He can't remember either and doesn't want to, and why don't we play Dark Nights. Charlie loves Dark Nights, though nothing much happens and I hate being shut up. All we do is sit in my wardrobe and close the door and scream as loud as we can and don't let Duncan in. Charlie gets so excited he sort of fizzes.

Now he goes every six months to the hospital where they make false feet so Mr Salter can check to see if he needs a new one with a bit longer leg.

'Mustn't have you lop-sided, must we, sonny?' says Mr Salter, and Charlie smiles though he hates being called 'sonny' worse than anything, like I hate 'princess'. He hates his shiny pink foot too. He buried it once by the potatoes but Dad dug it up and cleaned it and told Charlie he must wear it always and always and always.

Mum tells him too. Does he want to be hopping about the place all his life, she says, and Charlie says no. Good boy, she says, good boy.

Every day when he was little she made Charlie practise going up and down stairs wearing his pink foot and not touching the banister. 'Go on,' she said, 'next one. Good. And another. And another. Good boy.'

Now Charlie runs everywhere and kicks balls and is an example to both Duncan and me and other kids as well. He is a little warrior, Charlie. Everyone says. He will make something of his life they say.

Dad comes home smelling of the office, and swings Charlie high in the air. They walk to the corner store together hand in hand for a peppermint frog or two.

'*Don't* hold his hand. I've told you a thousand times. He must walk by himself,' says Mum.

'He's only five.'

'Five is quite old enough.'

Dad drops down to mop. His knees stick up either side of his head as he gets Charlie to lick his handkerchief so he can clean his face. He is like a frog. Not Charlie, Dad. A sad frog.

'Come and turn, Charlie,' I yell, and we rush out to the skipping rope fixed to the car shed so you only need one to turn instead of two.

> *Apple, jelly, gingerbread*
> *How many whacks until you're dead?*
> *Four on the knee*
> *And three up the tree,*
> *And how many monkeys can you see?*
> *One, two, three, four . . .*

Skipping is the best exercise in the world, Dad says. Boxers do it by the hour.

By the hour. Hang.

Though not perhaps for Charlie, he says. So Charlie does, and gets good at it, but he's a boy so it doesn't matter. Not like when girls are better, especially Eve Porter who Washes her feet in dirty water and so she oughta, to keep 'em clean. Eve has secrets, and pinches. 'Can't take a joke,' she says, and bags to sit next to Miriama Laing who everyone likes best and whose hair is so thick and curly it has to be tied up in bunches either side so she can see.

Eve knows things, like Duncan. She knew when the Duke was coming. He had come from England, she said, and would drive past and give us a school holiday because Dukes are allowed to.

We waited for the Duke in Dad's office which is upstairs in a concrete building by the railway line and would get a good view. *Derek Hopkins A.C.A., Public Accountant* is painted on one of the windows in black and gold. It turns into *A.C. snikpoH kereD* on the inside.

'What are the little square holes round the top of the clock tower, Dad?' I say.

'Decoration,' says Dad. 'It's called fenestration from the French word "fenêtre" meaning window.'

'But they're tiny.'

'They're still fenestration.'

'From teeny weeny fenêtres,' says Mum.

The curved iron roofs below us keep the rain off the pavements, and the sun, which is hotter than ever this year. Eve Porter says the schools mightn't re-open in February because of the polio, and Mr Porter knows because he's on the Town Council and she's seen the Mayor's Chain and we haven't. Last time there was an epidemic it was called Infantile Paralysis, but this time grown-ups are getting it as well.

'The Duke,' says Dad, 'will drive past in a Rolls Royce. Duncan, go down and buy three flags so you will all have something to wave.'

Duncan comes back with a badge pinned to his blue shirt. It is a small tin button filled by a cross red face with a moustache. Where are our flags, we say. What are Charlie and me to wave now Duncan has pinched the lot?

'Duncan, don't you see?' says Dad. 'The money was for all three of you so you could welcome the Duke. Give me the Duke's button.'

'No.'

'Duncan, I will not tolerate such . . .'

Mum snaps open her handbag and gives me a florin. 'Oh for heaven's sake. Go and get some more silly flags.'

'I don't want the button anyway,' I say as we clatter down the marble stairs with Charlie swinging around the corners on the gold banisters and keeping up well.

'Why not?'

'He looks like General Sir Redvers Buller on the tea caddy,' I say, puffing out my cheeks to show.

Charlie stands staring at the silly little flags. 'But he's a hero. I like the heroes.'

He knows them off by heart, the heroes. Major General Baden-Powell is on the lid, Lord Roberts, Lt General Lord Methuen, Lord Kitchener and Gen. Sir Redvers Buller have a side each. The tin is battered and some of the paint has come off but they still look fierce.

The stairs take longer for Charlie going up. We hear people cheering from outside but not much. 'Hurray,' they say. 'Hurray.' We run to look as a black car slides by beneath the open window, its roof so shiny it winks in the sun. A hand waves. Charlie and I wave our flags.

'Is that it?' says Duncan.

'Never mind,' says Dad. 'You'll see him at the polo match tomorrow.'

'Are all Dukes ratty?' asks Charlie, staring at Duncan's button.

'Not all,' says Mum. 'All the ones I've met have been charming. I have paper at home for writing to them. It's called Duke's Ivory.'

I laughed, I got the joke. Mum smiled. This is what Mum likes best. Laughing and getting the joke.

Dad explains that Mum is being funny. Duke's is a brand name, a reputable firm, undoubtedly. He gives a funny sort of laugh. But the writing paper is not only for dukes. Any commercial maker of paper, however prosperous, could not afford to make a special line of paper for the use of dukes alone. There were not enough dukes to make this a viable proposition, not even in Great Britain. It might, of course, be possible for a duke to commission a certain line. Unlikely though, highly unlikely. And there aren't any in New Zealand. Dukes, he means. Mum was being funny.

Mum stares at the railway ticket office which is a soot-covered shed below.

'Three,' she says.

'What was that, darling?'

'The washing line. I always check.'

We look where she's pointing, and there behind a window all streaked with soot is a bit of rope with two socks and a tea towel hanging from pegs.

'Last time,' she told us, her eyes teasing, 'there was a singlet. You have to check.'

She lifts a hand to Dad's mouth.

'No,' she says. 'Don't tell me. I know there is probably nowhere else to dry them. I know they are not there just to look mucky. I know the railway runs slap through the main street because Mr Hicks sold his swamp land cheap, otherwise the route would have gone past the foothills on the other side of the plains and think how much better that would have been. I know. I know. That doesn't make it any better.' She swings round to us, still clutching our flags. 'You know this place was called Hicksville originally?'

'Hicksville,' we yell, laughing at Mum's joke and hoping we'd got it right and it is one.

We went to the polo next day for another go at the Duke but he was indisposed and unable to play, the paper said. He told the paper he couldn't have ridden a rocking horse in his present condition.

'Poor man,' said Dad. 'Exhausting business showing the flag. Exhausting.'

'Blotto,' said Mum. 'Completely blotto. Ernest Cunningham told me, and he should know.'

It is good when Mum is happy. Everyone likes her. Mr Blew at Material Modes likes her so much he tells her which material the other ladies have chosen so they don't wear the same thing at the Assembly Hall or the Municipal Theatre or at weddings. Weddings are so hard for Mr Blew he has a notebook so he can check. 'Not the navy and white, I think, Mrs Hopkins. I see here that Mrs Appleton has . . .'

Mum drops the navy and white, bang. 'In that case . . .'

'Yes, quite . . .'

Mr Blew winks at me as I swing around the high-legged chair where Mum sits before the counter. He knows Mum is pretty.

Mum has no behind at all. This makes her difficult to fit, but the Lady Dressmaker in town knows what to do. 'We work on it together,' Mum says. 'It keeps us off the streets.'

In the summer she wears tub frocks which are straight and have no sleeves and are run up by Miss Gish who is just round the corner in Pepper Street. They are good for the heat, Mum says, and boiling coppers and bottling fruit and getting your tomatoes down while the glut's on.

Some things finish Mum off. Like when we had lunch in the holidays at the Trocadero Tea Rooms where there was a big picture of a lady with her frock flying and her arms in the air and her bare feet shooting up from some rays at the bottom. A Men's Club were having lunch there too but we couldn't see any of them because they were hidden behind big brown screens, but they were laughing a lot and having fun it sounded like. Then all of a sudden they burst out singing,

> *Give me some men who are stout-hearted MEN*
> *and I'll soon give you ten thousand MORE.*

This finished Mum.

'That's finished me completely,' she said, crying and laughing and the tears running down. 'Yes, yes, have cake,' she said, nodding at the little cake with its cherry. 'Have anything. Can't you just see them? No, no, that's finished me. Finished me completely. Isn't life wonderful,' she said, still crying.

Mum is full of jokes. She should've been on the stage, her friends say. 'Isn't your mother a scream?' She is too, and funny as well.

When Charlie and me were little and hadn't got the hang of reading and she read to us, she made up different voices for hens, roosters, squirrels, everything, not just the Three Bears. Before Charlie could read he sat turning the pages of picture books and laughing like mad. He knew books went with laughs like skies falling on the heads of chickens, and bears called Bobby going to the moon and not coming back. The Water Babies lived under the sea, but there were not so many laughs there. Mum didn't think much of Mrs Be-done-by-as-you-did. She didn't like the sound of her, she said, waving pretend brooms and doors flying open and old ladies being whisked away.

The Beach is the best bit of every year, but especially this summer with it being so hot, and the polio, and no swimming at the Baths. Every year Dad rents Mr Rowan's bach at Laing's Point for a month. Laing's Point is the bit which sticks out down the end of the beach by the river and the Bully Pond, and there are only three baches on it. The biggest one belongs to Mrs Clements who is old. Her children, James and Isabel, still live with her though they are grown up. The other one belongs to Mr Laing and his wife and their daughter Miriama who is my friend and who everyone likes best at school. The rest of the baches and cottages are further along, down the flat part of the beach towards the rocks and Mr Clark's woolshed.

Every year when the car rounds the last corner of the hill and we can see the sea for the first time Dad pulls off the road and says, 'Look.' And there is the whole of the bay, the point and the beach and the sand all spread out for miles, and the frills of the breakers going out through the blue for miles, but not as far as the Island where there is no life at all. Sometimes when you're down at the beach the sea is so glittery you have to shut your eyes a bit, but not up here. It is just blue and flat. You can tell how hot it is because of the haze from the sun and the way things shimmer.

We start whooping and fooling about in the back till Dad says steady on and drives down.

The first thing Mum does when we arrive at the cottage, before she sweeps up mouse droppings or once a dead one, or unpacks, or anything, is to open all the windows wide, then take off her corsets quick as anything, put on her togs and head for the sea. We all do, Dad too, and Charlie hopping fast as he can.

Mr Rowan's cottage that we rent is big and bare and made of wood, with bunk rooms and wooden floors. There are lots of spiders and sand in the lavatory like they all have.

Dad comes out every Friday with new food and books and things, and goes back to town on Sunday night. He kisses us before he goes, and sings his song.

Clap hands for Daddy,
His duty he never will shirk.
If it wasn't for dear old Daddy
We'd all have to go out and work.

Mum is different at the Beach. She forgets about Mr Blew and Material Modes and things matching. She swims and reads and has a nice time.

The three Laing's Point baches are right on the beach, so you run across the hot sand and fall straight into the sea. The land in front of them is disappearing year by year because the river is changing its course. Eventually the houses will have to be moved, people say, but we know this is nutty. It is good right on the beach.

Every Thursday the Catholic seminarians come down from their summer camp by the bridge to get enough fish for Friday. They fish like pictures in *The Bible* with nets. The best swimmer swims out beyond the breakers, dragging a huge one. The other men, all dressed like him, in black togs down to their knees, shout and dive through breakers and come up laughing way out beyond them.

Beyond the breakers. Wow. Shark bait.

They are practising to become Fishers of Men, Dad says, but not us.

They are nice men, but sort of mysterious. For the rest of the week we don't see them; they stay hidden in their camp in the silver poplars by the bridge over the river.

They laugh and joke and tease us, and tell us to watch out for the crabs trapped among the flapping snapper and terakihi when they tip them from the net onto the sand.

'One bite from a good Mick crab and you're ours for life,' says the best swimmer.

I know he is joking, but step back anyway. So does Charlie.

'Yours how?' says Charlie. Duncan is herding crabs into a bucket. He lifts one, wiggles it in Charlie's face. 'You'll be turned into a Roman Catholic and have to go to confession and have candles and all that.'

'Candles how?'

'Lit ones. You'd have to light them.'

'I wouldn't mind. I'd like it. Better than kerosene lamps and moths bumping about. Anyhow, your mouldy old crab's lost its tooth bit, hasn't it, Annie?'

'Yes.'

That night Charlie and me brushed the sand from the bottom of our feet and climbed into our bunks all happy and talking away when Boy, what a fright! Slow scratchy terrible knobbly things were brushing and groping and nipping our legs. I jumped yelling from the top bunk. Charlie wet his bed, which is worse at the Beach because of Mum having nowhere but the bath for washing.

Mum didn't fuss much apart from the sheets. It was funny, you see. She was laughing when she told Dad. 'Duncan,' she said when he arrived next day, 'is a kind and loving boy with a lively mind. It's just that he doesn't see the consequences of his actions.'

'Inconsequentional,' said Dad, pulling on his long floppy khaki shorts.

'That's what I said.'

'Not in so many words, darling.'

'Your father,' said Mum, 'is a stickler for accuracy.'

Dad patted Mum's arm and told her about a man in town who had been sailing pretty close to the wind and had had to pull his horns in.

Mum said oh dear.

Most evenings the grown-ups on Laing's Point go to each other's houses for a sundowner, Mrs Clements calls it. The afternoon sun misses the verandahs of the houses and they lie in the shade in deck chairs and drink beer.

Charlie and me and Miriama Laing from next door muck about nearby in our togs.

'C'n I have a drink of Fifty Fifty,' we say, and someone nods and we skid to the kitchen and grab the sticky bottle and brush off the flies. Its label has half oranges and half lemons on it so you can work it out. Charlie got it years ago.

The big kids, Duncan and his beach friend, Mike Girlingstone from the Store, aren't often there. They are exploring the beach, or the Bully Pond, or the rocks at the far end. Anywhere. Sometimes they ask the Maoris for rides when they race their horses through the shallow waves. And get them.

Miriama Laing has shorts this year. I have never seen shorts before and boy do I want them. Now Miri can climb trees or cliffs and jump off or stand on her head even, and the boys can't shout, *penny for the poppy show*.

'Why,' said Mr James Clements who lives with his mother, 'is the fly at the back of that child's shorts?'

'Perhaps it's a bot-fly,' said Mum.

Everyone laughs. Miri crashes to the ground from her handstand and laughs too. Miriama laughs at everything, but it puts me off the shorts a bit.

Mrs Clements' and the Laings' baches are also wooden and sandy and smell of the dry sacking on the bottoms of the bunks like ours.

Mr Laing, Miriama's father, is called Harry and is tall and has black hair. He does not talk much. Mrs Laing is called Jean. She talks a lot more than Mr Laing and comes up to his shoulder.

Miri tells me that he is finding his ancestors, checking up on his whakapapa he calls it. His mother was a Maori princess who married a white man after her Maori Chief husband died. His stepfather, Mr Laing, Miri says, 'gave Dad his name'. Mr Laing was brought up away from his own people, she says, and he wants to find his real history. He teaches ordinary history at the high school, where Mum's father, Grandad Brownlee, taught English till he died, and in summer he hunts for his own. He sits at a table in a small back room at the bach and reads books and makes notes and doesn't notice the beach hardly at all.

He visits the local Pa and talks to the old Maori men there and is learning to speak Maori. He will teach Miriama when he is good enough, and me too if I like, he says, and did we know that the Maori name for the beach means moonlit waters and we giggle because a bit of phosphorus got stuck on Charlie's bottom last time we went swimming bare in the moonlight with the grown-ups.

Mostly Miriama and me muck about down on the beach but sometimes we play at the Laings'. Miriama doesn't mind having Charlie as well. He puts Patch, Miri's dog, to bed in the wicker doll's pram and covers him up with a blanket and pushes him round and doesn't mess things up at all.

Mum comes over to the Laings' too. Jean is a joy, she says, and so is Bella Clements.

The three ladies see each other nearly every day and swap books by people they like and wonder what's happened to Jack Buchanan who was a matinee idol Bella Clements met when she was in London and he gave her his picture and signed it. She had dancing lessons from Victor

Sylvester too when she was there but Mrs Clements said they were a waste of money.

Mr James Clements is interested in lots of different things and his mother calls him darling. 'Darling,' she calls, and he comes sometimes.

Isabel she calls Bella or Bel. Miriama and I used to laugh at the name Isabel because of *Is a bell necessary on a bicycle*, but we don't now because we like Bel, and besides we're used to it. Like the whoopee cushion, funny names are not so funny when you get used to them. Not even Fay Sidebottom in standard two, though this took longer. We call Isabel Bel because she asked us to. She is thin and flat and her dress is the colour of sand. She started to train as a nurse like Mum but Mrs Clements needed her so she stopped. She does the cooking.

There are things you have to remember at the Beach. The sea can be dangerous for swimming if you're not careful, and we're not allowed in without grown-ups except Duncan sometimes. But the Bully Pond is very dangerous. It is so deep it goes down for ever and is bottomless. Children have drowned there, their wide hair floating if they are girls, sinking down, down for ever.

Dead bodies, Duncan tells us at night in the bunk room, sink first and then float up to the top, no matter how deep. He has seen a dead sheep floating. They blow up and smell yuck. That is what will happen if we drown at the Bully Pool.

I wonder which would be the worst, the sinking or floating yuck.

'No,' I say.

'Yes.'

Charlie is allowed to use his ski pole thing instead of his pink foot at the Beach. Mr Salter at the limb place put a special bit on the bottom of the bit that straps onto his stump, like a ring filled with netting so it won't sink in the sand. It's like the crocheted covers ringed with beads which keep flies off sugar and jam and milk, but Charlie's netting is tough and made of black rope and the ring is steel.

Mr Salter told Charlie he would be a new man with his ski pole, he calls it. And so he is at the Beach. He is another kind of person there, like Mum only different. He is quicker for one thing, scrambling and swinging across the rocks and its pools or climbing the sandhills where the sand slides away beneath him. Charlie loves the Beach better than any of us. Even Mum, when she's 'got rid of the smell of town' she calls it.

The only thing Charlie hates at the Beach is Duncan's Go Home shout. It can happen anywhere: the sandhills, the rocks, the woolshed, anywhere.

'Go home, Charlie. You can't keep up.'

'I can. I can.'

'Go home, Charlie.'

And Charlie goes, the high-tide mark on his whole leg dark from paddling, his head tossing from side to side to show he doesn't care.

Sometimes I go home with him but not always.

This time I do and I look back to poke my tongue out at Duncan. He stands there with his legs apart and arms folded and eyes squeezed against the sun. Sometimes Duncan disappears all day on his own – 'Mucking about,' he says when Mum asks him where he's been and what's he been doing. 'Just mucking about.'

Lorna

I used to be a nice woman, kind and pleasant, a dear girl once, I swear. When I was young, younger.

Now I sit in a deck chair in the cool of the evening with Mrs Clements and her daughter Isabel who are both reasonably pleasant people, especially Bella; I am offered my choice from Huntley and Palmer's Cocktail Assortment, and find fault in everything. I make a fist to prevent my shouting 'Stop talking' at Mrs Clements, who is explaining with much detail and many diversions how she came across the vodka we are about to drink. She was down on her benders this morning, she tells us, making sure there was enough beer because if there's one thing James hates it's a drought. He is not a toper as we know, but, like all young men, he likes his beer. So there she was, head down bottom up, when lo and behold she came across this old bottle. Goodness knows where it came from. But now she comes to think of it the Parkinsons might have left it when they stayed that time before Harold died.

Jean Laing and I smile at the bottle as if it is an unexpected guest to be made welcome. Harry Laing stares at the sea.

My husband, Derek Hopkins, is not here. He works in town during the week but he will be here on Friday, as the night the day. Nothing is surer on God's earth or beyond. Nothing.

'Heavens above,' says Mrs Clements, 'that must be six, seven years ago. How old is Charlie now, Lorna?'

'Five.'

'Is that all? I suppose it seems longer because of his foot.' She says dusting the bottle with quick, decisive hands. 'Anyway, I thought we might as well try it. Lorna?' she says, hefting the bottle in my direction.

I leap up. 'Thank you, Mrs Clements. Lovely.' I feel tempted to say 'Too kind. Too kind,' like Florence Nightingale in her bedridden dotage as she accepted the Order of Merit from one of Her Majesty's emissaries. Like me, she gathered, if nothing more, that someone was offering her something with amiable intent and reacted accordingly. Too kind. Too kind.

Warm vodka will probably be worse than warm beer but at least it will be different. It will make a change. I would like a change. Even the sea looks boring, which I would not have thought possible. It is flat, oily, calm and predictable. The cliff face of the Island beyond is stark and white like a tooth snapped from the mainland. On the seaward side of it, they say, are trees. Trees would be nice.

Cushioned by hillocks of couch grass and dusted with sand my younger children, Ann and Charlie, plus Miriama Laing, loll in front of the verandah. They lie torpid, sated with sun and sea, and glad to be here. Occasionally one of them lifts a hand in a doomed attempt to swat a fly.

The flies are bad this year, but then we say that every summer. They are large, these flies, sticky-footed beach ones which cling. Like children, they cannot be flicked away or ignored. Ann is now making a fuss about them, slapping arms, legs. She has not had time to get used to them and will have to do so. I open my mouth to tell her so, but shut it again because I see Mrs Clements' pale eyes watching me and I don't want her to hear my being irritable. I treat Mrs Clements with respect, which is the wrong word because there are aspects of Mrs Clements which I do not; nevertheless she is a woman of great presence and I am aware of this. She is a large well-powdered woman, not shiny with sweat like the rest of us. Perhaps you sweat less when you are old but more probably it is because she keeps well away from the coal ranges and heated flat irons of beach life when the temperature is in the nineties, as it has been for weeks. What are daughters for, and Mrs Clements has Isabel.

We talk about the real beach weather we have been having, we tell each other that it is perfect for swimming but that the nights are almost too warm. I mention that the children mutter in their sleep as they toss in their bunks with only a sheet for cover.

Mrs Clements says that she is interested to hear this. That James and Isabel were just the same at their age. She adds that it is different in the Riviera. The nights are cooler there.

Isabel, lean and sharp kneed, her eyes gentle, sits on the steps and strokes Charlie's pale hair. She has strong features, like her brother who is the most handsome man in the Bay by a long shot, but a good nose and strong eyebrows are no help to Isabel. Her hair is black and short and straight. There are no chestnut romps as in James's hair. Mrs Clements has told me frequently that it is a pity things are this way round and that Isabel should have her hair permed, that she won't *try*. Isabel says no. She refuses, she likes to be free. She swims without a bathing cap, her seal head ducking and diving beneath the waves as she laughs.

Charlie is now almost asleep against her angled knees. Isabel's head is bent to his. Mrs Clements hisses in my right ear, 'Poor Isabel, she's potty about that child. Of course she'll never have one of her own.' She sighs.

Some childless couples in Malaya, I am about to tell her, adopt orphaned baby orangutans. They shave off their body hair to make them look more like human infants and dress them in appropriate clothes and are happy.

I open my mouth, and, thank God, shut it again.

My mother stressed the importance of the sorting room which, she told me, lies between the thought and the tongue. If I had remembered about the sorting room I would not have made gaffes like shouting at the school sports at Arthur Smedley who was coming last as usual – 'Come on Arthur, you'll win if you don't lose.' In a loud voice in front of everyone.

Nowadays I have given up on the sorting room. I will say anything for a laugh and sometimes do, but I am glad the orangutans are safely stowed.

Their story does not end there. When the baby orangutans are about three years old they become obstreperous and violent. Some surrogate parents hand them back to the forest rangers from whom they came, whereupon the doubly orphaned *Pongo pygmaeus* cry day and night and refuse food for weeks. Other parents abuse them or hack them to death in despair at their recalcitrant behaviour.

Mrs Clements thinks, and I know she thinks, that Isabel's fondness for Charlie is because of his foot. But I know that both Isabel and Charlie are made of sterner stuff. People stop Charlie on the beach. They ask him where he lost his foot.

'I didn't lose it,' he says. 'They cut it off.'

His left foot went the wrong way. It was all they could do.

It is essential for him to be tough and he is, thanks to me. I have made him so. Somebody had to.

James Clements reappears from the back door. A small child with school sores dabbed with gentian violet has brought him a telephone message from the Store. His cousin, Garth, who lives on the hills behind the beach and owns the house we rent, would like him to have a meal with them next Thursday. There's some cousin from Shropshire and would he ring back.

James leans against the verandah post and rubs his back against it like some large and beautiful animal. He is incapable of making an ungraceful movement, which is unusual in so tall a man. Even the way his heavy cotton shirt hangs from his shoulders moves me. It is James I come to watch. He is the author of the heaviness in my chest, the tightening in the groin. Even, perhaps, the clenched fist.

James is not pleased by the Rowans' invitation. 'Put on a tie and drive for miles in this heat for dog-tucker mutton with Midge and Garth? Let alone some dim Rowan cousin. Bugger that.'

Mrs Clements smiles. Her grey curls frame her face like the frill of an antique bonnet. She smiles.

'Then don't go, darling,' she murmurs.

James tells us that even the thought of trailing down to the Store to tell them so makes him feel tired.

His mother is delighted at such indolence. She knows James doesn't mean it. That he will be there and back in a flash. 'Don't forget the bread order,' she laughs.

'I've done that,' says Isabel.

Mrs Clements nods.

I want to tell Mrs Clements to stop being ridiculous about her son. That she is spoiling him rotten. What would she do if she had Charlie? She would ruin him, turn him into a cripple. She has already squashed Isabel, or thinks she has, but not from kindness.

Mrs Clements did her best for Isabel when she was younger. She has told me so herself. Take the case of the evening shoes. There were no size sevens to be had after the War, let alone without heels. Mrs Clements bought a pair of men's leather slippers from the Farmers and Isabel painted them gold for the Ball Season.

She and I met at a dinner party before the Black and White Ball, which my father called the Tight and White. Mrs Newman, our hostess, was large and golden and loved fun and games. She was an icebreaker.

I was a flapper by instinct and conviction, one of the first in the Bay to bob my hair. Straight beaded shifts, shingled hair and high heels suited me. I was a success.

Isabel wore a long frock of some dark crepe. Her hair was shorter than mine and better cut. She stood tall and straight and told me she wished to be elsewhere. That she had hidden the invitation, but that Mum had found the wretched thing and there had been a stink. She laughed, and watching her I wondered at what stage slim, like me, becomes skinny like her. I thought she looked good. Different, certainly, from the rest of us Cuddlepots and Snugglepies, but good.

After the meal Mrs Newman gathered us together to tell us her plan for breaking the ice. The girls would each throw one shoe into the centre of the room, then sit down carefully so as to hide the still shod foot. The boys would then come in, choose a shoe and come to find its mate, thereby claiming their partner for the first dance. I was not pleased. The second-best-looking man in the Bay (James had gone to Oxford after the War) had insisted on the first dance and I had hopes of more.

We tossed shoes. Among the silver pumps, louis heels, neat little brocades and pale satins, Isabel's Gent's leather lay like a gilded cattle truck.

There was an embarrassed pause, a titter truncated by Isabel who flung back her head, her short hair tossing as she laughed. I laughed too, seized her hand.

And then the men came in. And we stopped.

Mrs Clements has now given up on Isabel. For a time before she lost interest she scared the wits out of the one or two young men who hovered briefly and were never seen again. They were, she told us, unsuitable.

Harry Laing, I remember, rose to his feet the night she told us this. 'How would you describe such people, Mrs Clements? Would my mother pass muster?'

Mrs Clements gave a light laugh. 'Don't be silly, Harry. Your mother was a princess. A lovely woman. Lovely.'

Harry's mouth smiled. 'Ah, but all Maori women who married whites in those days were princesses. Didn't you know? I'm surprised there are any left,' he said, slapping a passing fly.

Sweet as a nut, I was once. Dear little Lorna Brownlee from up the Middle Road. The one who could dance all night and remember the words of the songs. Who loved old dogs and sick children and was kind and patient with incontinent old men in Men's Medical.

'I'm sorry, Nursie. I done it in a fit. I'm sorry, dear.'

'Don't worry, Mr Spence,' I laughed, game as Ned Kelly with sodden sheets.

So what changed?

I had been engaged before the War, long before I met Derek. Had written to my fiancé, Corporal Alan Webster, every week while he was overseas. The troopship berthed in Wellington and I was given special leave from the hospital to go down to meet him. I can still hear the nagging of the train. 'What're you doing, what're you doing, what're you *doing* you fool.' I stood on the wharf staring up at the face of the stranger beneath his lemon-squeezer hat and panicked. I ran, fighting, struggling my way through the crowd pushing against me until I reached the entrance to Queen's Wharf. I fell into the hotel, sobbing. The receptionist thought my fiancé had died en route and I wished he had, though not really.

That was when I began cheating. A girl who jilts a wounded war hero at the moment of his triumphant return to his homeland has to start somewhere.

Jean Laing told me that when she takes off her corsets at the beach and flops about, the sheer relief, the release from pressure, reminds her of the first time she saw Harry again, alive and in one piece after the War.

Not so for me. My downhill course began with that sick scramble among the hooters and streamers and the crowds in hats waving and shouting and senseless with happiness. It was then I learned I was bad medicine. Alan Webster told me so.

Lorna,
I cannot call you dear because you are no longer. Little did I think as I gazed at the snap I wore next to my heart all those years, that you were bad medicine. I used to think that you had kept me safe. Safe for what? You are heartless and fickle. You can keep the ring. I could not take it back if you paid me.
Alan.

And I didn't mind, you see. I was glad, yea, glad with all my heart to have got rid of him. Which shows there was something wrong, does it not, with both me and my heart.

I had boyfriends. Pretty girls did, plain girls didn't, it was as simple as that. I also had a reputation. I was now flighty, if not worse. Mothers throughout the length and breadth of the Bay cautioned their sons, who took no notice. They flocked, we Charlestoned. I was fun.

I did not go to bed with these young men. They were too young, too gauche. Their hair was smoothed down with hair oil and their hot dancing hands were encased in white cotton gloves to save us from sweat marks on our dresses. Their stiff little programmes, their wee gold pencils and their groping, now gloveless hands bored me beyond words.

The man I did love was married. We spent our time together at a hotel in Waipawa with no lift. There was a sign in the foyer saying *Commercials Welcome*. The last item on the menu was *Fruits in Season*.

You do not need the name of my lover. He is dead now. His shell-shocked mind caught up with him and he blew his brains out in the tractor shed not long afterwards.

I had not told him I was pregnant. What could he have done, out on the coast with his new bride and baby son and his whole life ahead of him?

And I still had his child.

Derek was slightly younger than I, and a friend of my brother's. Like Ian he had been too young for the War, a dubious privilege in the twenties. He worked in Dalgety's Stock and Station Agents and studied for his accountancy examinations at night, and had admired me from afar for years, he told me.

I smiled and said thank you and yes, I would be happy to go with him in my new apricot cloche to the Autumn Meeting. I like racing. The members' stand was full and we sat on the steps and I took covert glances at Derek's profile as he stared at the field through binoculars. He was not a bad-looking man. He had a moustache but he did not, as it were, use it much. It was just there.

He held my hand. I moved it to my knee. He glanced at me, his smile one of radiant surprise. I removed it as Mrs Cyril Bradshaw ran up the steps to tell me that people below could see my knickers, and the race began.

I knew I was pregnant. I knew what I was doing. I was bad medicine. 'You must have fallen on your wedding night,' said my neighbour when my elder son Duncan was born. He was a beautiful baby. His father had been a fine-looking man.

You must understand that, like Mrs Clements, I did try. I did not love Derek Hopkins but I was grateful to him. And at least I told him. 'I cannot marry you, Derek. I am pregnant. The father is dead.' I could not have made it clearer.

He was shocked, deeply shocked, what young man would not have been? But, and this perhaps is why I married him, he looked me in the eye and told me that he loved me and that if I married him he would give the child a name.

I wept. I don't think I had wept before. The baby has a name, I said, he has my name but not his father's because his father is dead and what about his poor little wife out at the coast, so tragic. And I meant it. It was tragic, tragic.

Derek, obviously, was a good man. He was also a hard worker and determined to do well. He saw his own brass plate shining before him like a vision at the end of a long uphill slog. *Derek Hopkins, C.A.* Something he would win for me and lay at my feet.

I knew I was cheating and still do. I know.

Ann was born two years later. A solemn baby and easy after Duncan who was difficult. Babies were either easy or difficult, as girls were pretty or plain. I had to watch Duncan as a small child and still do. He is very quick.

I look around, leap to my feet. 'Where's Charlie?'

Jean's hand touches mine. 'He and Bel have gone to the Store.'

'To give your message, I bet,' I say to James, teasing, flirting, oh the wit of it all to shield my rage.

'Aye,' he says stretching hugely with arms on high. 'We all take our pleasures differently.'

What does he mean by that? Furthermore what has all this nonsense to do with me? Why should I feel cross because Isabel has seen fit to walk to the Store to decline an invitation for her beautiful brother to eat tough mutton in the hills with Garth Rowan, his pigeon-toed wife Midge and a dim cousin from Home. I owe Bella a lot and always will, but this is ridiculous.

The Rowans, for heaven's sake. Why should I fuss because Isabel, who has not been included in this gaiety, has acted as James's runner? She is an intelligent woman, Isabel, as well as a good sort. Besides, as James said, and probably meant quite straightforwardly with no hidden subtleties for me to snatch at, Bella will enjoy her time alone with Charlie. I see them walking in single file to the Store where the beaten track through the stamped grass is thinnest, side by side where it widens. Charlie will be telling her things, he is a yarner. He will be swinging himself along on his ski-pole leg, his face glancing up at hers to make sure she has got the full impact of his favourite story from his weekly comic *Rainbow,* called 'Betcha Barnes and his One-Wheel Wonder', which his father will bring out tomorrow. He will also bring liquorice allsorts. Charlie doesn't like the black rubber ones but Annie does, and she lets him eat her hundreds and thousands which fall off.

Charlie has been known to hang around outside the Beach Store. He stands, his eyes sad beneath his floppy grey sunhat which all children wear because of the polio epidemic, and stares at strangers as they come out clutching Frosty Jacks or Eskimo Pies. His eyes widen as he stares at their bounty.

'Just what I like,' he murmurs, and some of them rush back to Mr Girlingstone sweating behind the counter to get something, anything, quickly, for the waif at the door.

I checked when Duncan told me this story. I spied on Charlie and told Derek when he came out at the weekend.

'Ten out of ten for initiative,' I laughed.

I do that, you see, sometimes. I exaggerate my lack of moral tone so that Derek will over-react, will respond with pompous platitudes and I can laugh at him.

I stoke him up. He seldom lets me down. Occasionally, but not often.

Nor did he this time. He told me that there is initiative and initiative, called Charlie to him, sat him on his knee and explained to him that he must no longer ask people for ice creams at the Store.

Charlie explained that he didn't ask for them, that people gave them to him.

Derek said he realised that technically this was so, but in actual fact Charlie was begging for them and it must stop.

Charlie said he liked ice creams.

Derek said he realised this but that Charlie was exerting moral blackmail and it must stop.

'How?' asked Charlie.

'Well, just stop.'

'No, I mean how blackmail?'

'Well you look sad and . . .' Derek waved a worried hand.

'The foot, you mean.'

'Yes, well . . .' Derek sat silent and wretched.

Charlie looked thoughtful. 'Oh,' he said.

I laughed.

'Charlie, don't you see,' persisted Derek. 'We are lucky. I have a job. Things must surely get better with Labour, but many people still have no jobs, their children have no money for ice creams.'

'Annie gave one of her dolls away,' offers Charlie. 'At school.'

Derek's face, his happy face. 'Did she?' he breathes. 'Did she say why?'

'The girl didn't have one. She had plaits.'

'The girl?'

Charlie's white-blond head moves. 'The doll. Elsie.'

I bite my lip, literally bite my lip, but fail again. 'She didn't like Elsie much.'

Derek's face.

Charlie is a truthful child. 'She did, Mum,' he says. 'She liked her a lot.'

Derek's eyes shut briefly. He tries again. 'Yes, well. So you won't do it any more?'

'Would it be all right if you didn't have a job?'

'It would be . . . it would be more understandable.'

Charlie swings around, looks up at him. He trusts his father. 'What about the foot though?'

Derek buries his head in the curve of his son's neck. His voice is muffled. 'No,' he says, 'the foot doesn't count.'

Charlie swings off Derek's knee, grins at him and scoots out the door. 'OK,' he says.

I keep my damp eyes on the sticky fly paper hanging from the light above the table where we eat. It is black with dead and half-dead flies, one still waving.

'I lied,' I say. 'Annie did like Elsie.'

'I know,' says Derek and is silent for a moment. He stands, looks at me thoughtfully. 'We really must stop the children saying OK all the time. And yeah.'

'Yes.'

The evening breeze stirs the tamarisks. The breakers no longer roar, their sound is muted as the waves retreat, are sucked back, return with more water. I don't believe the moon controls the tides. Waxing and waning, all that. It seems very far-fetched to me. On moonlit nights when we swim naked there is phosphorus. Phosphorus is mysterious and beautiful stuff, inexplicable as moons and tides.

James lights a Craven A and hands the match to Annie to blow out. She does so but James has got it wrong. It is Charlie who still enjoys blowing out matches. Ann teeters on the brink of becoming one of the big kids, and there are things she has put aside.

The smoke rises around James's shadowed head, the light is fading.

His face is all angles, hollows, manly beauty at dusk. I think of Jeanette MacDonald and Nelson Eddy singing their hearts out across mountains. *When I'm calling you, ooh-oo, ooh-oo,* they swoop, and I wish to do just that. I wish Mrs Clements and Isabel would go away and I could make things clear, or perhaps clearer, to James. I am not a good woman, though presumably even a good woman may feel this tightening of the crotch, this awareness that her heart is beating and has been for some time. For her husband only, of course.

James leans forward, plants a hand on each knee and tells us the news. 'I'm going to make a film with my movie camera this summer,' he says. 'Cowboys and Indians, goodies and baddies, that sort of thing.'

There is a brief silence. Movie cameras are comparatively new in the Bay and much desired.

'Acting, you mean?' says Mrs Clements finally, as though trying out a new word.

'Yes. You can ride, can't you, Lorna?'

'Yes.'

'And I'll need at least two men, bareback riders, for the bad guys.'

Harry Laing's head is bent as he examines a loose board in the verandah. 'With black hats?'

'That's right, dark sinister-looking coves. Moustaches.'

There is something pleasing in the timbre of Harry's voice. 'Isn't that a bit obvious?'

'Western flicks are obvious. That's the whole point. Their conventions are as rigid as morality plays. It is what they do with the essential formula of crime, pursuit, showdown, justice. And, of course, suspense. The climactic race to the rescue. Audiences must be involved emotionally. Participants, if you like.'

'Goodness,' says Mrs Clements.

'Who wears the white hat?' I ask, knowing already.

James has a wonderful smile. 'Me. I will be the rugged hero who is a law unto himself yet possessed of the nobility and courage of an Arthurian knight.'

'Yes,' says Mrs Clements. 'But who will work the camera?'

'Bel.'

'Ah,' says Mrs Clements and rearranges her skirt.

There will be parts for all of us: Mrs Clements will run a Wild West gambling den. There is a Madonna-of-the-plains type part for Jeannie Laing. Mrs Clements asks what that means. James explains in some detail that women also are stereotypes in Westerns. Either they're very very good and innocent or they're bad but spirited. Mrs Clements asks will Jean be the good woman?

James nods. 'As ever.'

With her usual amiability Jeannie laughs. She thinks the whole thing will be a hoot and so do I.

Mrs Clements says that she'd always enjoyed charades and dressing up, pretending to be somebody else, that sort of thing. She tells us she was a Mother Superior once at school, and what was James looking for? A tough egg. Well, she could try. But she wouldn't ride bareback.

'You can, Harry?' says James.

Harry stretches. 'Yes.'

'Well, then?'

'No.'

'Oh, come on.'

'I said no.'

'What about the bareback scenes, the drama, the thundering chase along the foaming surf?'

Harry shrugs. 'There's no surf in Westerns.'

Jean leans forward. 'Do you think any of the men at the Pa would be interested, darling? A homemade cowboy flick would be fun. Rehearsing, filming, the whole thing. I can just see it, and I haven't even heard the story yet.'

So can we all. We don't want to miss a moment.

Harry's face is now in deep shadow at the back of the verandah but we can hear his smile.

'Local colour, you think?'

Jean laughs, ducks her crisp curly head to his arm.

'Great idea,' says James. 'You could ask two or three, Harry.'

'As paid extras?'

'Well, this is just a fun thing. Wouldn't they be insulted? I mean . . .'

'I should know, but I don't. I'll find out.'

The tide is out on the beach below. Maori men and women are digging for pipis, their children play on the shining pewter sand. Somebody calls. The sound echoes, cuts across the brrm brmms coming from Ann and Miriama and Charlie who are pushing Dinky cars around the tracks they have made through the couch grass.

Duncan's father told me once, and he was right, that every person in the world when shown a snapshot of a group looks for themselves first, their own children notwithstanding. An odd word, notwithstanding.

'What's my part?' I ask calmly. 'Madonna or spirited?'

'Yours?' James looks at me as though I already know. 'Oh, you play the bad girl. The harlot with the heart of gold.'

'How do we know,' I ask even more calmly, 'that she has a heart of gold?'

'She saves me at the end. From certain death.'

I see Mrs Clements' pale eyes on me. She is no fool, Mrs Clements.

'I'm going to find Charlie,' I cry, leaping to my feet in demonstration.

But Charlie and Isabel, hand in hand and still talking, are coming through the gate past the large hole in the sand which James digs every year for the rubbish.

'Thank you so much, Mrs Clements,' I say. 'I must go.'

'Hardly a party, dear, just informal drinks.'

An informal ex-peanut butter jar of warm vodka.

Mrs Clements is now congratulating James. She thinks the film will be a triumph. She loves the idea of the Wild West gambling den. Does James remember the poem his father used to recite? More of a ballad really. Something about *Winifred the Wonder of the West* and how people say she had a hairy chest. And James has written the story himself? She shakes her head in wonder.

Isabel tells us that yes, James has asked her to be the cameraman and she would like to but she'll need lots of help.

'Just common sense, really,' says James. 'And I'll lend you some books.'

She smiles her slow smile. 'Then I should be all right.'

I call the children and we scramble through the fence where Charlie can slide through. I swing him upwards, hug his brown thinness, kiss his salty ear.

'Oh, Charlie,' I say.

Ann and Charlie have extended the Dinky car tracks from the long creeping roots of the couch grass in Mrs Clements' property to the front of our bach. There is now a hill town and a town on the flat; garages burrow into hillsides; a hospital, marked with a wilting yellow gazania, indicates where you are taken when you crash. As well as the cars there is a pick-up truck, a London bus and a British milk float. Each child operates three vehicles, leaving two stationary as they hurtle off with the third. The school bus has broken down. Brrm, brrm.

The thing I like best is their concentration, their complete absorption in the realities of their invented world.

Powered by Ann, an ambulance ploughs to the scene of a major crash. Invisible men jump out.

'Is he dead?' asks Charlie.

'Nearly. This may be a case for Betcha himself.'

'Betcha,' squeaks Charlie. 'But we haven't got a One-Wheel Wonder.'

'We have! Look!' Ann snaps a minute tyre from a red car. Charlie is suspicious, looks doubtfully at his plundered Austin. Betcha Barnes is his, not Annie's. She has pinched him.

'You're not allowed. They get lost. Dad says.'

Ann's bare feet wriggle deeper in sand. She does not like interruptions.

'Do you want a One-Wheel Wonder or not?'

'He's mine,' mutters Charlie.

'He can't be yours. He's in *Rainbow*. He's everybody's.' She trundles the wheel towards the yellow gazania. 'See. Now, he's rescued the man. He's all bleeding and Betcha's whizzing him to the hospital and . . .'

'No!' Charlie snatches the tyre and flings it into his mouth. He coughs violently, tears spurt from his eyes. I leap from the verandah, seize him above the knees to upend him, beat his back. He coughs, splutters, sobs with fright as I beat and beat and beat.

'Is he going to die?' yelps Ann as the tyre shoots from Charlie's mouth.

I hold Charlie, swing him upright. I tell him it's all right, all right, all right.

Ann tells Charlie he shouldn't have put the tyre in his mouth.

'He's mine,' gasps Charlie as the Buick turns into the open gate and Derek toots the horn in greeting. He has arrived bearing provisions and fresh meat, beans from the garden and treats as well: watermelon and a tray of white-fleshed peaches from Mr Morley's orchard, *Rainbow* and *Teddy's Own,* the week's mail and two yellow Gollancz detective yarns for me. All, all will be there.

'Charlie nearly died,' says Ann, picking up the sticky wet tyre.

Derek wants details. He takes Charlie from my shaking arms, and asks him why he put the tyre in his mouth. Daddy has told him a thousand times not to put things in his mouth. Charlie, limp with exhaustion, opens his eyes. 'Have you got my comic?'

Derek tells Ann that this must be a lesson to her. He has told all you children not to remove the tyres from Dinky toys. They get lost and as this incident has shown they can be very dangerous, though why in the name of heaven a big boy like Charlie would swallow a toy tyre is beyond him.

Charlie closes his eyes. Ann says how could she know Charlie was going to go all dopey and swallow it.

Derek looks at *Brave New World* lying face downwards in the sand where I must have flung it.

'Were you reading?'

'Have you any objection?'

'No, but . . . No.' He pauses, looks around. Is unhappy. 'Where's Duncan?'

'With Mike from the Store.'

'Where?'

'I've no idea.'

Derek puts Charlie down gently. 'I think I'll have a look around first before I unpack the car.'

'Where're the sweets, Dad?' cries Ann, scrabbling in the boot of the car.

'Yeah!' cries Charlie, flinging himself around Derek's suited legs. He sees the wreckage beneath the town shoes: the collapsed towns, the hospital. 'You've mucked it all up, Dad,' he wails. 'Look, all our roads, everything, all busted.'

'Sometimes,' says Derek, glancing around as though Duncan might pop up from behind a nearby sandhill, 'I wonder why I drive over that filthy road every Friday night and back every Sunday.'

Charlie has found his comic. He pats Derek's leg kindly. 'To bring me *Rainbow*,' he tells him.

And to make love to his wife on Saturday night. Derek is a meticulous lover.

Normally he rubs and squeezes and twiddles and asks me whether I like it and I say yes, and sometimes I fear he does not believe me. But he tries. And so do I.

Tonight is different. He is excited, perhaps, by the heat, the blackness, the slick of sweat. Union is achieved, fulfilment given, need assuaged. I have no longing afterwards, as I sometimes do, to leap from the sagging bed and the dead mattress and rush into the still night to find a man, any man, to finish me off.

I roll over. My hand brushes Derek's back. I kiss it tenderly.

'Darling heart,' he murmurs. 'Darling heart.'

Ann

'I know I said I would,' says Mum, putting a finger between the pages of *Body on a Plate*. 'But just let me finish this. Only thirty pages to go.'

Thirty.

'Give us a cuddle, Charlie, and I'll take you,' calls Bel from Mrs Clements' verandah steps.

Charlie looks at her, his face all screwed up. He stands scratching his bottom through his pants like Dad in his pyjamas in the morning. He wants to go to the Bully Pond, we all do, but he's not sure. It's not so much the cuddle, he does a good cuddle, but he's five now.

'It's a swap, Charlie,' I say. 'Go on.' He and I do a lot of swapping. We swap Dinky cars and comics and marbles like everyone, though not his best Taw, which is a big glass one with red and green ribbons twisted inside which he has to hide from Duncan, and I wouldn't mind either.

'OK,' he says finally and hops through the fence where the wire's slack.

Bel puts away her colander of peas all podded and green like gobstoppers and starts saying poetry. Miss Granville at school moves her hand in circles while she's reciting, to get the rhythm she says, but Bel just says it.

> *Cupid and my Campaspe play'd,*
> *At cards for kisses, Cupid paid:*

He stakes his quiver, bow and arrows,
His mother's doves, and teams of sparrows
Loses them too . . .

'Who's Cupid?' says Charlie.

'The God of Love.'

This might put Charlie off. 'Who's the other one?' I say quickly.

'A girl,' says Bel.

'How do you say it?'

'Cam,' says Bel, 'then paspee.'

'Do you want arms around?' says Charlie, and Bel says, 'You bet.'

'Good, this step's burning my bum.' He climbs onto her knee, wraps his arms around her neck and gives her a good hug.

Miri and I stand, not laughing because of putting him off.

Bel sniffs his neck. 'Nutmeg,' she says.

Charlie just smells hot at the beach. At school he smells of Miss Cridland's room like all the Primers. Miss Cridland has hair like yellow candy floss sticking out for miles and she smells lovely. Miri says her scent's called *Evening in Paris* and it comes in a purple bottle with silver stars so she's probably right.

All the Primers like Miss Cridland. We did too. One of the reasons is she sticks gold stars on the bottom of the page and writes Good Work. Once Charlie drew his own star but Miss Cridland could tell at once and told him not to do it again because it was cheating, and Charlie didn't want to be a cheat did he?

Charlie said he didn't know and Miss Cridland laughed and laughed.

'Let's go,' says Bella.

Mum says, 'Bel, you're an angel,' and lifts a hand to us, and says, 'Don't drown, mates.' She calls again, 'Does your mother know where you're going, Miriama?' and Miri says yes and Mum lifts a hand again and goes on reading.

Now Miri and me are jumping down the sandhills in front of the baches with the sand slipping and Charlie on his bottom with his ski pole in the air where it's steep, and us all yelling, except Bel, who is remembering not to help Charlie.

Miri and I run off still yelling when we get to hard sand. We tear along beside the river which keeps changing its course and eating up Laing's Point. Miri's father says the tides are higher than ever this summer. He wonders if the tide patterns are changing.

It is out now, the tide, and the river is cutting through hard little cliffs of sand, good for stamping on to see how much will fall in. It is not deep here, the river, not like further up at the Bully Pond. This is one of the reasons why the pond is so dangerous. It gets deep suddenly and the river is tidal as well.

The Bully Pond Rock is huge and made of papa rock. It sticks out from the river bank and has holes in it where limpets and their shells have sunk in for years then died and fallen out. At high tide the rock sticks out of the pond like a hippopotamus, just the nose and eyes and the top of its head showing as it waits for something to happen and keeps cool.

Grown-ups sit on the rock and watch we don't disappear where it's bottomless. We aren't allowed to dive in or jump, not even honeypots, because of banging into bits of the rock which are hidden under the water. Charlie has to wear his water wings and not go in the deep bit alone. He hates this, but No wings, no pond, Mum says. Even Miri and me who can swim two lengths easy at the Baths and have got our Dolphin Cards pinned up at home, even we have to have rubber rings. No rings, no pond.

We don't mind too much though. We bob about, give each other tows and pretend to climb out of our rings. Mostly we dog-paddle like Charlie, who whizzes about in his water wings with his legs banging. There's plenty of room, and often we have the pond to ourselves. Grown-ups don't like swimming there. They think it's mucky, but the water's just cloudy because of the rock being papa.

This time Miri and me charge around the corner and then stop. Charlie catches up.

'Hey,' he says, 'there's other kids here. Maori kids.'

It isn't kids. One is a man and the other is a boy about Duncan's age.

At the end of last term Eve Porter got crabby with Miriama after school and said she'd cheated at hopscotch when she hadn't. Eve got so mad she said she'd have secrets, but there was no one for her to have secrets with because of all of us liking Miri better than her. Then Eve shouted at Miri, 'You're only a dumb Maori kid anyhow, and I'm going home, so there,' and did. We all stood round saying, 'She's mad, Miri,' and 'You have first go, Miri,' and 'Eve Porter washes her feet in dirty water.' Things like that.

But Miri said, 'I'm going home,' so I said, 'OK let's go,' and Miri said, 'Go away,' and ran off. So we went on playing, but after a while I thought I'd go home too and then remembered Mum was taking Charlie to see Mr Salter and Duncan had footy practice and I was meant to go to Miri's till Mum picked me up.

I walked along, not running because I was working out what to say when Miri said 'Go away' if she did. Or even if she didn't.

The Laings' house has a pepper tree with a swing in the front. Miri and Mrs Laing didn't hear me when I turned round the corner. They were sitting together on the back porch in the chair with the cane undone down one leg and Miri was saying, 'I'm not a dumb Maori kid, am I, Mum?' and Mrs Laing was holding her. 'Whoever said that, pet?' she said and Miri said, 'Eve Porter.'

Mrs Laing said, 'Well now, what about a bit of a mop up round here,' and wiped Miri's face with her hanky and said, 'Dad's a Maori. And I'm not. Is Dad any dumber than me?' and Miriama giggled and said 'No', because Mr Laing knows everything. 'Right,' said Mrs Laing, 'and am I any brighter than Dad?' and Miri giggled again because Mrs Laing counts on her fingers and says, 'Don't look then' when Miri tells her that even the Primers aren't allowed to do that.

'So Dad's a Maori and I'm not and we liked each other so we got married, and then you arrived and you're half Maori and half pakeha, and we love you very much and you're not dumb at all. Added to which bossy little Eve Porter is thick as two planks, and you tell her to put that in her pipe and smoke it.'

Miri laughs because Mrs Laing's talking Standard Three Talk, she calls it. Mrs Laing laughs too and looks up. When she sees me her eyes are wet and so angry I almost jump. She blinks and sniffs and says hello Annie. How about a drink of Fifty Fifty? And I say yes.

I think about mothers and fathers liking each other and loving their children. With us it would be Charlie best because of his foot and Mum does kiss Duncan and me sometimes, though Duncan's gone off it because of the Iron Lung, he says.

It is hotter than ever at the Bully Pond because of being sheltered and no wind. Even the squashed straw grass is hot under your bare feet. You can hear the sparrows messing about in the silver poplars up the river.

The Maori boy is wearing pants not togs, and he is diving in and skidding out again onto the rock to take a good run up from way back in the grass. This time he does a honeypot, skiting I bet. He goes way back on the grass and runs fast across the rock so's not to slip, then jumps as far as he can into the pond with his arms tight round his knees and shouts 'Yeh!', then comes up spluttering right in the deepest part of all. The sparrows spurt from the poplars and Charlie and Miri and me yell 'Yeh!' too and Bella is laughing and so's the man, but not so much.

He has black curly hair and is wearing short pants too.

Bel smiles at him and says, 'How does he know where the rock lies underneath?'

'My tribe have lived on this river for hundreds of years,' he says. 'We teach our children things.'

Bella stops smiling. The man shouts at the kid in the river. 'Come on, Joe. Out!'

Joe is spluttering and yelling and keeping afloat all at once. 'Why? We just got here.'

The man's hand smacks the air. 'Out.'

The kid's face moves.

'He's saying Shit,' says Charlie.

'You're not going because of us, are you?' says Bel.

The man doesn't say anything. He looks at Bel and shakes his head like Mum does when I drop things.

By this time Joe is back and slipping about on the rock and staring. He points at Charlie. 'He's only got one foot.'

'How do you know where the rock is underneath?' says Charlie.

'I'll show you,' says the boy and dives in, but Charlie knows it's No wings, no pond and Mum means it.

Joe splutters. 'Why didn't y' come? Can't y' even duck dive?'

'Not in my water wings.'

'Take them off.'

'No.'

'Why?'

'Mum says.'

'Is that y' Mum?'

'No. That's Bel.'

Joe heaves his bottom up onto the papa beside Charlie. 'Well, then?'

Charlie shakes his head. Joe looks at him. His eyes are brown and his hair is black.

'I suppose it's because of only one foot?'

'Yeah,' says Charlie, looking at me so I won't say it isn't.

'Did a shark eat it?'

'Yeah.'

'Hey, did y' hear that, Tam? This kid's foot got eaten by a shark.'

'What!' says the man and looks at Bel who is now sitting smoking on a bit of the rock where it's dry.

'Charlie,' she says, shaking her head and trying not to laugh, 'what a whopper.'

'*Liar, liar. Pants on fire,*' yells Joe and dives for miles and comes up grinning.

Miri and me are bobbing around and kidding about which of us is

47

in the deepest part, and yelling 'Look, I got a cockabully' when we haven't. They're hard enough to catch with a net even.

Joe wants to know more about Charlie's foot.

'So what did happen?'

'They cut it off. It went the wrong way.'

'Shit. Y' hear that, Tam. This guy says . . .'

'I heard him and shut up.'

'What'd they do with it after?' says Joe. 'The foot.'

No one has asked Charlie this before. 'I don't know.'

Tam is on his feet. 'Shut up, boy.'

'Why didn't you ask? I would've asked. Could've had it pickled, eh,' says Joe and sinks below the water as though he's drowning standing up.

Bella is laughing and choking on her cigarette and trying to stop laughing all at once.

'I'm sorry,' she says. 'It's just, it's just. Oh my God . . .' and hides her head in her frock and laughs. 'Terrible,' you can hear her say. 'Terrible.'

Tam takes the cigarette from her fingers, takes a long pull, then walks off the rock and stamps it into the sand with his foot.

I am bobbing about in my ring and Joe's towing Charlie about in his water wings. I wiggle my legs in the deep bit and watch as Tam comes back and sits beside Bel.

'You part-Maori or something?' he says.

Bel lifts her face all red and wet and blows her nose. 'No.'

'Must be.'

'Why?'

'No one but a Maori would think it was funny.'

'I don't, or rather I do . . .'

And now Tam is laughing and he and Bella are laughing like mad and grinning at each other.

'Poor little bugger,' says Tam.

Bella says, 'No. It's not like that.'

Tam offers her a roll-your-own and Bella takes it.

Now Joe's towing Charlie over to the bulrushes at the edge of the creek by the poplars. He parts the rushes, and what do you know, there's a canoe. It's brown, a dugout, waka, the Maoris call them. With seats and paddles and everything.

Miri and me are still sitting on the rock, and we can hardly believe it. It's like the baby in the Education Series lady. All hidden and tucked away, then suddenly, Wow, there it is.

Joe is up to his knees in mud and pushing, and Charlie's trying to help him but not getting far when Slam bang, Tam dives in over our heads and comes up beside them saying, 'I told you it's too heavy for kids.' He picks up Charlie in his water wings and dumps him in the canoe and Joe in his wet pants which are almost falling off by now and dumps him in the other seat. He gives Joe the paddle and one almighty heave from the back and the canoe glides out with Tam following.

'I'll stay in,' he yells at Bella. 'Currents.'

She nods.

Miri and I are shouting. 'Can I have a go, Joe? Hey Joe, can I have a go,' and Joe grins and makes faces at us like the pictures of Maori kids diving for pennies off the bridge at Whaka. He and Charlie go sailing up the river with Tam swimming beside and Charlie sitting there grinning like the Laird of Cockpen and holding on tight.

Then Charlie has a go with the paddle. Tam tells him what to do but he keeps going round and round in circles. When he's getting the hang of it more, Tam says to Joe, 'OK boy. What about the other kids?'

Miri and me shout and wave and the sparrows spurt out of the poplars again and a fish jumps, just a little one, but quite high. The canoe goes all wobbly when Joe stands up and Charlie hangs on like mad, still grinning, but not so much. Joe shouts louder than ever and points at the two of us sitting there in our sissy striped togs. 'It's my waka. I'll give the Maori girl a go, but not the pakeha,' and Tam yells, 'You'll do as I say, y' little bugger.' Bella laughs and Tam pretends to sink standing up like Joe did.

I think of *Sticks and stones may break my bones but words can never hurt me,* and it doesn't work any more than it ever does, which is never. I look at Miriama sitting there all happy and laughing and I think, 'Bugger.'

'You said Bugger,' says Charlie, still paddling and getting better.

I told you the Bully Pond was the best part of the Beach but it has never been as good as today. Me and Miri are still sitting there when around the corner from upstream comes another canoe! This one is a bit bigger and also made of wood but not a dugout. It's built, this one, not hollowed out, and the colour is rusty-red like woolsheds. It has two paddles and Duncan has the one in front and Mike Girlingstone from the Store has the back one, and they are paddling along fast as anything and Mike yells, 'Hey, you Maori boy, get that wreck out of our way. Shift!' and he is waving his paddle and Joe is on his feet and the dugout goes all wobbly again and then Duncan sees Charlie and yells, 'What you doing in that old dugout, Chas? You want fleas or something?' and Bella is up and yelling and so's everyone else by now, and the red canoe is going to bang straight into the dugout and I jump into the water in my tube to get Charlie.

Then Tam, who Duncan and Mike haven't even noticed is still in the water, grabs the back of the red canoe and shakes it like Patch Laing with a rat. Duncan sits down with a thud and Tam drags the red canoe right away from the brown one and he holds tight and leans one arm onto the canoe and he looks at Mike and Duncan and says, 'You nuts or something?' and Duncan gawks and so does Mike.

I hold out my arms to Charlie.

He says, 'Go away. I'm staying with Joe,' and then I see Bella's jumped in as well. She's kicked off her sandals and she's paddling about in the Bully Pond in her sand-coloured frock and she says to Tam, 'How about you and Joe shove off home?'

'Your river, then?'

'I don't give a toss whose river it is. I want to get out.'

Tam dives under the red canoe and comes up alongside her. 'Get one of the kids' towels.'

She shakes her head.

Tam takes Charlie who's gone all shivery and hands him to me. 'You're a natural, Charlie,' he says, and Charlie's cheeks puff out like General Sir Redvers Buller. 'See yer both tomorrow, Tam,' he says.

'OK,' says Tam and looks at Bella still paddling her legs to stay afloat. 'Tomorrow then?'

She shakes her wet head at both of them. 'I don't think my nerves would stand it.' Charlie and me and Miri say, 'Aw Bella, please,' and Duncan and Mike sit in the canoe looking silly and Miriama hops about on the rock and says, 'We'll have to come, Bella, because of my go in the canoe with Joe. Eh Joe?'

And Joe says, 'Yeah.'

But we don't. Miriama has gone into town with Mrs Laing to do a Big Wash and Stock Up. It's just Charlie and me mucking around with our Dinkies. Mum said wouldn't Miriama like to stay with us and Miriama said no. I don't care, but I'm getting a bit sick of it being just Charlie and me. Charlie cares so much about everything. He cares about the garage being under the orange flower and the hospital under the yellow one and getting it just in the right place and going brmm brmm louder on the corners when he changes gear and I say Aw cripes, Charlie, because I'm sick of it.

Mum is having a word, that's what she calls it, with Duncan on the verandah. Charlie doesn't hear. He wouldn't hear if a bomb went off.

'I'll have to tell Dad,' she says.

'OK,' says Duncan.

'And stop picking your feet while I'm talking to you.'

'OK.'

'If you say OK once more I'll scream. Now, start at the beginning. Where did you make the thing?'

'In the Girlingstones' shed.'

'How did you get the money?'

'Mike's delivery money. He's got tons.'

'So it's his canoe?'

'No. I made it. He just stood around and held things.'

'How did you get the wood?'

'Mike and I went in the truck with his dad to the warehouse for stores.'

'When!'

'The day after we arrived.'

You can tell from the way Mum's smoking that she's ratty. She's sucking quick and puffing smoke out like she hates it and grinding the butt into sand fierce as anything.

'I trusted you, Duncan. How could you do such a thing? No wonder I couldn't find you to help unpack. Even Charlie was helping.'

And me.

'And when you finally did appear, all you said was you'd been mucking about with Mike.'

'So I had.'

'*Duncan.*'

'You should've asked. "Mucking about where? What at?" '

No one says anything. Then Mum says cold as the milk billy in winter, 'Tell me exactly what you did.'

'Mike and I went to the timber yard which is right next door to the grocery warehouse and I'd worked out how much wood we needed and how many nails and screws and that, and Mr McCready told us a lot of what to do. But I'd got a book from the library called *How to Build a Canoe* and I knew a lot of it already. He said to give him a ring if we got stuck, but I didn't have to.'

'So Mr Girlingstone knew all about it?'

'Sort of. He thinks it's mine.'

'Why didn't you tell me? Dad?'

'Because you'd have gone on about sinking.'

'And Mr Girlingstone didn't.'

'He knew we wouldn't.'

'*Will* you stop picking your feet.'

Mum lights another cigarette, ducking her head down to it like she's hiding.

A gull flies high up and drops a pipi on the hard sand below to bust it, then flies up again and again, dropping it until it does, then eats the inside yuck. There's nobody on the beach. No one swims at low tide because of holes, and the rips are worse then too.

Charlie is flat on his front burrowing out an underground garage.

'So,' says Mum. 'Mr Girlingstone was to think you owned the canoe and that we'd given you and Mike and the whole enterprise our blessing. And if we had found out, then the canoe was to be Mike's, and as Mr and Mrs Girlingstone are responsible parents we were to . . .'

'She's not Mrs Girlingstone.'

'Will you be quiet!'

'Well, she isn't. Mike says. His mother's dead.'

'Was that the plan?'

'Yeah.'

'You could have drowned. Both of you. Why didn't you tell me? Why?'

'Dad'll fuss.'

'Yes, Dad will fuss. And so will I from now on. No more sneaking off for days on end.'

'What's sneaky about a canoe?'

'You didn't tell me.'

'Well, I have now,' says Duncan.

Mum looks as though she's going to bawl. 'Duncan,' she says.

Lorna

'The working title,' says James, 'is *Lust in the Dust*.'

Harry Laing's legs shoot out from beneath the deck chair, the heels of his sandals crack the verandah.

'In the what?' says Mrs Clements.

I say nothing. I am not in good odour with Mrs Clements, having, through incompetence and lack of attention to detail, arrived early for James's discussion of the script.

'Oh Lorna. You're not very good about time, are you?' she said.

'No.'

'Was your mother punctual?'

'Very.'

'Odd,' she said, puffing slightly at such divergence. 'I'll go and freshen up. Bella's just finishing the sandwiches. Don't go and help her. She's much happier beavering away on her own. I'm exactly the same. Just relax and enjoy the view.'

I stare at the heat haze shimmering against the Island, the glint of silver on the pale horizon, and wonder how many peasants have laboured how many hours to gather the flowers to crush the fragrance to make the scent that Mrs Clements wears. This is not the type of thought which gets you anywhere. Nevertheless it is the type I have when I am with Mrs Clements.

She returns drenched in essence of lavender, fluffs her skirts slightly and settles herself, comfortable and expectant as a broody hen. She leans forward.

'What a worry for you, dear, that business of Duncan and the Girlingstone boy . . .'

'Michael.'

'. . . and the canoe. What did Derek say?' She gives her chair a small intrusive jerk forwards. 'I always say Derek's such an honourable man, don't you agree?'

'Yes.'

'And what did he say.'

'He said he was disappointed.'

'I'm sure he was.'

And if you want any details Mrs Clements, I would like to suggest, but don't, why not ask Derek himself. There will be no further bulletins from me.

Derek was indeed disappointed. I can scarcely bear to look at him when the children 'let him down'. The very phrase defeats me. It is a favourite of Mrs Clements also. It surfaced last year when the newly appointed young organist at the Cathedral became pregnant and had to be dismissed from her post. Miss Lawson, confided Mrs Clements, 'had let down the dean'. The ropes and pulleys which ensured upright moral behaviour from those within his charge had failed him, had dropped him in the mire of another's turpitude. Bang went the dean.

I do not mean to be snide about Mrs Clements, much less Derek, though I realise I am. It is right and proper that Derek should be disappointed, both by Duncan's behaviour and my lack of supervision. I will do better, I promise. But oh, that face! It looked as though it had been modelled from warm plasticine and fingers had dragged lines downward before leaving the mask of desolation to harden. There are muscles called Something *dolorosa* which normally do this job. I have forgotten the name for the smiling ones, but *humorens* comes in somewhere.

Derek and I talked the subject through. We came to some con-
clusions.

I am to keep a timetable pinned up in the kitchen for Duncan to
write where he is going to be each day and with whom. I will check this
every night and Derek will re-inspect it at the weekends. I agree. I
promise. My careless trust is doubly reprehensible in the circumstances.
If Derek were not a decent man he would tell me with some force that
Duncan is my responsibility. As he is.

Mrs Clements is now revisiting old bones. Isabel, she tells me, won't
try. She is not going to mention how many times she has tried to get her
daughter to make the most of herself, to get out of those sludge colours,
try a new lipstick. *Coral Blush* or *Cherub Rose* perhaps? But will she? No
she won't. And it's not as though Mrs Clements hasn't tried. When she
thinks . . . She continues in this vein for some time.

'But Bella's getting better looking every day. A tan suits her, she has
a wonderful figure, moves well . . .'

'*Moves* well?'

'Yes. She swings along like some graceful . . .' Graceful what? Birds,
those symbols of freedom and grace, don't swing along when grounded.
Oyster-catchers scuttle, reef herons positively slouch. 'Some graceful
free spirit,' I say, realising too late that this makes no sense. 'And she has
amazing eyes. So clear you can see right through them.'

Mrs Clements says that the eyes are the window of the soul. She
adds that she can't see what help clear ones would be to a girl, and
besides . . .

'Bella,' I say firmly, 'glows with life. Even her hair is lustrous.'

Mrs Clements, after one startled glance, disagrees. Sometimes, she
confides, she can scarcely bear to look at her daughter. So dowdy. Of
course Harold's sisters were just the same. Etty, did I know Etty? Even
worse than Gretch, if you can imagine. And as for the twins.

She sighs deeply and changes tack. She is now on to James. James,
she tells me, her voice dropping to confide, has had a difficult life.

I am surprised to hear this. I should have thought that James, heir

56

to that beautiful property in the hills, had fewer problems than most men in the district. Look at him now, relaxing at the Beach for a month while Bob Jackson, the head shepherd at Rongomaha, looks after things. Certainly James put the rams out before he came down, but Bob Jackson is completely reliable and knows the place like the back of his hand. And, as James says, Bob can leave a message at the Store in case of flood, fire or famine. Added to which James goes up to Rongomaha once a week to check on his orchids.

Mrs Clements seems to be expecting some reaction to her previous comment.

'Oh?' I say.

'He's so good-looking, you see.'

'Ah.'

'Always has been. Ever since he was a little boy he's been besieged by girls. All the birthday parties, everything. Right through his life. It was just the same during the War. Oxford. Everywhere. And now, of course, it's impossible. Girls seem to lose all sense of anything, let alone decorum, when he is around. They just fling themselves on their backs and kick their legs in the air.'

'How terrible.'

'Yes,' says his mother with a sharp glance. 'Poor James.' A thought cheers her. 'Of course he has his interests, he's quite a polymath in his own way. You should see his library.'

My main memory of Rongomaha's library is after the Earthquake. All I can remember is a shamble of bound *Punches* and fallen plaster.

'Drama, theatre, the Napoleonic wars, Japanese prints,' she continues. 'He never stops. This cinema thing is new but you may be sure he will have read all about it in depth. James never does anything by halves. It's just the way he is. A born student. Sometimes I think he should have stayed on at Oxford. But then of course there's Rongomaha, and one wouldn't have wanted him to marry an English girl.'

Wouldn't one? I should have thought one might have been quite happy with some delicately nurtured English rose at Rongomaha.

'Some of them,' continues Mrs Clements darkly, 'don't *settle.*'
'Oh.'

On time and smiling come Jean and Miriama. Harry will be over soon. I suggest Miriama might like to play with Ann and Charlie. Miriama glances at Jean for confirmation, Jean nods, Miriama departs. Mother and child are as one.

'Tea,' calls Bella.

Mrs Clements remains seated. Someone will bring her both tea and sandwiches. She knows this.

James appears, complete with bulky manuscript, a pen, three coloured pencils and several folders. He moves beautifully.

'Are we all here?'

We nod to demonstrate existence.

'Right,' he says, 'I haven't had a chance to ask you, Harry. How did you get on at the Pa? Any starters for the bareback lark?'

'Yes. One of the older men, Wiremu Ropata, his son Tamati, and grandson, a boy about fourteen, a good rider apparently, called Joe – I don't have his surname at the moment.'

Bel leaps to her feet. 'More tea, Mum?'

'No, no, child. Not now. Don't interrupt.'

'Joe'll do,' says James. 'And what about money?'

'They won't accept money but they would be happy to accept koha.'

'And what's that. Money?'

Harry's face is stern. I feel an unexpected frisson. 'A gift,' he says. 'Koha.'

James nods. Makes a note. 'Right,' he says, with that considered emphasis which goes with manly handshakes and deals advanced or concluded: a bull bought, a coffin interred, something achieved. He looks straight at Harry.

'Now the next point I'd like to make, or rather find out. How keen are we all on this project?'

'We're not all here,' says Harry.

'What?'

'The Ropatas.'

'They will be this afternoon.'

'Then why don't you wait till this afternoon?'

'Oh for heaven's sake, Harry,' says Jean. 'We'll never get anywhere at this rate.'

I am surprised. Jeannie doesn't often surprise me. Well, well.

Harry tosses one hand to indicate apology, rejection or just get-on-with-it. Mrs Clements opens her sandwich and peers inside. 'No mustard I hope?'

Bella shakes her head. 'Egg.'

Mrs Clements tells us she is allergic to mustard but this we know already.

'I thought you didn't want to be part of our little frolic, Harry,' says James.

Harry leans back to smile. 'Good heavens no, I'm all for it.'

'And what about the bareback?'

'I wouldn't mind having a lick or two with the Ropata men.'

'It's not a question of not minding. However infantile the idea may seem to you, I happen to be very interested in the cinema, and Westerns in particular. Do you realise they've been making them for over thirty years? One of the first, *The Great Train Robbery*, was made in 1903. Unbelievable when you think of it. Double exposure, primitive but effective editing, intercutting. They're all there. In '03.

'Personally,' he continues, 'I regard Westerns as a major contribution to American art and culture, as integral a part of American folklore as the Odyssey to the Greeks, the Samurai warriors to the Japanese. All countries need their heroes, their invigorating legends, their myths. Give me Wild Bill Hickok over Alan A'Dale any day . . .'

'Wild Bill Hickok,' says Harry, 'was a murdering, cheating thug.'

James flicks a dismissive hand. 'But the poetry, the amazing history of the West. Sagas, man, sagas.'

He sees our faces and pulls himself together. 'Of course it's just a fun thing but it will take a lot of time and effort and teamwork. That's why I have to know how interested you really are.'

We are immensely interested. We are as keen as Mrs Clements' non-existent mustard and raring to go. We say so in different ways and with different emphases but there is no doubt about it. We are committed; even, no, especially Harry. The younger children trail around the corner in drooping togs for their morning swim, but they will have to wait while James tells us of *Lust in the Dust* written and directed by James K. Clements.

Miriama asks what's the K stand for, and James says Kingston. The children sit cross-legged beneath their sunhats, quiet as the field mice which creep into the baches in autumn. Even the flies are still.

James explains that his plot is not original. That there are only about twelve Western plots anyway, and that includes the pioneering themes. The wonder is that they have been able to do so much with the chase, the fist fight, the gun duel.

So it is his intention, his deliberate intention, to make a pastiche, a medley if we like, from every known convention or bit of business from past Wild West films. Not every one of course, but from stock incidents involving the usual stereotype characters. How many of us have read Zane Grey? 'Only you, Lorna? No one else? Well, what's your main memory?'

'They were always "redding up the camp".'

He looks at me. 'And what about *The Virginian*?'

Jean and I wave busily. We would love to read it again, we say, but how sad if he seemed less perfect, less truly chivalrous. 'Personally I never liked the girl,' I say, 'but remember when Trampas is disrespectful about her . . .'

'Yes, yes,' cries Jean, 'and the Virginian stands up and drawls, "Rise up now and tell them you lie."'

'I'm talking about the *film*,' says James crisply. 'Gary Cooper. Slow paced, but it has its own integrity and a real sense of time, place and people. Did none of you see it?'

Not a soul. And furthermore I don't want to. I have nothing against Gary Cooper but he is not the Virginian.

I think about the Virginian and how courageous and honourable he was. Noble even, in his passion for that spirited prig of a girl. Why are there no chivalrous heroes in books now? The War, I suppose, the disillusionment and despair for men who died like cattle. Or perhaps men have never been as chivalrous as the Virginian.

I'm not sure whether this makes things better or worse. I think of Derek.

James also is on to honour and I gather has been for some time. I watch him with belated attention as he expounds and extrapolates about the legends of the Wild West and male camaraderie and honour. I watch the sweeping gestures of his strong bare arms as he demonstrates the wide arc of the sky and the endless space of the prairies, and I think how apposite is the working title he has chosen. His long bony fingers demonstrate as he explains why you must always keep the last bullet for yourself in Indian country.

Mrs Clements hisses 'Sssh, darling,' but the children sit bemused in the warm sand and James avoids any mention of the verb to scalp.

All this I watch, and hear as well, and I come to a conclusion which I find confusing. I do not love James Kingston Clements. I'm not even sure that I admire him much. My feeling for him is simply lust. Excessive sexual desire is sometimes condoned, or almost, in the male sex, though never in Westerns. Even the villainous Trampas wants to marry Molly. In real life men possessed of strong libidos are called womanisers, gay dogs or ladies' men. All of which terms have a lilting sense of *joie de vivre* which is missing from the frenetic abbreviated slur, 'nympho'. Nympho is a term of contempt, and furthermore I'm not. Nor is there a madness in the blood. I merely wish to go to bed with James Clements.

It was different with Duncan's father. He was my reason for being, the pulse of my life. I longed to rush to the coast, snatch up the gun and join him when I heard he was dead. Words, I know, are easy, but can be true.

And there was the child. And at least I told Derek.

Bella is still offering egg sandwiches. She walks behind James who is in full flight, puts her hand briefly on the top of his head as if tempted to pat it.

'Of course we're not attempting *Ben-Hur*,' says James. 'There'll be no epic grandeur, no tumultuous crowd scenes. No cavalry charge, Indian raids on the circled wagons, any of that.'

'Such a good idea, the circle,' says Mrs Clements. 'I wonder who thought of it.'

'The Romans had Tortoises,' says Bella, saving the life of the last sandwich.

Her mother sniffs.

Bella doesn't bother to explain that she didn't mean pet Tortoises, nor indeed any Tortoise as such. That her Tortoise is an ancient Roman military term for a group of soldiers standing back to back beneath their shields with swords at the ready. She had thought the systems of defence slightly analogous so had mentioned it in passing and what had *Ben-Hur* got to do with things anyway?

This is one of the things which interests me about Bella. She has a still centre. She realises that explanations, let alone arguments, will not get her anywhere with her mother. Even more interestingly, she doesn't care. She lets it pass, is at ease with her Tortoises and other small pleasures and private delights. Can puff away irrelevant misunderstandings with hard-boiled-egg-scented breath and does so. She holds her fire.

'So – no wagons. What I plan to do is shoot a few scenes, location shots etc. to establish period, mood, basic situation, then straight into the action, the speed, the suspense. Of course it'll be tricky playing the lead as well, but I'm sure you'll get the hang of things, Bel. There'll be a few close-ups for emotional impact. For example there must be some of me when struggling against my bonds . . .'

'What bonds?' asks Mrs Clements.

'I'll tell you later when I give you the plot. But otherwise mainly long shots. Nothing fancy. We'll do the editing together. And obviously there'll be no last-minute cavalry charge.'

'Obviously,' says Mrs Clements.

'Nor, of course, sound. Miming, extravagant gestures will be required. Slightly ham of course but that's all part of the fun. Gustav Pauli's *Under the Southern Cross,* that's the style I'm after. Beautiful stuff, great camerawork, and made ten years ago. The sensible thing is to use the advantages we do have. The river for one. And the beach.'

Mrs Clements nods approval. Harry closes his eyes, Jean pokes him.

'We could have a shootout in the woolshed,' he says drowsily. 'Ted Clark wouldn't mind.'

James is impressed. He makes a note, thanks Harry and promises to check. There is a small reshuffling of behinds on beach chairs at Harry's contribution. A muted sense of prodigals returning to folds, a pulling together. The children, having expected excitement and found none, have drifted away, but the adults are all ears and James knows it.

'Advantages,' he says. 'Think of them.' Buoyed up by creative enthusiasm, he tells us the bones of the story, the kidnapping of Jeannie by the Indians at Devil's Canyon, the chase through the sage brush by the Sheriff and his posse. Maybe a shootout in the woolshed if he can fit it in and Ted's happy. It's all very open ended at this stage. Then Jeannie's recapture, followed by the betrayal of James the Sheriff from inside, his capture and trussing up by the Indians.

Do they have betrayals from inside in cowboy flicks? Jean and I are worried and say so. What about loyalty, camaraderie of the range?

'Who commits this felony?' says Harry.

'My half-breed Deputy. You.'

'Uh huh,' says Harry amiably. Any moment soon he's going to chew on a straw. 'Why?'

'Because you and I are both in love with Jeannie,' says James.

A flick of envy, bright as sequins and as ludicrous, slips past me. Is rejected. 'That makes sense,' I laugh. So does Harry. Jeannie smiles. She smiles too much.

'When do I come in?' says Mrs Clements. 'What about my gambling den? Where is it?'

I refrain from thinking Mrs C is an importunate old bore because I want to know too. It is high time the harlot with the heart of gold put in an appearance.

'That's easy,' says James to his mother. 'I'll hire the Settlers Hall.'

'Why would you need to hire it?'

'Because I have to transform it into your gambling den for a couple of days.'

'There's no need to hire it, darling. I'll speak to Sid Russell myself.'

You can see why I am ambivalent about Mrs Clements. She is a woman of natural authority and acquired position who uses it for the common good, who can take charge and handle responsibility. Can deal with things. She is also generous and is kind to children. At the same time she is a martinet who runs her daughter's life, or attempts to, who sees no reason why she should not bully her daughter and anyone else, including the caretaker of the Settlers Hall. But why should I be surprised? People of natural authority know they know best. It is part of the gift. If only Bella would *listen*.

James is now on to what happens next. It sounds good. Mrs Clements appears to be safely corralled behind the bar, away from the gambling den action, but I am all over the place. I see my spangled stockings, my tempting cleavage, my heels, all the appurtenances of louche behaviour. I have always enjoyed showing off, especially in front of men. I am good at it.

I compose myself. Unfold my bare legs, sit up straight, or as straight as you can in a canvas deck chair. I nod.

And the last scenes are even better. James has excelled himself. 'Having been betrayed by Harry here,' he explains, his eyes gleaming, 'our hero is dragged to the river. No, on second thoughts, he will be trussed up and his horse led, then Harry and one of the Indians lash him to a post near the Bully Pond and depart leaving him struggling against his bonds. This is where the close-ups come in. You know how the tide rips up that creek?'

We do. We do indeed. To tell you the truth, my scalp crawls.

'Then what?'

'There'll be a chance for some great camerawork, Bel. Shots of the incoming tide, cutting back to me. Back to the tide. A terrific build-up of tension, and quite easy to fake.'

Bella can see it too. 'Yes,' she says.

'So. There I am, ravaged, desperate, half drowned – there's a bit which I think might be quite telling, when my hat floats away . . .'

'Your white one?' squeaks his mother.

'. . . just before Cantering Kate here and the Indian lad arrive on their ponies to rescue me,' smiles James.

I smile back. 'Then what?'

James is gathering his papers. He looks up in faint surprise. 'Jeannie and I ride off into the sunset, of course. And by the way, Devil's Canyon where Jeannie's abducted by the Indians. That gorge at the top of the valley by the Bull Paddock'll do beautifully, won't it, Bella?'

'You mean beyond the caves? We can't ride up through the bush track. Too narrow.'

'We'll come up the back way, Buck Louse. No bush in Westerns.'

James often calls Bel Buck Louse, or Buck for short. It dates from the time when Bel was small and James told her she didn't have the brains of a buck louse and Bel insisted she did.

Her smile is less frequent than James's but just as good. 'If you want a hideout there's always the glow-worm cave.'

'Yes. Lighting would be hell though. In any case we'll all have to spend a few nights at Rongomaha. That'll be all right, won't it, Mum? We can bunk down in the shearers' quarters.'

'Oh, that won't be necessary,' says Mrs Clements, 'there's plenty of room in the house.' A thought, smaller than a man's hand and less substantial, crosses her face. 'Well, not all of you, perhaps.'

Bella lifts her head, then returns her attention to her thumb which she suspects may have a splinter.

The thought of Rongomaha appeals to me. I can see no reason why we should not stay a few nights in the hills. It would make a change, and the children will love it and I won't have to cook. I'll help Bella, of course, but Rongomaha had electricity installed several years ago. All that will be involved is amiability in a large cool kitchen as we fling a leg of mutton into a real oven instead of a wood-burning range, turn a switch rather than light a lamp.

And the food. Good farm-killed mutton, like that from Rongomaha, dissolves in the mouth. My mother used to practically salivate when offered farm meat. She was a country girl herself and behaved like a White Russian emigrée deprived of her rightful heritage at the mention of it. Butchers' meat was a very different animal.

Rongomaha is a glorious place. Sometimes I think if I lived there I might learn to be good again, like Captain Stanhope of C Company in *Journey's End*. Shattered by three years in the trenches and virtually destroyed by drink, he dreams that perhaps, just perhaps, after it's all over, he could get away somewhere, could stop drinking and become a decent man once more. Only thus would he become worthy of the love of his topping girl (another Molly) who waits at home.

He doesn't of course. It is a heart-breaking story, and the comparison is not valid. I must not confuse tragedy with self-indulgence. Besides, I'm not sure I want to pull myself together, even if I could. It would be a case of changing a great deal more than my spots. Nevertheless there is something about Rongomaha which induces in me a wish to improve.

The homestead has not been there for ever. It just looks as if it has. There is calm and deep silence beneath large deciduous trees. Copper beeches, elms, an oak or two surround dappled swards, and I mean just that. The house is wooden and the verandahs are wide. There is a dovecot, delphiniums, a croquet lawn and vistas down to the sea. Mrs Clements and her family are surrounded by peace and plenty.

I won't go on about the '31 Earthquake. Reminiscences of such horrors from those who were there are deeply interesting if you also were present and can share the emotions and memories aroused, otherwise less so. Nevertheless I need to explain the immensity of my debt to Bella.

At the time of the Earthquake the children and I were at Laing's Point as usual. Derek was working in town, as were many other of the men, including Harry Laing.

Earthquakes are more terrifying than flood, fire or cyclones, none of which I have experienced, but still I know. The ground beneath does writhe and wrench, your heart does stop, giant hands do seize. Cars can and do disappear down chasms in roads. And the noise, dear God, the noise of a big one is the tearing roar of a world gone mad.

Charlie was a small baby, asleep in his pram by the water tank, when it happened. I can't remember my getting to him, what I had been doing before, anything. Just snatching him and sprinting beyond the range of the booming, lurching tank. Or trying to. I was knocked over, tried again, fell once more. Charlie was crying, and not only Charlie. People rushed from Laing's Point and from all the baches along the beach. Some floundered in from what was left of the sea. Screaming for Duncan and Ann, I grabbed Jeannie. 'They were with you. Where? Where?'

She looked at me blankly, sobbing, clutching her child as another tremor began.

'No,' she cried. 'No!'

I shoved Charlie at her and ran inside our fibrolite bach. Its timbers were groaning. Chairs rushed across the floor towards me, a half-finished jigsaw slid from the tilting table to meet jars of bottled plums cascading from kitchen cupboards. There was no one there, no one at all, just Patch Laing shivering and urinating in a corner. I tugged him outside, and ran senseless and whimpering towards the Clements' bach.

Looking back I see my memories as a dream, a vision of live children and Bella. Clutching Annie under one arm and dragging Duncan with the other, she stumbled from the Clements' damaged bach. Clouds of dust rose around them as the swaying chimney collapsed. Bricks fell as they ran, chasing them.

They were alive. My children were alive, and Bella had saved two of them. I can't remember many details after that.

Nor can I remember when rumours of a tidal wave began, but it was easy to see why they did. The day was humid and hot, the sky Gethsemane dark. The sea disappeared as we watched, its waters sucked back almost to the Island.

The Clements and Ted Clark from his homestead along the beach took charge. Mrs Clements, large, serene and completely in control, took a roll call. Heads were counted, terrors stayed, women reassured and permission to enter their houses, even for a moment, refused.

A small redhead stood clutching himself. Mrs Clements pointed to a tamarisk.

'Do you want to be squashed flat, Jimmy?'

'No.'

'Then go here.'

All he needed was the voice of authority. Someone to tell him what to do.

There were about forty of us holidaymakers turned refugees, including ten men. Our behaviour ranged from jittery terror to frozen calm. Mrs Clements told Jimmy's mother to pull herself together and help Mrs Stevens, who had six and could use a hand.

The telephone line from the Store was dead; the road to town, they said, blocked completely. We watched the astonishing sea, or lack of it, its absence as frightening as aftershocks. 'Tidal wave,' we murmured. 'Tidal wave.'

I don't know whose decision it was that we must leave. The Clements' presumably, or Ted Clark who farms along the far end of the beach. We would all go up the hill to Rongomaha. James set off to inspect the road, the Pontiac piled with shovels. Hours later he reappeared. He had made it but only just, had alerted the head shepherd and his wife, and returned immediately in the farm truck. He and Ted ferried us up the hill in relays. I remember noticing that the Maori Pa seemed deserted.

We drove across the Rongomaha cattle stop to peace of a sort and stillness, and no sea at all. The birds were settling for the night; starlings whirled in the air as Bob Jackson and his wife and Claude the rouseabout ran to meet us. I can see Claude now, old and small and muttering to himself as he ran.

We slept outside. The house might not be safe, nor the woolshed. I can't remember food or lack of it, just lying beneath the black sky with sleeping children and no Derek and aftershocks all night.

Next morning Bel disobeyed instructions and entered the house, got the wood-burning range going and produced tea and toast for everyone. The children discovered the ripe apricot trees and, convinced that communal camping was the best fun anyone had ever had, ran about amongst shattered parents. Charlie slept most of the time. Duncan, I remember, was wonderful. He knew Dad was all right.

The aftershocks continued for days but it is the peace I remember most, the feeling that the world, like the starlings, had settled once more. Like a large and tranquil woman, Rongomaha had come forward, opened her arms and welcomed us.

Bumping up the rough track from the gate comes a Morris filled with Rowans.

'Oh Gawd,' says James. 'Well, at least we've finished.'

Garth toots the horn, Midge waves. There is someone in the back seat.

James lopes off to meet the uninvited guests who pile out of the car with greetings and instructions about how Cousin Phoebe mustn't worry for an instant, that Midge has brought their own picnic but it was such a lovely day, real beach weather wasn't it, and seeing as James hadn't been able to come up last week and Angus had been so disappointed they, or to be exact Midge, had taken the bull by the horns and popped down on spec. And, for goodness sake, what were we all doing sitting around on such a lovely day? We should be having a swim and why didn't we all go right now? The littlies were panting with the heat, weren't they? The littlies, pulled back by the renewed action and slightly bewildered, say yes. Midge asks Charlie how he is. She always makes a beeline towards him to deliver herself of this inquiry. Charlie replies he is OK and how is Midge? Midge replies she is very well thank you and isn't Charlie lovely. Charlie looks at her thoughtfully and scratches the crotch of his knitted green and white togs. I enjoy small children in bathing togs, their pot bellies are endearing.

Garth Rowan is now introducing his cousin Angus from Shropshire. Angus Rowan is an attractive-looking man of average height, fairish but not blond, he stands ramrod straight and looks us in the eyes. We look back at his sharp blue ones, his confident stance, his fair moustache, the punched leather patterns on his gleaming brown shoes. Angus doesn't look like a dim cousin from Home. He is one of those men about whom you find out quickly. I do not mean that he is boastful, but when we ask him he tells us all. That he comes from a village near Wenlock Edge. That he has recently retired from a cavalry regiment having decided that a peace-time army career is a dull business after the real thing, and that he has accepted Garth and Midge's longstanding invitation to come out and have a look around New Zealand with a view to trying his hand at farming.

'Where?' asks Harry.

Angus smiles his friendly smile and says he has no idea at this stage but he likes what he has already seen. Some of it, he confides, looks to be what his father would have called beautiful cavalry country.

James says that if Angus was in the cavalry, presumably he can ride.

Angus chomps his moustache. 'Yes.'

James explains his need for bareback riders and Angus says he'd be happy to try. That he used to fool about without a saddle as a boy, of course. That he'd like another crack.

Marshalled by Midge and farewelled by Mrs Clements, who never ventures onto the beach, we head for a swim.

The sea is perfect, as it has been for weeks, its blues translucent, its foam whipped white, its temperature refreshing. Crisp but welcoming you could call it. A crisp sea.

Ducking, diving, shrieking, in ages from five through fifty we swim together. I keep my eye on Charlie. There are rips at this beach, even at high tide. Where's Duncan? I realise I can't remember where he is meant to be, let alone is.

We trail back. Midge insists that we pool our resources and why don't I hop through the fence and find something, anything, a loaf of bread would do, and we can all have a picnic on Mrs Clements' couch grass. The Laings decline, we don't.

Angus sits in the sand surrounded by food and flies. His bare feet are white as snow, their fine hairs sleek and dark as he tells Bella and me about Shropshire which is his county. He is, he tells us, a Shropshire Lad and do we happen to know the poetry of A.E. Housman? We tell him we do and he is pleased. He talks to us with ease and charm. I like him and so does Mrs Clements.

I also sense that Midge's assumption of command does not please her. Mrs Clements, like most of us, prefers to be captain of her own ship. And besides, the Rowans are mean as church mice and have legs on their stomachs from crawling. I know this because she has told me so. Call that a ham and egg pie, I hear her thinking. Half the size and not a patch on hers (or rather Bella's). However, youngish male cousins from Home are welcome, and Angus shows every sign of shaping up well.

'Thank you,' he says, handing up his plate. 'I should like another hard-boiled egg.'

Around the corner come two Maori men, and a boy about Duncan's age. Bella and Charlie leap up in welcome.

Mrs Clements lifts her head, cocks it slightly to one side.

'Yes?' she says.

Ann

We've been to the Bully Pond with Bella twice more, and Tam and Joe
have been there both times but Duncan and Mike not at all. Duncan
said the whole thing had got busted by Bella telling on them, and he
and Mike aren't allowed to take the canoe on the river unless Dad or Mr
Girlingstone are there. Ask yourself, says Duncan. The whole thing
stinks and who was that Maori kid anyhow? I said Joe, and he danced
around shouting Slow Joe, Slow Joe, laughing till Charlie punched him
and he got such a surprise he didn't hit back.

Joe calls Charlie 'Boy'. Charlie shivers all over he's so mad about
him. We have good times mucking about at the Bully Pond: mud-slides
on the papa rock, catching bullies, paddling the waka and duck diving.
Bella and Tam swim when we're in, otherwise they just talk and smoke
and laugh.

So Charlie is pretty excited to see the Ropatas. The last of his bacon and
egg pie falls down his bare front as he scrambles up.

'Joe,' he yells. 'Tam. Come in, come in,' but they're there already, us
being outside.

Bella is thanking them for coming and shaking hands. She asks
Tam if this gentleman is his father and he says yes and she says I'm
Isabel Clements. Tam says we know that, and there's more handshakes.

James Clements is also jumping about shaking hands and asking names. Ropata, he says, Ropata. Tam's father is called Wiremu Ropata. Joe's second name is Ropata too. His mother died when he was six.

'Died?' says Charlie, and I say yes, and we both stare at Joe because we don't know any other kids whose mothers have done this except Annette Ferris round the corner at home. Joe sticks his tongue out and we stop staring but it's still interesting.

'Can I have a go with your shanghai?' says Charlie.

'No,' says Joe. 'Where's the Maori girl?'

I say 'What?' and Charlie says 'Who?' and then I think does he mean Miri, so I shut up. Charlie never shuts up. 'What Maori girl?' he says.

'Miri,' says Joe.

'Miri's not a Maori,' says Charlie. 'It's just her father.'

'She's next door,' I say, and Joe jumps through the fence. Charlie hops through too but not me. I'm not going.

'Harry Laing told us to come,' says Tam. 'Where is the man? Running on Maori time?'

Mr Clements laughs Ha ha and says, 'Come and meet my mother,' and everyone is shaking hands again. Mrs Clements says how good of them to come and starts telling Mr Ropata and Tam all about the film and everyone is nodding and smiling. Mr Ropata is smaller as well as older than Tam, and he carries a carved stick to lean on. His hat has a duck feather in it and his legs are bandy.

Mrs Clements says won't they sit down and that she was expecting them later.

'It's low tide later. Good for pipis,' says Mr Ropata, lifting his stick and smiling.

Mrs Clements says, 'Oh.'

'Hop over and tell Mr Laing his friends have arrived, would you Annie?' calls Bel. Mr Clements waves a hand and says, 'Of course, of course.'

Mr Laing is in his back room. There is nothing there but him and his desk and a chair and books, and he is just sitting there staring straight ahead. The sun comes through the window in stripes like from the cloud with Jesus on it saying *I am the light of the world.* I knock and say, 'Are you busy, Mr Laing?' because he looks a bit funny.

He swings around and smiles and says, 'Busy? Never. Just thinking.' I tell him about the Ropatas and he says, 'Already? Good on them. Thanks, Annie,' and pulls himself up, grinning.

'Forward to the lace counter,' he says, and drops down till he's level with me and says, 'You're a good girl, Annie. You know that? Straight as a die like your mum.' Then he rubs my hair and goes.

No one has ever said I am like Mum before.

Miri and Charlie and Joe are playing Maori stick games out the back with Bel's kindling. Miri is better than Charlie. 'Gee, you pakehas are useless,' says Joe, and Miri laughs and her hair bangs about even more.

'He's only five,' I say. 'Give me a go.'

I get quite fast, but Joe's quicker. 'Slow down a bit,' I say, 'till I've got the hang of it.'

'You ought to see the little kids at the Pa, they can lick me easy,' says Joe. 'You should come to the Pa, Miri. See them.'

'You got to be asked. Dad says.'

'Next time he comes, you come too.'

Miri says, 'Gee,' and giggles.

'Me too, man, me too,' says Charlie.

'I can't have pakehas lying around all over the Pa,' says Joe, and goes on telling Miri all about the piano and guitars and the meeting house and the marae and chickens and puppies and pigs even.

'Gee,' says Miri again.

Charlie stands up and hops for the fence. 'I don't want to see your sweaty old Pa anyhow.'

Liar, liar, pants on fire, yells Joe.

'Nor me,' I yell, and jump through after Charlie who's swishing his head about to show he doesn't care.

Mr Clements has got to the part in the story where he's tied up near the Bully Pond and the tide is roaring in and Mum is riding, riding to save him, and so is Joe.

'Where is that boy?' says Mr Clements. 'He should be here. Hop over would you, Duncan?' And he does.

'Is Joe going to be in the film?' says Charlie, and Mr Clements says, 'Yes, yes of course,' and Charlie says, 'Shit.'

'Why's Joe going to help save the Sheriff?' asks Mr Laing. 'He's one of the Indians, isn't he? Dark, swarthy, eyes too close together?'

'Yes, but he's seen the light. Bad case of hero worship, I'm afraid,' says Mr Clements. 'Contracted while I've been their prisoner.'

'Ah,' says Mr Laing. 'So the boy's a traitor? A kupapa?'

'No, a loyal Maori.'

Mr Ropata and Tam and Mr Laing laugh.

But not Joe. He says he's not going to do it. He doesn't mind the bareback, but if he's an Indian he's not going to rescue a pakeha. Not if he's an Indian. He stands there with his legs apart and arms folded like Duncan and says, 'No.' Everyone goes quiet. I can see Mrs Clements' eyes sticking out and Mrs Rowan's and everyone huffing and puffing. Mr Ropata bangs his stick on the verandah and says, 'Come on, boy. This is just pretending,' but he is laughing inside I can see. Mr Laing and Tam are not bothering to keep it inside and nor is Bella. The Englishman says how would it be if he rode to rescue James with Mrs Hopkins, and Mum says Lorna, please. Mr Clements says no, that wouldn't be nearly as dramatic. Mr Laing says it would be a damn sight more likely though, and why pick on Joe.

'This is my film,' says Mr Clements. 'And I'm directing it.'

'What's the trick in bareback riding?' says the Englishman, and Tam says, 'Taking the saddle off first.' Bella laughs and Mum, but not Mrs Clements.

The Englishman, who's called Angus, says, 'Right. How about my first lesson later this afternoon?' Mr Ropata says no, it's a good low tide

75

and the pipis won't wait and maybe they'd better be getting along. They could ride over tomorrow afternoon maybe. Angus says, 'Excellent.'

All this time Joe is looking ratty and standing close to Tam and Mr Ropata. People are getting up and sitting down, and Mrs Rowan just keeps on talking like she does all the time.

We all want rides and start asking Mr Ropata. Mrs Clements says of course not. Charlie whispers she won't be there anyway because her legs swell up on the beach and maybe we'll get a go. Yippee.

Then there's handshaking again and the Ropatas go. Bella and Mr Laing and us kids walk down to the yellow truck with them and they shoot down to the beach, rattle rattle, brmm, brmm.

'What are you going to do with that wretched child, James?' Mrs Clements is saying when we get back.

'Forget it, Mum. It'll work out.'

'I hope you know what you're doing. They seemed pretty uppity to me.'

'Let's go down and help them, fellas,' says Bella.

Mrs Clements says, 'Bella', and Bel says, 'Why on earth not?'

We go down to the hard sand where the yellow truck's parked with all the gear, buckets and sacks and stuff, and the Ropatas mucking about.

Bel goes up to Tam and says, 'Can we help?' Tam looks at Mr Ropata and he's not laughing at all. He shrugs and heads off for the sea with Joe. His legs are more bandy than ever in short pants.

Bel says, 'Doesn't he want us?' and Tam says, 'Ask him,' and takes her hand.

'Ouch!' she yells, and Tam drops it like a hot potato. 'What the hell?' he says.

Bel's got a splinter of wood in her thumb from when she was stoking the range the other day and she can't get it out. 'Give us it,' says Tam and squeezes her thumb between his thumbnails.

'*Caramba*,' yelps Bel.

'Do you want it out or not?'

'Yes, yes, go on.'

He tries again and you can see it hurts like mad, and finally Bel goes Aaah and out comes a big black splinter all covered in pus.

Charlie likes it when they pop out. 'Give us a look. Wow.'

Tam stands there grinning. 'What a fuss, woman,' he says. 'My great grandfather would have eaten the lot of you.'

Bel grins back. 'Not me. Not fat enough.'

'The leaner the sweeter,' he says, taking her hand again and turning it over. 'Crunchy little fingers and all. What's that Englishman doing here?'

'He thinks he might like to try farming.'

'Good on him. I must show him my part of the Ropata holding sometime. All three bloody acres of it.'

Bel doesn't say anything.

Charlie unstraps his ski pole and hops. Charlie can hop for miles, but gathering pipis is tricky for him. You have to squat in the waves and he keeps getting knocked over, so he punts around on his bottom.

Joe doesn't talk to him, or Mr Ropata. They just keep digging for pipis and throwing away the small ones and not saying anything. Nor does Miri.

Collecting pipis is good fun. You can feel the pipi trying to dig deeper as you tug on its shell. Sometimes they get away, but not often if you hang on tight and pull like mad. Sometimes when you throw it in the sack the big white tongue it's been digging with is still hanging out and it slides back so quick and easy. You wouldn't think there'd be room.

Mum won't cook them though. They're Maori food, she says, like muttonbirds and sea eggs.

Mrs Clements comes next afternoon to borrow *The Story of San Michele* which Mum can't find. Mrs Clements says don't worry. That it doesn't sound her cup of tea really, but everyone's going on about it and she thought she might give it a go. '*Why* are Maoris so useless about time?' she says.

'I suppose they're not panicked by clocks. No tick, tick, ticking inside,' says Mum, coming up from under the bed, covered with dust and holding the book. 'I'm useless too, remember.' She whacks the book and hands it over.

'But at least you *care*. They don't. They were meant to be here at three.'

'It's only half past.'

'Half past is half past.'

'Look,' I say, pointing. And there they are, all of them, Mr Ropata with the feather in his hat, and Tam and Joe sitting up on his pony which is called Jackie.

Jackie and the two bigger horses, a black and a brown, are stamping their hooves and swishing their tails and moving their backsides from side to side and snorting like horses do. The harness jingles and Patch Laing makes little dashes at their hind legs and backs off quickly.

Everyone from the Point is there except Mrs Clements who is watching from her kitchen window. Duncan and Mike are leaning against the fence and pretending they're not watching. All the Laings are there, Miri with her mouth open and Mrs Laing trying to shut Patch up and Mr Laing just standing. Charlie is there, and Mum by now, and Mr Clements and Bel and Angus. The Ropatas and their horses are just inside the gate by the rubbish heap. The flies have disappeared, with the snorting and jingling, I suppose, but it's good anyhow.

Tam and Joe jump off their horses. Mr Ropata climbs down slowly.

'Lesson one,' says Tam. 'Saddles off,' and Angus laughs.

Off come the saddles but not the bridles and they're all piled up against the fence and down we go to the beach, Charlie sulking because he wants a ride.

The tide is out, stretching for miles, and the sand as hard as it can get.

Away go the men and Joe, their horses charging off towards the rocks, the men gripping tight with their legs like they're glued on. The horses seem to get longer as they gallop, their manes and tails thin in the wind. They race through the shallows with water spouting, the men yelling and whooping like in Cowboy and Indian flicks at the Cosy in town, and sometimes here at the Settlers Hall. Then they wheel around at the rocks and race back and we're all saying, 'C'n I have a go?', all jumping about and Duncan and Mike as well.

We don't get one, though, not even Duncan and Mike who have before, often.

'You going to ride in them?' says Tam, pointing at Angus's pants.

'What else?'

'Pretty flash aren't they? Get dusty.'

'Yes,' laughs Angus. 'I notice you don't overgroom your horses.'

'What's "grmm"?' says Charlie.

'Maybe the Indians didn't either,' says Tam. 'Give you a leg up.'

Angus shakes his head and jumps up quickly. The horse, Tam's black one called Rewi, is away like a bomb and everyone's yelling to Angus to grip, and Angus is doing it, you can see, all the way down to the rocks. On the way back the horse shies and Angus comes a cropper outside Colonel Holdaway's cottage and lies still. Rewi turns round and trots back to Tam and everyone tears up the beach fast as they can. Bel gets there first, then Tam.

'I'm fine, fine. Just a bit winded. Right as rain,' says Angus and sort of crawls up.

'Why didn't you show him how before he started?' Bel snaps at Tam.

'Those pants gave me the breeze up. I thought he could ride.'

'He can ride. Bareback's different.'

'How the hell do you know?'

'All kids ride bareback.'

'Then you can help Charlie's mum save the Sheriff. Joe'd be pleased.'

'I'm the cameraman.'

'Woman.'

'Have you any objection?' says Bel, and they're really mad at each other, you can tell.

Mr Clements is fussing around Angus who's still saying, 'Quite all right. Quite all right.' Mr Ropata and Joe sit on their horses and don't say anything.

Then Angus has another go on Rewi, and another and another, and Mr Ropata says he's a natural. Tam and Joe don't say anything until the end when they're up at Mrs Clements' house and saddling up. Tam tightens the girth on Rewi and says, 'If you're serious about this bareback business you lot should come down the coast to the Races next weekend. You'll see bareback there that'll curl your hair, won't they, Dad?'

'Only two races.'

'Whole truckload's going from the Pa. There'll be a hangi after.'

'A hangi. A real one?' says Miri. 'With stones?'

'No other sort,' says Tam.

'What's a hangi?' says Angus, rubbing his arm.

'Maori oven,' says Mr Laing. 'Food cooked underground on hot stones. Not to be missed.'

Angus says, 'Well, let's not.' And we're all agreeing and wanting to go and Joe's still on his pony not saying a word. Mr Ropata says, 'If you would like to come you would be welcome. The races are open to all.'

'It's the racing you should see,' says Tam. 'You'd get some great shots there, Bella.'

Bella nods.

'The sundering gallop by the thurderous murf,' says Mr Laing, but no one laughs.

So then everyone is thanking the Ropatas again and they canter off. Mr Ropata waves his hat.

'They went thatta way!' yells Mr Clements, but that one doesn't work either.

Mrs Clements is having a rest in her bedroom. You can hear little puffing snores and sometimes a whistle.

'Let's have a look at that arm, Angus,' says Bella.

'No, no. Just a scratch.'

'It's bleeding. It'll mess up your jodhpurs. Come on.'

Angus rolls up his sleeve. 'They're messed up already.'

'Let me,' says Mum. 'Flesh wounds to an ex-nurse are like trumpets to an old war horse.'

'I'll leave you to the expert,' says Bel, laughing.

'No, no,' says Angus. 'This is serious stuff. Stay and hold my hand, sing me comforting songs, calm my nerves. Not Housman. Not much comfort in Housman.'

'Tell us Cam-paspee, Bel,' says Charlie who likes the bit about the arrows.

'Campaspe only comes with cuddles. You know that, Charlie,' says Bel, and Charlie hops on her knee.

Bel hugs him and says,

> *Cupid and my Campaspe play'd*
> *At cards for kisses; Cupid paid:*
> *He stakes his quiver, bow, and arrows,*
> *His mother's doves, and team of sparrows;*
> *Loses them too; then down he throws*
> *The coral of his lip, the rose*
> *Growing on's cheek (but none knows how);*
> *With these, the crystal of his brow,*
> *And then the dimple of his chin;*
> *All these did my Campaspe win:*
>
> *At last he set her both his eyes –*
> *She won, and Cupid blind did rise . . .*

'What a pig of a lady!' I say. 'You didn't say before about his eyes.'

'Why'd she want his eyes?' says Charlie. 'What'd she do with them?'

'Maybe she wanted to pickle them, like Joe and your foot,' says Bel, and she and Charlie laugh like mad.

'What?' say Mum and Angus.

'Nothing.'

Bel and Angus and me are doing a jigsaw. It is called *Crumplecot Cottage* and is a proper wooden one, quite old, with a thatched cottage with a garden and two ducks on a lawn. I always start with the ducks, Bel starts with the hollyhocks and Angus starts on the edge like Dad does. We had another wooden one once called *Lady Betty's Bunfight* with men and ladies in wigs but it got lost.

Angus tells Bella that she has the most beautiful hands he has ever seen.

'Lucky old me,' says Bella, sounding sniffy.

James comes from his bedroom, stretching and holding a piece of paper in his hand. He picks up the piece with the smaller duck's behind on it, the one I've been looking for, and drops it into its place. 'Listen,' he says, and starts reading.

Programme for one of the First Maori Race Meeting at Otaki 1868
Come, come, notice to all. This notice is to all friends in the East, in the West, in the North, in the South –
Oh friends, Listen. Horse races will be held at Otaki. These races will be run under the Patronage of the King of the Maori People.

Stewards of the Races
Chairman – Enabia Te Waro and his friends.
Starter – Hoai te Waru and his friends.
Clerk of the Course – Hohepa Te Hana.
Clerk of the Scales – Tuia Hoanui.
Handicapper – Honoiti Ranapui and his wife.
Treasurer – Hiwi Piahana.
Secretary – Puke Te Ao.

Rules of these Races.
1. Men owning horses and wishing to enter them must deposit money

in the hands of the Secretary.

2. Don't bring any drink to these races.

3. Men who have taken too much drink will not be allowed on this course. If any disobey this rule he will bring the whip of the club down upon him.

4. No girls will be allowed to ride as jockeys in these races.

5. Jockeys must wear trousers in all events.

6. No jockey must knock any other jockey off his horse or touch the reins of any other jockey, or strike any horse other than his own, or swear at or threaten any other jockey.

7. Any other jockey breaking this rule will be driven from the course if he does not pay 20 shillings to the Treasurer.

8. You must not change the name of the horse, or suppress the fact of a win at any other race meeting. You can be expelled or fined not more than 50 shillings if you break this rule.

9. Persons allowed to see these races must not say rude words to the Stewards or swear at jockeys who do not win or otherwise behave improperly.

Mail Print.

'What a gem,' says Angus. 'And to think that's less than seventy years ago. "The whip of the club", "trousers must be worn in all events". Beautiful, beautiful. Where on earth did you find it?'

'In a tin box at Rongomaha. I knew Father had it somewhere. It was one of his party pieces.'

'Genuine, you think?'

'Oh yes. I imagine so. He used to declaim it occasionally. You remember, Bel?'

'Yes.'

'Well, they've certainly come a long way in that time,' says Angus.

'No they haven't,' says Bel. 'Not as regards their land.'

'Oh for God's sake, Buck. Anything more phoney than someone sitting on that land moaning about the deprived. They wanted to sell,

Grandfather leased it first, gave them a fair price, and they sold.'

'It's not as simple as that.'

Angus says, 'Why Buck?'

'Short for Buck Louse,' says Bel.

'Good heavens. Ah, here's a beak,' says Angus and drops it into my duck.

'You realise that it's a Maori Race Meeting, Angus?' says Mrs Clements.

'Yes, I thought that's what would be interesting.'

Mrs Clements says that perhaps it's difficult for Angus to understand, not being born and bred here, but there is a certain something about the whole thing, not James's film of course, they must have the men from the Pa for that, but she is not happy about other aspects. There's something a bit too casual about the whole thing for her taste. The race meeting will be a very mixed bag and she's not sure she will go.

Charlie looks up from his comic. 'What's a mixed bag?'

Mrs Clements gives a sort of laugh and says, 'Not now darling,' then asks Angus if he'd like to stay for a meal.

He says he would like to very much but how can he let Midge know?

'The Store has a telephone. You'll take a message, won't you, Ann?' says Mrs Clements. 'Mr Girlingstone will ring them.'

I say yes, especially as Mrs Clements always gives you a penny for messages, but Angus says, 'No, no, let's walk. Come and show me the way, Bella.' And off they go.

Mrs Clements wriggles her bottom further into her chair. She smiles and says, 'Well.'

James looks up from the paper.

'Such a nice young man. What age do you think he'd be?'

James says, 'For God's sake, Ma,' and goes on reading.

'I think I might come to the race meeting after all.'

'It's a hell of a road.'

'Twenty years ago, possibly. Not now.'

'It didn't exist twenty years ago.'

'Nonsense. We used to ride over for tennis with the Bartons.'

'Yes, and you'd still be better off on a horse. Pot holes you could bury a pig in. Hair-pin bends. Shingle.'

'I'd have you know I was one of the first girls in the Bay . . .'

'. . . to get your licence. I know, but that doesn't make the road any better. I'm taking the truck.'

'I shall drive the Pontiac.'

'Good. There's always some child who's car sick.'

Mrs Clements says if they get car sick they'd be far better off in the truck. They can just lean over the side, and besides they'll be in the fresh air. However, there is something more important she wants to talk to James about. That it's all very well for Harry Laing, but she feels all this carry-on is getting a bit much. That they'll be asking us to the Pa next.

James says he wouldn't put money on it.

'Digging for pipis, riding bareback, where's it going to end?'

'When *Lust in the Dust* is finished and we have a dance at Ted Clark's woolshed, present our gift, then go our several ways like the guests at *Johnny Crow's Garden*.'

'I know that one!' I say.

> *. . . but before they went their several ways*
> *They all joined together in a hearty vote of praise,*
> *For Johnny Crow and his garden.*

'Exactly,' says James. 'Only this time it'll be for Jimmy Clements and his film. Won't it, Ann?'

'Yes.'

'I think, Ann,' says Mrs Clements, 'that your mother will be wanting you at home.'

I dreamed that night that a buck louse was riding Tam's black horse. Not Bel, a real buck louse sitting straight up on Rewi's back and galloping down to the rocks with all its legs waving except the front two which were holding the reins tight. I told Charlie about it but he didn't believe me. Charlie doesn't have dreams.

Miri is telling us about the Pa and the marae and all about when she goes with her father and how good it all is and what a pity we can't go because we'd love it.

Charlie and me don't say anything.

'There are houses and there's the meeting house where they meet and the elders and other men speak on the marae but not ladies because they're not allowed.'

'Not at all?'

'Oh, they can *talk*, but not make speeches and walk up and down and bang their sticks and go on in Maori, Joe says.'

'Where does Joe live?'

'He lives with his Grandad and Tam who's his uncle.'

'Who cooks their dinner?'

'Tam does and sometimes there's a hangi, and there's a sort of kitchen place and a place where everyone can eat. But Mr Ropata's house is best,' she says. 'It's the loveliest house I've ever seen, and when Dad has his lessons with Mr Ropata, Joe shows me *everything*.'

'Like what?'

'Everything. The piano. They've got a piano and Joe's allowed to play it, and a guitar and he's teaching me to play, and there's a lovely photograph big as anything and all framed of Mr Ropata and Mrs Ropata getting married and she's *lovely*. All her hair's up on top and it's got three feathers in it and all the bridesmaids have bouquets and Mr Ropata's as proud as anything, you can see.'

'When did that one die?' says Charlie.

Miri doesn't know, but the photograph of Tam's sister, who was Joe's mother, is even prettier, but not as big. Joe was only six when she died and he doesn't remember his mother much.

Charlie says he'd remember if Mum died, and Miri says no he wouldn't, he wouldn't at all, and that we should see the kiwi cloak which is very precious, and the taonga which are sacred treasures which belong to the tribe but they're kept in the Ropatas' house because he's a chief. They're in a glass case, except the cloak, and they are sacred because the spirits of their ancestors are in them and because they're so old and beautiful though it's mostly because of the ancestors and the mana of the tribe. There are greenstone meres and adzes all made by hand and then rubbing on sandstone for years and years and then finally they rub them on their legs.

'And the treasures Mr Ropata brought back from Egypt after the War are all there too. Fat squashy pouffes with camels and cushions with leather pyramids and a little red hat called a fez, Joe says.'

Charlie says Egypt's where Mustapha Bun from *Frolic and Fun with Mustapha Bun* in *Rainbow* lives.

Miri says that's different. Charlie says how can it be different. Egypt's Egypt. Miri says she's not talking about Egypt and what a pity we can't go to the Pa and see everything but she's glad she can.

Lorna

Startled sheep scatter as the Pontiac drops down the last incline to the sea. I had forgotten this magic place. Or rather I have memories but no name for this long sweep of beach, this surf foaming and slapping and liable to dump the unwary.

Waimaire, you tell me. 'Tranquil waters,' you say. Well, well. Nothing has changed in the thirty years since I was last here. The cliffs are the same, the two pohutukawas still cling to them with roots like hawsers, their crowns a burst of summer flame.

'They're early this year,' Bel tells Angus. 'That means a long hot summer, according to the Maoris.'

'I suppose they have to say something,' says Mrs Clements.

Why did I come here as a child? It was something to do with the fact that I was a fair child and my hair was useful for making fishing flies. I can remember the obligatory Ouch as my father and his friends plucked a strand or two. But even more I remember that my cousin Nancy's hair was dark, and thus useless, not even glanced at by fishermen.

These are the threads of memories which cling. *Who loses and who wins, who's in, who's out.* The pangs of rejection are as sharp in childhood, the moments of bliss as ephemeral. True bliss comes in packets, sealed, complete and liable to self-destruct.

But children do not know this. More vulnerable and nearer the ground they conduct their arcane rituals, chant their chants, learn the arts of survival, but expect the good bits to last.

Like dogs, they are sensitive to tone. The lilting upbeat approval of *Good*, the sad lowering of *Bad* are recognised at an early age. They learn when to be present and, more importantly, when to absent themselves. Or some do.

I lay on the hot sand, I remember, and turned to Nancy who was demonstrating the splits in an effort to catch up. 'I'm glad I've got fair hair,' I said.

'Huh,' sniffed Nance. 'Mine's curly.'

Mrs Clements has taken charge of the Passenger List.

'You girls must come with me in the Pontiac. The children can go in the truck with the men.'

Jeannie explains that Miriama might be car sick, and that she should travel with her in case.

Mrs Clements looks thoughtful. 'I take your point,' she murmurs. 'The fresh air would be beneficial.'

My children have never been car sick and there would be mutiny if I suggested they miss bucketing about on the tray of the farm truck over thirty miles of shingle road. Anyway, they have not been invited into the Pontiac.

'You come in the front with me, Lorna. And Bel, you might as well go in the back.' A thought appears on Mrs Clements' face. It comes up, not like thunder, more as a gentle pearly flush. 'Angus,' she says.

Angus demurs. No, no, one of the children perhaps?

The children jump nimbly onto the tray of the truck. Duncan gives Charlie a leg-up. 'I'll mind him, Mum,' he says. Derek smiles proudly at me and I grin back, waving hard.

'How civilised,' says Angus, as we set off through a swirl of dust.

What is Mrs Clements hoping for, I wonder, with this back seat congress. Propinquity is useful as a starting point, but little more. What is Angus expected to do? Fling himself on his knees? Fascinate? He asks the name of the different crops in the paddocks as we pass.

' "Choumolier",' he says. ' "Rape." I always enjoy the fields of mustard at home. So vivid.'

'Mustard,' snorts Mrs Clements on cue.

'Look,' says Bel, as we pass a yellow truck. 'The Ropatas. Slow down, Mum, you'll drown them in dust.'

'How can I pass them if I slow down?' says her mother reasonably. 'Tell us more about Shropshire, Angus. Are your parents still alive?'

Both parents, sadly, are no longer with us. Angus is an only child.

'Ah,' says Mrs Clements.

The Ropatas' truck thunders past us. Men, women, children and babes in arms wave and shout.

'Honestly,' snorts Mrs Clements. 'Do you know,' she says peering through clouds of dust, 'I think they're getting darker.'

Bella explodes with laughter. Angus looks puzzled. 'Darker?'

'Darker,' says Mrs Clements with conviction. 'The Maoris. They're getting darker.'

Charlie's bum, he tells me, is numb but nobody has been sick. Not even Miriama though she looks far from well. Derek tells me the children have been good, although it is difficult to see how they could have been otherwise on such a journey.

James is now tutoring Bel. 'Remember, we're not attempting to film a mad stampede of fifty covered wagons.'

'Good.'

'But today's work will be very useful. You've read the books I gave you?'

'Yes.'

'Shots of the riders from different angles are out. It certainly adds to the speed, but we're not in that class. What we're after is the *effect* of speed. You'll find we can get a lot from imaginative camera placings, horseback pursuit shots, that sort of thing. Also I hope to get some stock footage during the races which we can use later. Action stuff during the bareback races. Long shots, of course.'

'Yes.'

'And you can practise smooth panning, that sort of thing. Also try and keep clear of stewards in white coats and the wrong type of hat. Glaring anachronisms can be edited out later, but avoid them if you can. Remember, the first Westerns were made in the East, and damn good they were too.' James claps his hands, flings them apart. 'Now, a few location shots first. Bring the tripod.'

They depart, followed by a gaggle of excited children in varying shades of browns, pinks and scarlets. Unlike the white, the brown appear to me to be no browner.

The camera crew and their followers progress along the hard sand to the other end of the foreshore, to rough grass, tin sheds, horse floats, horses groomed and ungroomed, and groups of men in huddles. The yellow truck has arrived. My father told me once that yellow is a good colour for a motor vehicle. Apparently it is easily seen and thus less liable to be banged into. My father was proud of what he called his fund of useless and unverifiable information. He and Derek treated each other with affection and polite incomprehension.

I take Derek's arm.

He turns to me, smiling. 'Why do women wear corsets? You're lovelier than ever at the Beach. More bounce.'

My eyes fill with unexpected tears. 'I've been here before.'

'Tell me,' he says. I tell him the little I can remember. I leave out the bliss.

Angus, I see belatedly, is wearing jodhpurs and riding boots. He hopes there might be a chance of a ride – somebody pulled out, fallen over, you never know. He excuses himself and sets off, his back straight, his Panama at an angle.

It is hot and very dry. The surrounding hills are no longer straw-coloured; lack of rain has bleached their stubble to platinum. 'Poor parched hills,' my mother used to call them, which irritated me as a child. How did she know they minded?

We stroll up the other end of the beach to the site of the hangi. Steam rises from the pit in puffs around the watchers and workers.

Derek talks with the man in charge, a large shining mountain of a man with an impressive puku beneath his shearer's black singlet. Derek seeks information. The process is explained in detail. They nod, yarn, wave their arms.

Charlie appears to tell me he has found a corker dead fish with maggots. He turns the fish over with a stick to facilitate inspection of the white writhing heap. Disturbed sandhoppers shoot upwards. I pop black bladderwrack pods with my sandal. Anything is better than maggots. From the nearby hills comes the flat buzz of bleating sheep, the insistent chivvying of dogs. Someone must be moving a mob.

'Where's Duncan?'

'Up there with Joe,' says Charlie, 'grooming Jackie and putting bets on.'

And so they are. Jackie's coat gleams. His grooms are deep in the conversation of men with shared interests. They nod amiably, keep talking as I appear.

'Why'd you put money on that old wreck?'

'He's local. See. It says. I bet he practises here.'

'Naa. Wear him out dead.'

'Duncan,' I say, 'where did you boys get money to bet?'

'Bel gave us five bob each. And Dad gave us another, so we've shared that. Beaut eh. Keep it for the bareback race. Going to put it on Tam, aren't we, Joe?'

'Yeah. Can't lose.'

'Where are the girls?'

'Dunno.'

I scan the beach. There is no sign of Miriama. Ann is attempting to leap on the reflections of clouds sailing before her on the shining wet sand. As always they move on ahead of her. She will never catch them. She knows this but keeps jumping.

We line up to watch the first race.

Colonel Holdaway's shooting stick is propped alongside Mrs

Clements'. Colonel and Mrs Holdaway are well-respected members of the Beach community. They have been coming to their little cottage along the beach for as long as I remember and have always been good friends of Mrs Clements and her late husband Harold. The remaining three exchange pleasantries, their sticks teeter towards each other as the conversation becomes more animated.

Bella and James and their equipment are poised on the hump of a nearby sandhill. The Laings, with Miriama in tow, stand talking to Mr Ropata who wears an Official's badge. Derek heaves Charlie onto his shoulders.

They're off!

There is a hush. A gull screams. Thundering down the sand comes the field, Maoris and whites bunched tightly together. Hell for leather and few holds barred they storm down the beach, encouraged by the shouts and roars from Mrs Clements' mixed bag of onlookers.

A Maori boy on a piebald breaks from the bunch, is overtaken by a chestnut, doubles his whip and pulls free again. Men, women, children and dogs leap, shout, dance with delirium. Duncan and Joe race for the betting shed.

The piebald passes the post, the Maori boy stands in his stirrups, clenches his fists. 'Hai!' he roars. He's won. And so have I, five shillings. Ann stands silent beside me, her hands still clasped in wonder. Charlie, having almost broken Derek's neck, is lowered once more.

James is right, the chase is the thing. All you need is speed and skill and strength and courage. Chariots, wagons, cyclists or runners, all are exhilarating, but men on horses win hands down. The flashing hooves, the floating manes, the sheer beauty of animals at speed is the bonus.

This is how races should be seen. Only yards from the action, close to the sweat and oaths of the protagonists, on a course encompassed by sea, sky, hills and sheep.

The Maori boy, small, dark and about twelve years old at a guess, but can't be, is now receiving his winner's envelope from Mr Ropata. They exchange words. Applause is general. Nothing can erase that grin. Hone Hopi is stuck with it.

Angus appears, his grin as wide as Hone's. He has achieved a ride in the Men's Open and the second Bareback. Incredible bit of luck. Some poor chap has had some sort of hernia blowout. All right now apparently. Angus hops about in his trim boots. 'Where's Bella?'

'Panning at the hangi.'

Angus laughs at such wit. He is a kind man, and unlike me, who keeps my distance from the vast teeth and skittish hooves of unknown horses, is exhilarated. Angus is a real horseman. 'Jolly good,' he cries. 'I must go and tell her my luck.'

I hope Mrs Clements notices. She seems to have retired to the Pontiac with Colonel and Mrs Holdaway. A pre-prandial spot, perhaps.

There are long gaps between races but no longueurs. We lie torpid beneath the pohutukawas. We eat bacon and egg pie and drink warm beer. We discuss form.

Angus sits beside Bella, his face glowing. She smiles, offers him an Anzac biscuit. He has had a long talk with the Clerk of the Course. Female jockeys, he tells us, are still not allowed. The handicapping system is rather unusual. Difficult, obviously, one can see the problems. Great day though. Wonderful.

Mrs Clements is pleased at his reaction.

Angus says he can't remember a more beautiful day. Not even on the Riviera.

Mrs Clements nods in agreement. 'Juan les Pins,' she mumbles through meat paste sandwiches.

'Exactly,' says Angus.

The sun shines, a faint offshore breeze dusts pohutukawa stamens onto Bella's asparagus roll, drops one in my beer.

I watch James as he squats on his heels checking his gear. Concentration in men is always attractive, if distancing.

'How did the Maoris get their horses here?' asks Mrs Clements.

'Horse floats,' says Duncan, chewing hard.

'Expensive, surely?'

'Everyone shares. Joe says.'

'Still. A horse float.'

'Yup.' He shoots off to what Mrs Clements calls the Maori end to liaise with Joe.

'Where are the Laings?' I ask Annie.

She nods her head in the direction of Duncan's sand-spurting heels. 'Up there.'

Angus is not fussed by the fact that his two races follow each other, nor that they are the last. He follows James and Bella about, holding things, carrying the tripod, chatting. James is pleased with the footage he has achieved, especially of the first bareback race. He intends to shoot more at this afternoon's one. And the close-ups and panning have been good practice for Bel.

The last two races, the Open Sprint and the Eight-Hundred-Yard Bareback, Angus tells Mrs Clements, are the most prestigious. Officials at the betting shed have told him. The Bareback seems a bit odd to him, but why not. Apparently there is even a small cup for each, donated years ago by the late Mr Barton.

'Quite gaga,' says Mrs Clements, picking a small leaf from her chocolate lamington. 'Has been for years. Ever since . . .'

Bel raises a cautionary hand in passing. 'Mum.'

'Since what?' says Annie, full of sun and sea and cold sausage rolls.

'I wasn't speaking to you, dear.'

Mrs Clements leans closer to Angus. I resist the temptation to tell her she has a thread of coconut on a front tooth. She whispers in his ear.

'What curse?' says Angus.

'Oh, some nonsense. You know the sort of thing. A Maori maiden defiled by a member of the household. Chief's daughter, of course. The usual thing.'

'And what happened?'

'Oh, I can't remember. One thing after another. But at least the house didn't burn down. That was something.'

'There must be few old wooden homesteads in this area which haven't burnt down at some stage,' says Derek. 'They're all fire traps.'

'My point exactly,' says Mrs Clements.

The shadows of the oyster-catchers lengthen on the sand, the breeze freshens. Time now for the experts. *All the tried and trusted riders from the stations near and far have mustered at the station overnight.*

Well, sort of. I watch Angus at the starting line. His borrowed horse seems restless.

I admire Angus. He reminds me of the schoolboy at the circus I took the children to last year. All the essential elements were there. The Big Top and the usual oom-pah, the faded splendour and the bored lions. Annie clung to me when the lion trainer inserted his head between the yawning jaws. Charlie watched calmly at first ('It's only pretending, isn't it, Mum.') before burrowing his head deep in my lap. Duncan stopped breathing.

How do lion trainers practise, for heaven's sakes.

But more than the children's reactions, more than the clowns, the equestrian by-play of spangled blondes or the death-defying activities of trapeze artistes, I remember the boy from a local boarding school. About ten or eleven, I suppose, his grey uniform shorts long, his grey socks with striped tops held up by garters, he accepted the Ringmaster's invitation to ride the huge bony animal held by the two men beside him.

Come on down, you heroes, you champs! Leave your ladies and hurry on down. You'll see nothing on the outsides! Stay on the Widow Maker here for ten seconds and the bag's yours. Ten Jimmy o' goblins for ten seconds. A pound a second. Money for old rope. Thank you, Sir, give him a big hand! Asked y' Mum, have yer, sonny? Not here? Well, she'll be proud of yer, come on down. AND another. My word, watch 'em rolling. Three, four. You'll see nothing on the outsides. AND another cowboy!

Down came the locals, the experts, the rough riders, the farmers and their lanky sons in woollen farm pants and flannelette shirts. He didn't win, the calm child fiddling with his snake-buckle belt, nobody did, but he lasted six seconds on the Widow Maker and his bucking strap, which was better than most.

I would feel the same concern for Angus except that he is a good rider, utterly confident and properly dressed. If Angus were arrayed as an Old Testament prophet he would still be at ease. He cannot be responsible for the lapses of others. And so he sits, serene, confident, and trained to win.

The crowd gathers at the winning post. Excitement mounts. There is a hush, a roar.

They're off!

And again the thunder and the tension and the glory of the chase rips down the churned-up sand. Tam appears from the bunch on Rewi, followed by Angus and Bob Jackson, the head shepherd from Rongomaha. Mrs Jackson jumps screaming beside me, her bosoms bounding. Now Angus is ahead, a hair's breadth, a head, then over!

To my astonishment and the bitter disappointment of the children, the overdressed ring-in, the greenhorn from the Old Country, has won the Men's Open. There is stunned silence for a moment, then applause.

Charlie is almost in tears. ' Tam,' he sobs, 'Tam should have won.'

'Why?' I ask.

'He should, he should. He just should.'

I stare at Tam, who obviously agrees with Charlie. There are congratulations, handshakes; men and horses mill about, then canter back to the far end once more.

The presentation of the minuscule silver cup follows. Mr Ropata addresses Angus. He is courteous and congratulatory to this guest at his party, this stranger on the borrowed horse who has licked his son.

Angus, sweating and ecstatic and clutching his prize, moves towards Bella. He dips his head and hands her the cup.

'I'd like you to accept this, if you would,' he says. 'With my compliments.'

A surging blush sweeps up Bel's neck, stains her face. Even her shoulders are appalled by this old-world charm.

'No, no, I couldn't. Not possibly. Please.'

'I've asked Mr Ropata. It's just for a year. A keepsake.'

Goodness me, I think. Goodness me.

Mrs Clements, assisted by Colonel Holdaway, stumbles to her feet, snaps her shooting stick shut and bears down upon her daughter.

Bel stiffens. 'Thank you, Angus. I'll be happy to keep it for you.'

He grins, runs to his horse, turns to wave. 'I'll be back after the Bareback,' he calls.

'Fat chance,' sniffs Charlie. 'Tam'll eat him.'

'How did you meet Tam?' asks Derek.

'At the Bully Pond,' says Charlie with a quick upward flick of wrist to nose. 'With Bel.'

With Bel. Goodness me once again. I change the subject. 'Let's go and look at the horses,' I say to Derek.

Mrs Clements waylays us. 'Isn't it exciting! What a coup. And a borrowed horse. Training tells, and of course Shropshire has always been horsy.'

I did not know this but can well believe it. I see horses and empty stirrup cups on high stone walls, hounds milling, rose-lipt maidens and lightfoot lads thundering across fields to brooks too broad for leaping. I see them crashing, lying still.

All the riders in the last race are Maoris except Angus.

Bob Jackson, his wife and I agree that Captain Rowan is a good sport.

'How many times has he ridden bareback?' asks Mrs Jackson. 'Once! My word. It just goes to show!'

She smiles her good-natured smile. Everything about Mrs Jackson is wide, generous and friendly. I still see her as she ran towards the beachcombers, as she called us, when we arrived at Rongomaha after the Earthquake. In her floral cotton, snowy ankle socks and black Cuban heels, her all-embracing warmth preceded her as she ran towards us with her husband and Claude the rouseabout puffing in the rear.

'Look, Bob,' she cries. 'They're off!'

Horses and riders are bunched tight, the shouts are louder than ever. This is cowboy stuff, or rather Indian, elemental in concept and execution, and wonderful to watch.

A horse stumbles, knocks against Angus's. Both riders fall. They duck and roll and run to safety as Tamati Ropata thunders past the post, his arms held high, his 'Hai!' a roar of triumph. I run to help the fallen but am beaten to the post by First Aid Officials. No damage, they say, everything is ka pai, the sand is soft by now. Angus thanks them, shakes hands all round and limps back to the prize-giving.

Mr Ropata presents his son with a cup identical to that of Angus. He is proud of his son, very proud. They beam at each other, speak in Maori, shake hands.

Tamati gives one final shake and lopes over to Bel who has been filming. She stops, looks up.

He holds out his cup. 'Here,' he says. 'This is for you.'

She shakes her head, angry, confused. 'Don't be ridiculous.'

He shoves it forward. 'Take it. From me.'

She takes it suddenly, almost snatches it. 'Thank you, Tam.'

She smiles, walks over to Mrs Clements who is once again lumbering upright from her stick. 'Here you are, Mum,' she says. 'Here's another one for your collection.'

Duncan and Joe Ropata stand side by side. Joe looks at his grand-father, Duncan at Mrs Clements. 'Crikey,' they say.

I see what they mean. It is hard to know where a bystander should look at this time. Mrs Clements seems about to throw Tamati's token on the sand and jump on it, or else fling it at her daughter's smiling face. Her hands twitch and clutch around Tamati's eggcup-sized trophy, her voice stutters. Colonel Holdaway offers support, Mrs Holdaway hovers, making small mewing noises of concern.

Mr Ropata's rage is equal but different. His face is a mask of stone, his hands clench his carved stick. He waves it at Tamati's departing back as he canters up the beach. 'Joseph,' he says. 'Tell Tamati to come to me. Up the other end.'

United as ever and happy as well, the Laings appear. 'We've been with the elders all day, haven't we, Miriama?' says Jeannie.

'Yes.'

'No races at all?' asks Derek.

'Some.'

Miriama hops on one foot, changes feet. 'We're going to stay for the hangi,' she lets slip, 'and go back with the Ropatas after. Dad says.'

Ann's face, her give-away eyes.

How can I convince her that this exclusion will not last for ever. That an idyllic childhood is a contradiction in terms for the shy. That this too will pass. What about the Ugly Duckling, I could say. Look at Duncan the Bad, Charles the Bold. See if they care. I feel a surge of love for my solemn child, my dumped Annie.

I take her hand, pull her to my side. She pushes me away with a long disgusting sniff.

'Hey Mum, Dad,' says Duncan, appearing from nowhere, 'Joe says I can stay for the hangi and come back in the yellow truck. I can, can't I, Dad?'

'I don't see why not,' says Derek. 'Do you, love?'

'No,' I say. 'Why not?'

The homeward journey usually seems shorter than the outward bound, especially in the dark. Not so this time. It is endless. We sit as before, me in front with Mrs Clements. Bel had offered to drive. Mrs Clements had declined this offer with a genteel snarl and shoved her daughter in the back with Angus. The atmosphere inside the hot Pontiac is frigid. Angus, having launched a few conversational streamers and seen them wither in the gloom, goes to sleep, worn out, presumably, by both physical and emotional exertion.

Bella, a silver eggcup in each hand, sits curled in her corner. One of the cups drops from her fingers and falls with a small clatter at her feet.

Angus's or Tam's? Which bower bird's offering is sculling about the feet of its recipient? It is a relief when she picks it up.

'Whose?'

'I've no idea.'

'I hope it's not dented.'

'Hh.'

I think of the farm truck and its long drive home. Of Ann and Charlie rattling about. Of Derek guarding offspring, wrapping them up, keeping them warm. Of Duncan in the yellow truck.

A morepork calls in the dark; haunting, insistent and clear. Morepork, it begs. Morepork. The loneliest sound in the world.

Mrs Clements drives on, skilfully avoiding pot holes where possible. In bristling rage and total silence she does her duty by us all.

Lorna

James has decided to shoot the gambling den shots first. Mrs Clements thinks he should start at the beginning and shoot through to the end. James says that is not how films are made. His mother says she knew Sid wouldn't mind about the hall. Not only does Sid not mind. He has jumped at the chance of a bit part, the barman who ducks beneath the bar whenever shots ring out. Other extras have been recruited from the Pa for the gamblers. Supply exceeds demand. Stage props are handed out; toy guns, unloaded rifles, a pair of sheepskin chaps, the contents of Rongomaha's ancient wardrobes and Dressing-Up Cupboard are to hand. My frock was once a fancy dress of Bella's. I am a Dutch Girl, fortunately minus hat. Not quite what I had in mind, but flattering in an odd sort of way. Mrs Clements is busty in red velvet.

James gives us a brief burst on the art of mime. We have all seen Charlie Chaplin. We know what humanity, what pathos Chaplin can wring from gestures.

Gestures, he tells us, must be generous but not ridiculous, especially as there'll be no captions.

'But how will they know what's happening?' asks Mrs Clements.

'By our actions, our facial expressions, the way we move. That is the original genius of silent films. Think of it as ballet plus drama, action, the chase. We *see* the story. I'm still not entirely convinced that sound is necessary in Westerns. Certainly you hear the gunshots, galloping hooves, the sound of frying bacon, etc., but as for dialogue . . . I hope to hire a silent Western from the manager of the Cosy in town . . .'

'. . . Trevor Warwick,' murmurs Mrs Clements. 'His father used to be at Rongomaha. Excellent stockman, but he left to become an auctioneer at the sale yards of all things.'

'. . . which we can show here in the hall, so you can see what I mean. We might run it through several times, so that I can demonstrate, make my point.' He pauses. 'Gamblers in place? Right. Now the essentials, Bel, are clean background shots. The action comes later. Ready, Lorna? Right. Camera!'

I am good at acting. I knew I would be and I am. I prance around in my ex Dutch Girl garment, flirting, being wanton and enjoying myself. Ann watches me with pride, Charlie with puzzlement and Duncan with something else. Derek went back to town last night.

I am impressed by James's expertise. He appears to know what he's doing. He does not refer to his script. It is all in his head, he says, a matter of instinct.

The Settlers Hall is transformed, though little has been added except an air of sleaze, booze, beat-up men, Mrs Clements and me. We rise to the occasion. Nothing can touch us; we are born again, transported. New. We are pretending to be someone else. Think, when we talk of harlots, that you see me printing my proud hoof etc., and so I do, on the seat of the chair as I deal drinks to the goggle-eyed gamblers. I am a harlot, a certified harlot, and licensed to behave as such. Down goes my bosom as I pass glasses of gut-rot cold tea. James appears, in his guise as Sheriff. I throw myself at him, wrap my spangled leg around his startled one, melt against him. He responds.

Mrs Clements appears from the Ladies' toilet at the back.

'Cut,' she roars.

Bel, startled, does so.

We disengage.

The children have taken on the role of an offstage Greek chorus.

They tell us what's happening, what they think will happen. *Who loses and who wins.*

James has done a deal, he tells us as we meet at Mrs Clements' house that evening. Trevor Warwick from the Cosy has a copy of *Arizona Gold* he's willing to lend. We will have to pay for admission but James thinks he can subsidise the cost. There's no need to make a profit. He can pick up the slack.

Films have long been shown at the Settlers Hall on alternate Saturday nights. A truck drives up to park behind the projector holes hacked in the back wall of the hall. The projector and its operator are mounted in position on the tray of the truck, a few minor adjustments may be necessary to the indoor screen or the placement of the truck, then the lights go down and the evening's show begins.

The whites sit at the back and the Maoris on forms in the front. We are united in our enthusiasm for all films, but especially Westerns. Derek and I have had fine nights at these sessions. First with Duncan asleep in my arms, then Ann, then Charlie, I have booed and cheered and wept with the best. Derek has offered to take a turn with the baby but I have declined. I need something to hold.

Most of the beachcombers are there for this treat, plus what looks to be most of the inhabitants of the Pa. There are few seats left at the back by the time the Laing family arrive. I wave my hand to indicate this fact to Jeannie. 'Here. Come back here.'

The Laings stop, stand together in their usual serene trio. Harry murmurs something to Jean and heads for the front benches. She gives one startled glance then follows. They sit alongside Tamati Ropata and Joe. They nod. Joe changes places to sit beside Miriama.

A whispering sound like the soughing of wind in the poplars drifts from the back of the hall.

'Why're they sitting down there?' says Ann.

'Quite,' snaps Mrs Clements.

Three young seminarians sitting beside us, with brutal haircuts and dark suits, watch the situation with interest.

Bel has been talking to the projectionist on the truck. She and Angus come in last of all, glance around for seats as Jean waves.

'Oh good,' says Bel and moves to sit beside her.

Angus remonstrates, I can see him doing so. 'No, no. Let me. There's one left at the back.'

'Then you go and sit there,' smiles Bel.

Tamati Ropata is on his feet. So is Mrs Clements. Impeded rather than aided by her stick, she surges towards her daughter. 'Bella, come back at once. You're making an exhibition of yourself.'

'In what way?'

'You know perfectly well. Come back immediately.'

Bel stands. 'I'm quite happy here, thank you.'

Mr Ropata is also on his feet. 'May I suggest, Mrs Clements . . . ?'

'Not at the moment, thank you.'

'. . . that it is you who are drawing attention to the fact that Maori and pakeha normally sit apart.'

Mrs Clements glances around the packed hall. Moist brown, startled blue, eyes old as the hills meet hers. She gives a shuddering gasp, a gasp tugged from her by rage, humiliation and possibly shame.

'Tell her,' she hisses at Mr Ropata, 'tell her she can walk home.' She blunders towards the door, assisted belatedly by Angus.

Tamati Ropata smiles.

Bella's head moves. 'I'd better go to her.'

Tam says something.

Bel sits.

My scalp crawls.

'What's going on?' says Derek.

The lights dim. The audience is hushed, the world still.

Sex was last night. Derek and I lie flat on our backs in the dark.

'Tell me all,' he says to the blackness.

'I don't know any more than you do.' And I don't. Not a word.

'Those two identical cups. Bizarre really. I wonder how Mrs C will play it tomorrow. And how will Bel get home?'

'I've no idea. I suppose with the Laings. James was going to run the film again to demonstrate various points.'

'Interesting.' Derek flings a sweaty arm across me. 'Not that it's anything to do with me.'

Not me either. Nevertheless I should like to know. Not for any worth-while or valid reason, just as a sop to my reprehensible and life-saving love of wanting to find out. I don't hand it on, this beautiful knowledge, this scuttlebutt, this gossip. It's just that I like to know what's going on. And I am very discreet. Quite admirable really. A good girl at heart.

We kiss good night.

Mrs Clements plays it as you might expect. Escorted by Bella and James she presents herself next morning at what is once again the Settlers Hall cum gamblers' den. Powdered, constrained, yet gracious as ever, she ignores Bella, and speaks frequently to James and anyone else within range. She moves among the assembled cast and onlookers like a local Member of Parliament among her constituents, a word here, a nod, a patted head. She acknowledges the presence of the gamblers lounging on their battered chairs, smiles at their blank faces and moves on to sink down onto an armchair beside Mr Ropata. She leans towards him. Apology? Time of day? Hard to tell. In any case, he rises, nods and moves away. She puts a hand on his sleeve, murmurs something. His reply is brief.

Mrs Clements straightens her shoulders, lifts her head hero high and smiles at the assembled company. Some smile back.

I prance around in my Dutch Girl disguise. This is not me, you understand. This is a harlot pretending to be me. I smoulder across the hall at James but the moment is ill chosen. He merely looks distracted.

Not so Duncan. From the corner of my eye I glimpse his face as he heads for the door. I move to follow him, call his name, but my progress is impeded by the Laings who are making their entrance – and I mean just that. They move forward together, their grouping formal as a War Memorial sculpture. Harry has his hand on his wife's shoulder, their child stands between. They are a unit.

They are followed by three Maoris whose names I don't know but whose faces I recognise from our day at the Races. These are men of distinction among their own. They stand behind the Laings in silence.

The crowd stills, stops talking, stares. A glass crashes from a table. A lean and hungry dog skids outside. A baby cries.

'I have something to say,' cries Harry Laing. Eight feet tall and totara proud, he steps forward, speaks for a few minutes in Maori, then switches to English.

'Last night I came to a decision. I decided later, much later than I should have, but thank God in time enough. I am Maori and I am not and never have been pakeha. I am Maori and have been since birth. My mother was Maori, my father was Maori. My stepfather Walter Laing gave me his pakeha name, taught me his pakeha ways, his pakeha speech, sent me to board at pakeha schools away from my own people. But I say again, I am not and never have been pakeha. My name is not Laing and never has been. This day I give Walter Laing his name back. I do not want his name. From this day on I am Hare Henare. No te tangata whenua ahau. I am Maori. From now on I align myself, my wife, my child and my life with Maori. These are my people.'

He continues in this dignified, stern and impressive vein for some time. He will try to forgive his stepfather, he tells us, for his lost heritage and his lonely childhood, his sense of alienation and loss. He has come home to his people, and his wife and child are proud to join him.

The gamblers, the Indians, the shifty and the proud erupt into a roar. Small bewildered children look on in awe. The rest of us stand hesitant, filled, on the whole, with good will. After all, it's not us. I look at Jean with new eyes. Bel rushes forward with arms out to embrace her. James moves forward with his hand out, followed by Colonel Holdaway and his stick.

'What on earth's he talking about?' says Angus.

There is no sign of Duncan. I must find him, talk to him, explain that I am playing a part. Which he knows already, or should.

But first I congratulate Jeannie and Hare. I fling my arms around them both, wish them every possible happiness in their new lives. Hare replies with his usual calm dignity. Jeannie, also as usual, is all smiles. 'It won't be so much different,' she says, 'as *enriched*.'

'Will you live at the Pa with the ponies?' asks Ann.

'And the dugout?' says Charlie.

Jeannie smiles.

I watch Miriama surrounded by her new friends, dancing about the hall like a pea on a drumhead. I look at the envious faces of my children, at Joe who looks as though he will burst with pride.

'And obviously Miri's very happy?'

'Wouldn't yours be?' laughs Jeannie.

There is no sign of Mrs Clements.

Once again I am pushing my way against an enthusiastic and emotional crowd. The glare of the sun outside is so strong I am unable to focus for a moment. Then I see them. Mrs Clements, her behind propped against the tank stand, her face collapsed and her speech hesitant, is attempting to explain something. Duncan, uncomprehending but sympathetic, is doing his best to comfort her. I run towards them.

'Oh Lorna,' she gasps, rocking backwards and forwards, backwards and forwards. A single tear runs down her face. 'What's happened to everything! It's all gone mad. Stark raving mad, the lot of it.'

'No, it hasn't, I promise.'

'You don't know. You don't know anything,' she moans. She turns to Duncan. 'You're a good boy,' she says. 'Good and kind like your father, aren't you?'

Duncan shakes his head.

'But you can go, dear, I'm quite all right now, thank you.' She gives a little heave against the tank stand to demonstrate. Smiles, sniffs.

I touch his hand. 'I'll see you later.'

He turns without a word.

'It's Laing's Point, Lorna,' keens Mrs Clements. 'Laing's Point, don't you see?'

Lorna

'But what do you mean?'

'Think, girl, think! What do you think I mean.'

'But Mr Laing bought the land years ago. We've always known that.'

'No. It was Harry's mother's gift to her new husband at the time of their marriage.'

'I thought Maori land was communally owned.'

'The lease of it, child. It's Maori leasehold.'

'Then why's it called Laing's Point?'

'The Maori name's one of those long-winded nonsenses meaning Bush Pigeon Sitting on the Cliff above the Sparkling Waters or somesuch. Kereru something. But that's not the only reason. Anything Walter Laing owned or leased or inherited or even got landed with, like Harry, was his, and named accordingly. Subtle distinctions never made a whit of difference to Wally. As far as he was concerned the land was his. He let his cousins, my Harold and Garth's father, build cottages, but would never let them buy. He couldn't, I suppose, but he made it seem as though this was due to his generosity. Laing's Point was his kingdom.

'And as for his beautiful skelp of land over at Rissington. People say,' her voice drops, 'he used to put his stallion out to a mare to entertain his guests. Right outside the front door! They were on the verandah of course, the guests, and there were stable hands, but even so. I've never known such a patriarchal man.'

She pauses, her hands quiet at last, her mind far away. 'He was a racing man of course, like Harold, but you have to wonder.'

You do indeed.

'What was Mrs Laing like?' I ask.

'Hinemoa? Oh, she was a lovely woman. Lovely in every way. It's not her fault, all this unpleasantness.'

'But surely Harry's not going to send his father's friends and relations packing?'

'Stepfather. And it's leasehold, I keep telling you. Leasehold! And now that Harry's gone back to the mat . . . You heard what he said. "I align myself and my life with Maori." What does that sound like to you?'

'That he wants to find his childhood, the culture and beliefs of his own people. Think if it had happened to you.'

Mrs Clements does not bother to answer.

'The Laings won't go and live at the Pa,' she continues, 'so the obvious way to do this *aligning* is for Harry to make some gesture, and to be seen to make it by the members of his tribe, and the obvious way for him to do that is either to tell us to get off his mother's land (or tribal land or whatever) or else to let every Tom, Dick and Harry from the Pa come up here and build their whares. How would you like that? Chickens, pigs, dogs all over the place. At Laing's Point! But by then it won't be Laing's Point. It'll be some wretched Bush Pigeon Sitting on the Cliff above the Sparkling Waters and everything'll be ruined. *Ruined.*'

I try to reassure her. I tell her I'm sure nothing so drastic will occur. She asks me how I know. I tell her I don't, but I am sure that her fears are misplaced.

'You don't know them like I do. It's not like it used to be, you know. When I think of the good relations the Clements have always had with them (and the Rowans too, I have to say), I could scream. Ever since my Harold's father, George, built his first cottage. He loved the Maoris, they were his friends. He spoke their language, took an interest. And they loved him back, don't tell me they didn't. They helped him at the start. Look at that flax cloak! Not many people got a flax cloak. And the children's names. Harold, all his sisters, all of them, were given Maori names as well by the chief. It was a great honour.

'And the help we've given them since. The hours I've spent training the girls, the whares we've built for the stockmen. Everything, everything. And now look at it! And if James thinks I'm going to let them come and stay in the shearing quarters after all this kerfuffle he is very much mistaken. And furthermore,' she says, huffing herself to her feet, 'I'm not staying here another minute. Not a minute. And you can tell him I said so. Goodbye!'

She clambers into the Pontiac, turns the key and lurches across the paddock with the exhaust smoking.

James appears at the door of the Settlers Hall. 'Lorna, you're on. Whatever are you doing?'

I run across the rough grass. 'Coming,' I say. 'Coming.'

'They can come up by the day,' says Mrs Clements, 'but they are not, I repeat, not going to stay in the shearers' quarters. The whole thing has gone far too far in my opinion, and if it wasn't for your precious film, James . . .'

'I'll have to pay for their petrol, coming up here each day.'

'Then do that. Do that!'

Never have I seen Mrs Clements so vehement towards her son. James is surprised and says so. Mrs Clements sniffs.

The Laings are conspicuous by their absence as we smoke and drink beer and watch the white cliff face of the Island turn pink from the reflected sunset. Oyster-catchers at the tide line below take flight. All grace and beauty now, they skim the waves calling *Keep, keep.* There is no wind, not a breath.

'So when can we come up to Rongomaha, Ma?'

'Any time you like. I've told you that. Oh this heat! I'm dripping.' Mrs Clements, her face its usual soft powdered self, sighs, leans back. 'Disgusting,' she mutters.

'Next week? The saloon takes should be in the can by then.'

Mrs Clements nods. 'As you will. Bella,' she calls, 'did you hear that? Four adults and four children extra next week.'

'Yes,' replies Bella from the kitchen.

'You'd better give Hilda Jackson a ring about the beds. We may need to take extra sheets.'

Bella, her face damp, appears with a small silver cup in each hand. 'OK,' she says.

'OK. Why is everything OK! And anyway it's not. What are you doing with those silly little things?'

I feel a twinge of sympathy for Mrs Clements. A small twinge, but nevertheless present. Her daughter's acceptance, albeit reluctantly, of a token of esteem from a suitable young man has been nullified by her even-handed acceptance from the unsuitable. Bella has extinguished her mother's chance of a maternal glow. Her offhand laugh, her triumphant retelling, 'Oh, Midge, it was priceless! Such a gracious gesture. I didn't know where to put myself. There we all were, and suddenly over he comes . . .' will never see the light of day.

'Just giving them a buff-up,' smiles Bella.

To James's relief the Ropatas have agreed to appear at Rongomaha each day in the yellow truck. They will be made welcome.

'Won't Joe be there all the time?' asks Charlie.

'Not at night.'

'Why not?'

Because, Charlie, Mrs Clements has drawn the line. Things are bad enough in her opinion and anything more would be intolerable.

'Because,' I say, 'Bel already has eight extra to cook for.'

'She wouldn't mind,' says Charlie. 'And you can help her.'

'She might make pikelets like after the Earthquake,' says Duncan.

Charlie dislikes mention of the Earthquake, a time remembered with enthusiasm by the other kids. He has no recollection of it and feels he missed a good party.

I am glad Duncan is having a break from Mike Girlingstone's company, and I don't doubt the Girlingstone parents or parent will be equally pleased. Duncan and I will see more of each other, talk more, and what is more I will behave myself. I wish to erase the memory of his face at the Settlers Hall that day. He can be very loving, Duncan, and he shares my affection for Rongomaha. He also shares Charlie's affection for Joe, I notice, which puzzles me. From Bella's account I understood there was no love lost between them at the Bully Pond, but children are notoriously fickle. *Now my sworn friend, and then mine enemy.* And vice versa.

Charlie sits on the back step rubbing his stump, which is usually a sign of unease. Normally he ignores it unless attaching or detaching his pink foot or ski pole. He can't go, he tells us, and leave Patch behind. He'll have to stay here and look after Patch.

'Listen, dummy,' says Duncan, who is longing to get off, to be driven up the hill by someone, anyone, who cares, just so long as he can be with Joe and the bush and the caves as soon as possible. 'Patch isn't your dog. He's Miri's and she wouldn't leave him starving to death. Look at her. She's more dopey about him than you even. Besides, he stinks.'

'He doesn't,' yells Charlie. 'Does he, Miri?'

'No,' says Miri dispassionately.

Charlie is outraged. 'Why don't you care?'

Miriama kisses a black patch between the ears. 'Duncan's just being silly,' she says sweetly.

'Don't you call me silly.'

'She just has,' says Ann.

And now they are rolling on the couch grass like cubs exchanging cub-like blows. Derek distrusts such behaviour. He calls it mauling. I tell him that all small mammals play roughly in this way. It sharpens their senses, teaches them tips they will need later in life. He tells me that I can be trying sometimes, but this I already know.

I am opening my mouth to tell the children how much we have to do, when Miri releases Patch. Charlie gives him a quick embrace and returns to the attack with the same finesse.

'He does not pong.'

'Why would I say he pongs if he didn't? He does.'

'So do you, you mouldy pig.'

'Like him. Phew! Stink the place out.'

'Duncan! And you, Charlie. Of course you can't take Patch. He's Miri's and he is going to stay at the Pa.'

Charlie says why can Patch stay at the Pa when he can't.

Duncan says because they'd be ponged out.

Charlie says that's pretty jolly funny coming from Duncan seeing he was the one who said Charlie'd get fleas from Joe's dugout, and now he's all over him like a soppy tart.

Surrounded by newly ironed shorts, shirts, shifts, tub frocks and sheets, by the obligatory bacon and egg pie, the sausages, the cooked cold beef and four hot bickering children, I over-react. I drop everything.

'Did you say that!'

'Yes.'

He is a good-looking child, Duncan, but can be sulky. He stands in front of me, smouldering. 'I didn't know him then.'

Derek would know what to say now. Something appropriate, wise. Something friendly but firm.

Suddenly I don't want to go anywhere. Not even to Rongomaha. I want everyone else to go up the hill and leave me alone. No children, no Derek, no Maoris, no whites. Just me and the sea and a decent book.

'Two toys each,' I shout, 'and two books *only*. And don't forget your togs.'

I haven't a good book left, I remember, and even if I had I wouldn't stay here. Who would? Who could? It was just a thought.

Mrs Clements arrives in the Pontiac to sweep us up the hill. She is calm as I pack our chattels in the boot, but cannot for the life of her understand why I wish to ring Derek from the Store when I could so easily ring him from Rongomaha. I try to explain that I want to tell him we're leaving, not that we have arrived. Understandably, perhaps, she finds this senseless, but stops anyway and produces small change for ice creams. As I say, Phoebe Clements is a generous woman.

Derek tells me it is good of me to ring. He is all right, missing us all, will see us next weekend. It will probably be the last of Morley's white freestone peaches soon and he will bring a tray. Mrs Girlingstone, two feet from my ear, nods smilingly. I thank him, am about to replace the old-fashioned receiver on the cradle above its wooden box, when he calls, 'Lorna.'

'Yes.'

'Be careful, darling.'

'Yes, yes we will.'

His voice drops. There must be someone in his office – Miss Murphy, perhaps, his typist who makes a good cup of tea.

'You are all very precious,' he says.

I climb back in the car, feeling strangely moved by this comment. The children sit licking voraciously in the back. They are glad of the ice cream and express thanks. However, Charlie tells Mrs Clements' broad back, he would have preferred to travel with the Henares and see the Pa. Ann and Duncan stop licking momentarily to agree. I tell them they would not see much, that the Henares would probably deposit Patch and come on straight away. Duncan says how do I know, they'd probably stay for hours and see everything. Mrs Clements says she had not realised the children would rather have travelled cheek by jowl in Harry Laing's funny little Morris, and why had I not told her. She adds that it's a bit late now.

'Henare,' says Duncan.

Mrs Clements says she would have thought that Duncan would have had more manners than to interrupt her. She wonders whether she has brought her Queen Anne chocolates with her from the Beach.

I turn my head to grimace at my son's surly, troubled face. Behind his head lies the whole length of the bay, the surf creaming in for ever, the sand silver, the Island shadowed by cloud.

116

'We won't be able to swim in the sea,' says Ann.

True. True.

The main road into town turns to the right by a hill topped with limestone outcrops. Mrs Clements swings her cargo to the left along a road which is little more than a shingle track, turning and twisting through the bleached bones of the surrounding hills.

'No pasture left,' says Mrs Clements. 'None.'

'What do the sheep eat?' asks Charlie.

'You might well ask. However, we are fortunate. Rongomaha has artesian wells. It's never as bad as it looks here.'

The road narrows further. I am glad to hear about the wells. At the moment things look bad indeed. Green pastures have turned to a desert of bare hills. There are a few cabbage trees, but little else. Willows droop beside trickles of water in shingle river beds; sheep nibble endlessly. A couple of magpies, raucous and outraged as ever, fight it out in a pine plantation as we pass. Some of the trees lie uprooted, their dead trunks contorted, severed by storms or tossed aside by winter gales.

We pass the mailbox with its waiting milk churn and mailbag stamped *Rongomaha*. There is no other name on either it or the open gate. Why should there be? Everyone knows. The cattle stop rumbles beneath us, and before Charlie has finished telling us he can feel it in his bottom, we turn the corner into a different world.

In the nineties James's grandfather, George Clements, a man of vision, and by this time some means, had had the small four-room cottage he made on arrival from the West Coast torn down and a large homestead built in its place. He then turned his attention to the garden, and to the astonishment of his neighbours engaged a landscape gardener to transform the slopes of his bare paddocks into a garden worthy of the Old Country.

Huge stones were transported for miles by bullock wagons or drays. A pergola was built. Stone walls and steps ascended gradually up terraced gardens to what are now enormous old trees. Wisterias were planted, gardens made, a tennis court achieved and a nearby creek dammed for a swimming hole beneath a waterfall. The water is icy and the stones sharp beneath the feet, but even in a summer as dry as this one the moss will be green velvet, the spray drops bright against the fern fronds. Fantails will dip and flick their tails at the overflow. It is hard to believe that fantails are not playing games. Their fan play, like coquettes', seems designed to please.

At the turn of the century George Clements employed four gardeners. There are photographs of them up to their bootstraps in mud, their shovels to hand, their faces moustached and their heads hatted, pipes clenched between their teeth and their trousers tied with boyangs, these are the men who changed the landscape. Single men mostly, they lived the whole of their working lives in the back country, as Rongomaha was then. When they retired they went to live in boarding houses in town. They were hard workers, James's father Harold told me once when we inspected the old prints together. To me these photographs are one of the pleasures of Rongomaha.

The ones of the station at work now line the walls of what is still called the Smoking Room. This pleasant room has been taken over by James, and a small conservatory built from it where he attends to his orchids. Orchids do not enchant me but they are interesting. Very interesting. I suppose their appeal comes from the astonishment of their flowers. Such blatant flaunting swans from such spiky ducklings. Like mushrooms, and pearls from oysters, orchids have the glamour of the unexpected.

Of the three, I prefer oysters. My father used to say it was a brave man who first ate an oyster, but thank God he did.

I visit the photographs each time I am at Rongomaha, stare at the faded sepia, the funny hats above the solemn faces, the starkness and the tree stumps against the sky. The bullockies and the hand shearers, the brown faces and the white, the stockmen and the rouseabouts all interest me. What did they think of their lives? What did they know?

There is no woman to be seen in any of these photographs except for an old sepia print labelled *Mum and Dad, late afternoon 1905* of Mr and Mrs George Clements riding along the brow of a hill, silhouetted against a pale sky. They were taken almost within shouting distance of home, their son Harold told me, after their thirty-mile ride from the railway station. They had shipped the horses down to the Manawatu Show by train and done quite well, but of course they had to ride them home from town. Still, two cups were not to be sneezed at.

I also admire the wedding photographs, or rather the newspaper clippings of them. James has collected these for years, many of them from before the War, and has stored them in discarded chocolate boxes. These yellowed cuttings from the *Auckland Weekly News* and the *New Zealand Free Lance* are buried treasure to me. I beg James for them, devour their smudged images, their unusual captions, their *Broad Acres United*, their *Titian Bride Weds*, their *Bagpipes at Craigieburn*. I mouth the names, compare the bridal gowns, the floral work, the retinues; even the marquees demand my attention. This *Broad Acres United* world was beyond me and I knew it, but the fascination remained.

The other part of Rongomaha I like best is what Mrs Clements calls the Backquarters.

'How many staff did you have then, Mrs Clements?' I asked her once.

'Oh, three or four, and of course Claude did the birds.'

I did not discover until later that Claude the rouseabout had many other duties besides 'the birds', but I did find out where he did them. Amid the rabbit warren of short and long passages, of store rooms and sculleries, serveries and sinks, hidden behind cold rooms and the sink for flowers, was a dark low-ceilinged concrete cell with an open doorway and a window with no glass, its only furniture a low wooden bench. 'What was this room for, Mrs Clements?' I asked.

Mrs Clements sighed. 'That's where Claude did the birds. But those days are gone. Alas.'

Alas. I have always liked the weary tolling of 'alas'. It has worn better than 'alack'.

Last night, on arrival at Rongomaha, we had what Mrs Clements called a scratch meal with the children and more or less fell into bed. This morning Bella and I sit at the scrubbed pine table amongst the remains of breakfast. Above us, hanging from the overhead light, is the ever-present fly paper. The rubber fly swat is to hand and the flit gun is not far away. Mrs Clements does not like flies. She gives them no quarter, nor does she distinguish between the surfaces on which they land. A stinging slap of the swat on a bare leg must be disregarded. Vigour of despatch is all, each small black shape spinning on its back a trophy.

I ask Bel who does the birds now? She looks faintly surprised and said who did I think did the birds? She adds that birds are no longer such a feature of life at Rongomaha as once they were. Apart from the odd pheasant, and of course the duck season, they jog along quite happily with an occasional chook or two.

I ask Bel about Claude, the rouseabout. He is a gentle kindly man, she tells me. Quite lovable really, but liable to go walkabout occasionally and drink himself silly. It is an extraordinary business. She can never understand it. There he is, a good worker for six months at a time and as pleasant a man as you could hope to meet, then suddenly, instantly, this compulsion for whisky and quantities of it appears, and he is off. Not tomorrow, or the next day, but instantly. Once he departed leaving a half-plucked duck. He doesn't come back till he's sober, though, which is something. He lives in a whare up the hill and doesn't do much now except the scraps and the wood. Bel grins. 'He told Mum a few years ago he could no longer do the birds because after all these years the pulling and that gave him the dry retches. He did say he'd give me a hand with the plucking if I was pushed.'

'Didn't your mother object?'

'Certainly not. We know our Claude.'

It is just as well the kitchen is cool. I have underestimated the workload. I can see Bel and I and Bel's young helper, Rua, plus Jeannie when possible, will be spending some time in it. It is a big room with three large windows and three doors; one opens to the back courtyard with its various buildings, one to the dining room, and one onto a back verandah covered by a wisteria which must be beautiful in the spring. A lot happens in this large room and most of it takes time and tastes delicious. Breakfast this morning was comparatively simple: cream, strawberries, bacon and eggs for the men, toast and homemade butter and Bella's marmalade.

Jeannie and the rest of the team, escorted by all the children, are now filming on location, a phrase I am less at ease with than James. I'm not sure I will ever manage 'in the can'.

The Ropatas arrived after breakfast in the yellow truck, were offered tea, and declined. The loaded farm truck, escorted by the mounted contingent, set off in convoy for Devil's Canyon to film the abduction of Jeannie.

Why, you ask, is Bel not filming? Because, as James says, Rua can't be expected to cook for eight extra unaided, so Bel and I can stay home this morning to give her a hand and get ahead of the game. Angus has shown great aptitude and interest in the camerawork and he's very happy to take over for the morning. We can come up later in James's old Dodge.

'On that track?' says Bella.

'Well, ride then.'

'OK. You're sure you've got all the lunch?'

Mrs Clements departs after breakfast to do the flowers. I see her drifting past the door to the verandah occasionally. Framed by wisteria leaves and shaded by a becoming straw, she carries a flat trug laden with delphiniums, roses and native foliage for background. She looks like something from a calendar called *Country Gardens of Great Britain*.

Bella is planning ahead. Rhubarb Crumble for pudding today, but what about tomorrow? Lemon Delicious always goes down well, though it uses every bowl in the place. There is no need to discuss meat. It will be farm-killed mutton or possibly lamb if one has been injured and has had to be put down. A man who kills a perfectly good lamb for the house is regarded with suspicion by any true farmer. There is a whiff of bad husbandry at the thought of such extravagant waste.

So it's just puddings and smokos for us this morning. We beat and whisk and roll and slice. Puddings line up in the cool room, the pig-bucket fills with peelings. I am pleased to have time to talk with Bella. We are at ease together and she talks sense.

We discuss what we have been reading, how Dorothy Sayers must surely have been in love with her aristocratic sleuth, Lord Peter Wimsey. How the snobbery of her books is part of the fun, how brilliant her plots are. We move on to what Mrs Clements calls all that nonsense about Harry. We wonder how Jeannie's life will change. We find this topic interesting and discuss it at some length.

'I'm sure Jeannie's happy,' says Bel, peering at her rhubarb which is in danger of boiling over. 'Closer contact with things Maori will enrich her. It's not as if it's Mum.'

As usual Bel has put her finger on it.

'I do feel though,' I say, 'not so much with Hare but with Jeannie, as if there's a sort of film or something between us. I know it sounds ridiculous. Do you feel that?'

'No,' she says, still crumbling. I should not have asked.

I tell Bella of her mother's concerns about Laing's Point.

She rinses her hands under the tap, ducks her head to drink. 'I don't know anything about Maori leasehold,' she says, 'but if it's Hare's land, why not?'

'Why not what?'

'Let him do what he wants with it. Would the sky fall?'

As far as Mrs Clements goes, yes. I do not say this. I do not say anything. I retreat into another batch of scones. Bel thinks we'll get away with them not being fresh tomorrow if we keep them in the Westinghouse overnight and put them in the oven tomorrow to freshen. We discuss such things with care. We are good providers.

The enormous Westinghouse gives a deep rumbling grunt. Bella takes a tray of egg sandwiches and fresh lemonade to her mother, who is now resting in her room. I am impressed by such solicitude, but, as ever, Bel has combined grace with good sense. She and I will be able to sit undisturbed over our sandwich at the wisteria-shaded table on the verandah.

It is very still. A shining cuckoo calls. Duncan's father told me that the rhythm of their song can be translated as *Tah tah tah tiddely pom*. I suppose many have thought of this, but it was he who told me.

'How are things,' I say as we light up, 'with you and Angus?'

Bel blows a beautifully formed smoke ring. Not many women bother to practise, but Bella has always had time for small skills. 'What do you mean, things?'

'He's very attentive.'

'There's no one else to be attentive at.'

There is something disturbing about that word 'at'.

'There's me,' I say, 'and Jeannie of the thousand smiles.'

'You're both married.'

This is unanswerable. Nevertheless I know the signs of the attentive male. They listen to what you have to say, for one thing; they leap to sit beside you. Tentative fingers brush. Eyes move. You can tell.

Angus, I tell Bella, is coming along nicely.

She leaps up, stubs out her cigarette and, to my astonishment, flings her head between her hands. Her shoulders heave, presumably with laughter. She lifts her head and mops.

'He asked me,' she snorts, 'he asked me last night in the garden . . .' Her eyes sparkle, literally sparkle. 'Oh, dear Lord, I'll never feel the same again about night-scented stocks. He asked me whether I had "a romantic attachment with anyone at the moment".'

'So what? Obviously it's a good idea to find out if the field is clear. You should be flattered.'

'Don't you think it's hilarious?'

'The phrase yes, but not otherwise. Why should I? You're an attractive woman.'

'Don't be ridiculous,' snaps Bel.

'So what did you say?'

'Nothing much. I just bolted. It was such a shock. He seemed quite rational this morning, though, didn't he?'

I see Angus at breakfast, the competent despatch of bacon and egg, the quick herding of marmalade to toast, the strong bite. Angus is as energetic at breakfast as he is everywhere else. As the head shepherd's wife says, he's a ripsnorter of a chap, a real goer. I tell Bel this.

She sidesteps. 'Good old Hilda.' She draws deeply, sighs the smoke out. 'I bet you we'll be left with Blackie and Bess. They'll have taken my Thompson and all the good hacks.'

Even I have not the bare-faced gall to mention Tamati Ropata.

Blackie and Bess it is. They are old and tired. They have mouths of iron and are full of guile. Eventually Blackie realises that Bella is not going to be dislodged, however often he attempts to rub her off against wire fences, and Bess learns that I am not fooled by a sudden false stumble. We progress. It takes time but the heat is lessened by the breeze, and the space and quietness is true joy. As we pass beyond the Bull Paddock and its incumbent, the valley narrows to a ravine, the limestone cliffs rise high and steep on either side; there are outcrops of rock high above, no vegetation except a few cabbage trees and thorny matagouri bushes. The sheep have retreated and there are no goats. The Devil's Canyon is perfect for its role. High, steep, mysterious. No birds.

Charlie and Ann run to us, begging for rides. Bella swings Charlie in front of her, Ann hops up onto the now resigned Bess. They tell us all, including that fact that it's spooky here, eh? That we have missed the beginning scene when just Mr Clements and Mrs Henare come riding into the canyon together all happy and unsuspecting and not knowing *anything*. Mr Rowan filmed that bit. But boy oh boy, wait till you see the Indians! When they come screaming down from right up there! They did it this morning a couple of times but Mr Clements wants you to make another take, Bella, and he can tell you where to stand and that. If there's time they'll do the part where the Indians snatch Mrs Henare right off her horse! Mrs Henare is not so keen about that bit but Mr Clements says . . .

Everyone should have the company of a small child occasionally. They are good at wonder and their enthusiasm is at the ready.

The men greet us. Bel is welcomed with courtesy and no sign of embarrassment from Angus and with brisk efficiency by James. She does not waste any time. Having been briefed by James as to angles, camera replacements and similar technicalities, she drops Charlie, takes over the gear from Angus and heads Bess up a rudimentary zig-zag track after the mounted Indians. Mr Ropata leads, followed by Hare Henare and Joe. Tam stops, exchanges a word, takes the tripod from Bel. She looks well on a horse. Thin women do.

We wait while Bel takes preliminary shots. And wait. And wait. James shouts.

Doing? doing? returns the echo.

Nothing happens. They don't even wave. Bel dismounts, repositions herself. We can see nothing.

The children are fidgety. 'Where are they, Mum? Where are they?'

Suddenly, roaring, whooping, high wide and hellish fast come the Indians, their steeds surefooted, their riders limpet tight. The impact is astonishing. From stillness to turmoil in seconds, such violent action, such intensity, such skill and rage and triumph all combined. Battle cries and oaths split the air. I shiver. How, how in the name of all that's merciful, can horses and men survive such hurtling precipitate speed. Dislodged stones, a small rock or two crash straight down to fall at our feet. I have never seen anything so dramatic in my life, nor have the children. Charlie is speechless. Duncan yelling.

'It's like *The Man from Snowy River*, on the cover,' whispers Ann.

> *He hails from Snowy River, up by Kosciusko's side*
> *Where the hills are twice as steep and twice as rough,*
> *Where a horse's hoofs strike firelight from the flint stones*
>   *every stride,*
> *The man that hold his own is good enough . . .*

'They had saddles, stupid,' says Duncan. 'They weren't bareback. Look, look!'

'Magnificent, quite magnificent,' cries Angus. 'Who needs a cavalry charge?'

James agrees. He glances at his watch, tells the panting Indians and their horses how well they have done and that we'll have smoko before we head back. Bel takes over thermoses, assisted by Angus. We hand round mugs and rock cakes to men who now stand yarning together, stretching and mopping and lighting their smokes. Dogs and children mill around.

Tensions, if there were any (and as Derek says, I tend to exaggerate) seem to have melted. Mr Ropata, Tam and Angus discuss the finer points of bareback riding. Bel, Hare and James agree the abduction of Jeannie should wait till tomorrow.

Angus offers to ride Bel's horse back to the homestead. She shakes her head. 'No, thank you. I enjoy the ride. Would you like a ride home, Charlie?'

She leans down. He puts his good foot on her boot and swings the ski pole over like an expert. 'Bye, Mum,' he calls, his face ecstatic as they ride off.

The rest of us collect gear, whistle up a dog or two, stand around, pile into trucks. Angus appears at my elbow. Could he not ride Bess home for me? I must be tired.

I am not fooled by such concern but I have not the heart to decline. 'She has a pig of a mouth. And she's slow, but if you want to . . .'

He's up, off and disappears in pursuit. Bess is in for a shock.

I sit next door to Jeannie in the truck. We prop ourselves against the back of the cab and I discover again that I am not entirely at ease with her. Presumably Jeannie also feels this. Which is ridiculous. Jeannie is a friend, a true friend.

Tired, hot children lie about. Duncan can't see why he couldn't have ridden home on Mrs Henare's horse. It's always Charlie who gets things.

Mr Henare was leading a horse. What a waste. And Mr Clements is in the cab of the truck. Look, you can see. What about his horse?

Ann yawns. 'Mr Jackson's riding it home.' She curls up beside Miriama as the truck starts.

I make conversation to Jean. I ask about this, that, the other thing. Jeannie smiles, agrees, confides her delight in Hare's decision.

'It's just so wonderful for Hare. He's a different person. Totally relaxed. He feels he has come home.'

I open my mouth, shut it, try again. 'And what about you?'

'I'm happy if he is.'

I duck my head to avoid her gaze, scratch around for something soft to sit on. I haven't ridden for some time. I tell Jeannie I wish we had a cushion or two. She tells me there aren't any and also that Hare doesn't think they'll stay on at Rongomaha. He senses that Mrs Clements feels he has let the side down in some way and he's not going to put up with that nonsense. They'll come up from the Beach by the day. And besides, Miriama is missing Patch. Jeannie hopes Mrs Clements won't take it the wrong way. Hare will tell her tonight.

'You call him Hare all the time?'

'Yes.'

'Even in bed?'

She glances towards the sleepy children. 'No,' she says, 'not yet.' She giggles. 'It's like, oh I don't know. Not a different person or anything. I don't mean that. Just an extra. Something you hadn't expected.'

I find this comment both crystal clear and a relief.

'Jeannie,' I say, 'you're wonderful.'

Jeannie demonstrates this once more by taking the older children to the swimming hole while I head for the kitchen where Mrs Clements stands wondering what to do for the best. She didn't know when we were going to arrive home, or how many. And now Rua's disappeared. She hasn't returned after her day off. 'Gone,' she cries. 'Just like that.' She gives a brisk wriggle of her shoulders, pulls herself together. As if things weren't bad enough. Just when the child was beginning to be of some use to Bella. No notice, no farewell, just sneaked off when she's most wanted. They just melt off without a thought. Mrs Clements adds that she is not at all sure she would have agreed to have had such hordes in the house if she'd known Rua was going to let her down. In the meantime perhaps I could make a cup of tea while she sets the table. James will be in the Smoking Room.

She drifts towards the dining room, pauses en route to say that she supposes she could add more knives and forks later, but that she does like to know what she's meant to be doing in her own house. A cotton cloth would have to do, she supposed. Or were the children being fed first?

Mrs Jackson, apparently unfazed by Rua's defection, appears at the back door with the day's take of eggs.

'Where are you going with that tray?' she asks. 'Mr Clements? I'll pop it in. It won't take me a sec.' She holds out her capable hands, smiles her capable smile.

'No thank you,' I say, with that small flash of assertiveness sometimes felt by the less efficient in the face of arrant competence. There is nothing silly about me. I too can carry trays. Besides, this one is for James.

And I will see the photographs again.

Lorna

James is stretched on the ancient leather sofa which he has had moved to the conservatory from the Smoking Room. His head lies against one arm, the synopsis of the film is propped against his stomach. He adds notes with coloured pencils, deletes, adds more. He glances up, smiles, makes a half-hearted attempt to rise.

'No, no,' I say, placing the tray with teapot and scones and two cups to hand.

The sofa sighs as he leans back once more. The soughing of expelled air from leather cushions is welcome made audible.

Surrounded by orchids, books and tea cups James is expansive.

'Grab a stool. Let's talk. It's going well, don't you think?'

I agree. My praise is extravagant but not forced. I think James is doing a wonderful job, and say so. Frankly I am astounded, not from doubts as to James's ability but at his knowing where, let alone how, to start. It is an astonishing achievement. All this I tell him as I perch on a cane stool at his feet.

We talk about the film, relive the hurtling descent of the mounted Indians. Did we notice Joe? We certainly did. Quite a feat for a fourteen-year-old. James says that the actual snatching of Jeannie from her horse may be tricky, but she will have complete faith in Harry's ability, which is the main thing.

'Hare now. Long a.'

'As you will. Obviously he's the man for the job as well as an excellent rider, but the whole thing will have to be rehearsed most carefully. Normally of course they'd use a stunt woman. Fortunately Jeannie's a tiny little thing.' His hand flicks. 'Plucky too. All this fandango.'

'Do you think Hare will hand over Laing's Point to his tribe?'

'Why on earth?'

'Your mother seems concerned.'

'Oh, you know Ma. Coming up to the set tomorrow?'

'I think I'll have to help in the kitchen. Rua's disappeared.'

He nods, drinks his tea, asks for more.

A Greek goddess called Hebe was cup-bearer to the gods. That is all I know of her.

'Should be quite interesting. Plenty of action.' He reaches out an arm for his smokes, offers me one, lights up. His face through the smoke is dreamy yet intent. His eyes gleam.

'The part I'm really looking forward to,' he says, 'is the river scenes. Quite tricky but intensely dramatic. Yours Truly bound to the post and the tide screaming in.' He sits up, flicks ash into a saucer. 'Tense, wouldn't you say? If Bella can get the close-ups right.'

'James,' I say suddenly. 'Why have you never married?'

He puts down his cup and swings his legs off the sofa. He is in no way discomfited, has in all probability been asked this question before. He pats the sofa cushion beside him. I jump from my stool, am welcomed by warm leather. James leans towards me.

'Do you really want to know?'

'Yes.'

'I have this problem, you see.'

'Oh.'

'I'm not proud of it, anything but. However, I have to admit I'm a perfectionist. In everything. Everything I say or do, or want. Things matter to me, things which may seem ludicrous, things which others dismiss without a thought: small flaws, a lack of symmetry. The mess and muddle of other people's lives can keep me awake at night.'

'How on earth did you survive the War?'

'That's very perceptive of you, Lorna.'

He is silent for a moment, staring at a magnificent pale-pink cymbidium at eye level.

'God knows. God knows. And worse than that. Being a perfectionist oneself is bad enough, but I have this dream of the perfect woman. Someone as kind as she is fair, as loving as she is true. Tall, slim, elegant, beautiful skin, limbs, with that . . . how can I put it. Who was it who said, "She was the type of woman to whom one gave orchids." '

My voice is doubtful. 'A corsage?'

'No, no, I can't stand the things. All bosomy cattleyas, florist's wire and maidenhair. Terrible. No,' he says firmly, 'more draped. Species probably. White dendrobium from head to toe.'

'Smothered in them?' I whisper.

His hand brushes mine as he puts down his cup and turns to me. 'Don't you think, Lorna, that somewhere in the world there must be a woman who, if a man saw her standing on the steps of Shepheard's, would know she was the one?'

'Shepherds?'

'Shepheard's Hotel, Cairo. With an 'a'. I spent quite a lot of my leaves there.'

'And you never saw her?'

'Once. Or so I thought.' James's eyes are far away. They stare beyond and through orchids and bright glass, oceans and time. 'She was a young Hindu woman. In a sari of course, slim as a reed. Calm, serene, beautiful as the dawn.'

'On the steps?'

'What? Oh yes. Yes, she was, as a matter of fact.'

'And then what?'

He leaps to his feet. Picks up a dim little re-potted thing, stares at it briefly and replaces it. He turns to me again, his face a tragic mask. 'She was wearing sandals, you know how they do. As I passed her, I nodded. She, of course, made no response. I dropped my eyes and . . .'

'Yes?'

'One of her feet, her beautiful slim brown feet, the left one, had six toes.'

There is nothing to say.

'I found out later she was a Maharajah's daughter.'

Still silence.

'I have always known,' he says eventually, 'that the woman I love must be more than beautiful, must look and be perfect at all times. Someone who can look both divine in tweeds and melting in evening clothes.'

He gives a short bitter bark, stands and stretches. 'I must go, I've promised to have a word with Bob Jackson. Bobby calves.' He turns at the door. 'And thank you for the tea.'

I make no reply. The arrogance, the overweening conceit – but most, oh most of all, the absurdity of the man have silenced me. This is a man I wished to lie with. Carnal knowledge was what I had in mind: exploration, intimacy, lust fulfilled. I lie back to the sighing exhalation of the sofa, unsure whether to laugh or howl. Disillusion, self-hate, anger, all, all are mine. Derek comes to mind. I see the Vision of the Steps and have a thought so beautiful I laugh aloud.

James will never know what she would have looked like in tweeds.

I lie still, my behind and thighs stiffening by the minute. It is some time since I have ridden a horse.

I wake up, aware instantly that I am not alone. Angus and Bella are in the Smoking Room next door, engaged in a private conversation which I cannot avoid overhearing. They stand close together. Angus is in full flight, Bella obviously confused. He is proclaiming his love for her in no uncertain terms. He is saying . . .

I leap up, or attempt to, wave hysterically. 'Stop,' I cry, 'stop talking, I'm here.'

Not unnaturally, they retreat. I am alone. I walk stiffly to inspect the photographs. The faces stare back at me with the non-committal gaze of the dead and buried. They take no interest in now. Do what you will.

Owing to Rua's untimely disappearance Mrs Clements has decreed that we girls should feed the children in the kitchen, then serve the adults' meal after we have put them to bed. In the meantime she and the men will have a drink on the front verandah. Ice will make a nice change.

The children are to sleep on the Bachelors' Balcony. I find this term deeply romantic with its connotations of importunate young men leaping and prancing about. There is something twirled moustache about the phrase. It comes from the days when young unmarried men, living alone in some distant hut, would ride for miles to enjoy the hospitality of James and Bella's grandparents, George and Grace Clements.

George, as a young man, had joined the thousands of hopefuls who rushed to the West Coast in the sixties in search of gold. Like other astute diggers he soon realised that his chances of making a good strike were slim but that the gold-rush towns were thriving. Whereupon he sold his claim near Stafford and moved into Hokitika, bought two draught horses and a dray, and set up business as a carrier. He and his Clydesdales were a familiar sight around the town, Bel told me. All three wore similar straw hats, the horses' slashed appropriately to accommodate their ears.

Grandfather George's origins before his arrival in Westland were not discussed. It was not, Bella believed, that there was any dire skeleton clanking, just that there was not much point in mentioning the past. Like many men's, George Clements' history began when he prospered.

And prosper he did. He married Grace Stacpoole, the sprightly younger daughter of the original grocer in the town, by whose good offices (as his proud son Harold told me) he produced a son and four daughters. Having made his modest pile, George and his family came north seeking land. With his usual good sense and good fortune, his arrival in the Bay in the 1880s coincided with the development of refrigeration which enabled the transportation of frozen sheep carcasses to Britain and the consequent increase in the prosperity for farmers in the area.

George and Grace's bachelor guests I see as lean and hard, and smokers to a man. Lonely men and far from home, they came to play tennis, to dance all night, to meet and greet and flirt, and sleep on the Bachelors' Balcony. They could smoke there, talk, swear even, could indulge in high jinks and horseplay and I imagine they did. And next morning there would be more fun and games with those good sports Ettie and Gretchen and the twins. And, of course, their brother Harold, from whose bedroom the balcony opened.

Rongomaha has always been known for its hospitality. No swaggers nor anyone down on his luck has ever been turned away. Both George Clements and his son Harold were generous men. They could afford to be, but the wherewithal and the impulse do not always go together.

The four iron bedsteads on the balcony look as though they could well be the originals. There is no other furniture apart from a few hospital-type lockers and a rolled tarpaulin blind. The waist-high wooden balustrade ensures safety. The wide overhanging roof protects from driving rain but little else. The balcony now has the stark clinical air of one in a Tuberculosis Sanatorium whose consultants and directors are committed to the beneficial effects of fresh air and the spartan life.

Charlie is half asleep at the kitchen table. 'May I carry him?' asks Bella innocently.

'Just this once.'

He opens his eyes as I tuck him into bed.

'Will there be stars?'

'Of course.'

'Beaut.' His mouth brushes mine. 'Night, Mum.'

'Blanket,' says Ann, who hasn't seen one for weeks.

Duncan wants to know how echoes work. 'Ask Dad on Friday,' I say, kissing his proffered cheek.

If Derek were here he would wait till it was dark enough and point out the Southern Cross, but now is not the moment. We have work to do. Bel and I restraighten blankets and prepare to leave the four beds and their slight forms, the toes pointing to the darkening sky.

Jean is hearing Miriama say her prayers,

Gentle Jesus, meek and mild,
Look upon a little child;
Pity my simplicity,
Suffer me to come to thee.

She glances up from Miriama's bed, her face dreamy with love. 'I think I'll stay a moment till she's completely asleep.'

This suits me as I have not yet had a chance to apologise to Bella. I begin as we pass the woven Maori cloak which hangs on the wall of the top landing.

'Bel, I must explain. I'd gone to sleep. I had no idea.'

Bel smiles, pushes back her hair. 'I was glad to see you.'

'I felt such a fool.'

She runs briskly down the stairs, pursued by me. 'Not as much as I did.'

'Why don't you like him?'

She turns to me, her face flushed. 'Not now. We've got to dish up. Come on.'

Mrs Clements has given some thought to the placing of the guests at her table. She sits at one end, with James at the other in the carver's chair. On her right with his back to the kitchen sits Angus, on her left Hare Henare.

'You girls,' she says, as Bella and I bring in the last plates piled high for the men, 'had better sit near the kitchen. It will make things easier for you, especially since Rua's departed.' She snaps her lips together. 'If there's one thing I can't abide it's the whole table leaping up and running off to the kitchen every five seconds to *help*.'

I move to sit beside Angus. Mrs Clements' hand rises palm outwards in an unexpected benedictory gesture.

'No, no, Lorna. Bella will sit there. You sit beside James, and Jean can sit beside you,' she says to Hare. 'If and when she arrives.'

This comment is unlike Mrs Clements and I fear she realises it. Irritation, unhappiness and her fixation about punctuality have defeated her momentarily.

Jeannie slips into the room and sinks beside Hare, all fresh pink lips and pretty apologies.

'She wasn't quite asleep,' she explains.

Mrs Clements does not pursue the topic. She achieves a watery smile. 'Eat it up while it's hot, dear.'

I sit beside James, glance at his beauty with the peeled and angry eyes of the disillusioned. I dislike us both, but surely he is the more ridiculous. Lust, after all, is *real*. Immoral, selfish and wrong, but definitely real. James seems to me to have lost his reality, to be no longer worthy of belief. The sharp angle of his wrist, the beauty of his hands as he carves, remain the same. It is the man himself who has disappeared.

The french doors to the verandah are open, the evening breeze gentle. I am breathing deeply, angrily, as I sniff the fragrance of Shot Silk and Crimson Glory, watch the reflection of their pink and burgundy petals and the sheen from the silver bowl in the polished wood beneath. The Rose Bowl was awarded to Harold Clements when Panache won the Cup many years ago and has been in service ever since. Mrs Clements feels there is something about roses in a silver bowl. We agree.

The meat, the gravy, the vegetables are all cooked to perfection. Even the mint sauce tastes better than usual.

I think of my mother, a handsome woman and a good enjoyer. I see her grey hair piled high and gleaming beneath the light. 'Farm lamb!' she cries. 'I can't believe I'm me.'

I used to wonder who she thought she was, but her comment was rhetorical and the question never asked.

My father, on the other hand, ate in silence. He could never understand why farmers ignore the best bits when carving, the knobbly bits, the sweet and nutty bits close to the bone. It puzzled him.

James is telling us that Bob Jackson has been a bit slack over the bobby calves. They should have gone to the works last week at the latest. That he can't understand what Bob was thinking of.

Angus eats his meal with his usual industrious enthusiasm and appreciation. He tells Bella the food is delicious. She says thank you. They sit side by side in creaking silence. There are long pauses all around. Despite the excellence of the food and the balmy night and the fragrances flowing, the atmosphere at Mrs Clements' table on the second night of our visit to Rongomaha is strained. Very strained. No one will *try*. People, perhaps, are tired. Or angry. I think of a long hot bath, wonder whether Mrs Clements' allergy to mustard will mean supplies are limited. And does mustard in fact remove stiffness? Has anyone ever actually known someone who has had a mustard bath? Like the moon and tides it seems highly unlikely. Keep calm, Hopkins. Calm.

Angus, having mustered his plate clean, asks James to tell him more about the bobby calves. James replies that there is not much to tell. That nobody wants hundreds of gash bulls eating their heads off. He adds that we should run through tomorrow's shoot while we're all here. The point as he sees it is how Jeannie feels about the kidnap itself. It will obviously have to be well timed and well rehearsed but he doesn't want her to be apprehensive. We could possibly think of an alternative. He adds that he can't think what it could be.

Jean smiles and says as long as Hare does the actual snatching she's happy. She adds that she trusts Hare completely.

Mrs Clements says who on earth did Jeannie think would do it otherwise? Mr Ropata perhaps? That wretched child?

Bel lifts her head. She has not eaten much. 'Why not Tam?' she asks gently.

What on earth does Bella think she's doing? This needling, this picador business will not help. Bella, my love, this is no way to behave. Where is your judgement, your grace, your sense?

There is scarcely a face around the table which is not either mildly irritated or positively affronted by her question. Angus's lips purse, Jean looks startled. Hare's expression indicates that his enthusiasm for his own race may not extend to Tamati Ropata. The pleats of Mrs Clements' neck shake, she swallows air, makes odd noises in her throat. Eventually she draws a deep breath.

'May I ask, Isabel, why you make such an extraordinary suggestion?'

'Because Tam's a much better bareback rider than you, isn't he, Hare?'

'No,' lies Hare, 'and if anyone's going to snatch my wife off a horse I would prefer to be responsible, rather than some hack from the Pa.'

'Hear, hear,' glows Jeannie.

'Speaking of which,' says Hare, changing the subject, 'I've been meaning to mention something else, Mrs Clements. Jeannie and I, and of course Miriama, want to thank you very much for your hospitality to us over the last few days. However, I think, on balance, it would be better if the Henare family went back and stayed at the Point.'

Mrs Clements, torn between a possible impugning of her hospitality and increasing dislike for the man and his concerns, pauses for a moment, then opts for affront.

'Why on earth?'

'There are several factors involved. We have had a very happy time and are most grateful, but among other things Miriama is pining for Patch. She hates not being with him. She's quite distraught at times, isn't she, Jeannie?'

'Yes.'

Mrs Clements is not placated. 'Never, in all my days, has anyone *left* Rongomaha.' She remembers, gives a quick sniff. 'Not a guest, I mean.'

Hare's face is stern. 'I should perhaps have mentioned this first, should have thought it through when we were first invited to stay.' He rubs his fingers on the polished table and stares at them. 'I feel I have put myself and my family in a false position by staying at Rongomaha. We should be with our people.'

'At the Pa?'

'No, but I feel . . . I could bring Wiremu Ropata up each day. Tamati and Joe'll still have to ride the horses, but there will be no need for the truck.'

James nods thoughtfully.

'Is this more of your *aligning?*' inquires Mrs Clements.

Hare is himself again, serious, dignified, a man not distracted by petty sarcasm. 'If you choose to see it as such,' he says gently.

The men require second helpings. I avoid Bella's eye as we scuttle in and out, am saved by the mundane. 'Is there any more mint sauce?'

'No,' she snaps. 'Let them eat redcurrant jelly.'

'What have we for pudding?' asks Mrs Clements on our return.

Bel replaces the replenished gravy boat with care. 'Rhubarb Crumble and cream.'

Mrs Clements rises. She is in command once more. 'Not for me thank you. Coffee in the other room?'

She turns at the door. 'I suppose, Jean, that your family will still require breakfast and a packed lunch before you return to the Bush Pigeon on the Cliffs above the Sparkling Waters?'

Jeannie's lip wobbles. She jumps up, slaps about her front in search of a handkerchief. 'Oh thank you, yes,' she cries. 'Thank you so much, Mrs Clements. That would be wonderful.' She sinks down beside her husband, snuffling like a small disconsolate animal.

We stare in silence as Mrs Clements departs.

I am woken by the song of tuis or possibly bellbirds. I am never quite sure which is which. At intervals since dawn I have been aware of small bare feet padding or hopping through my room from the verandah on their way to the lavatory and back. They like the lavatory near the Bachelors' Balcony. Its porcelain handle labelled *Pull* has long since disappeared and has been replaced by a stirrup. Added to which there is reading matter for all ages, including, Ann tells me, *Seven Little Australians*. Charlie tells me at about 6 a.m. that there were stars and it was corker. I tell him I'm glad to hear it, and roll over.

I wake again at seven and go to rouse them. Their clothes and Charlie's ski pole have disappeared. The beds are made and some attempt has been made at redding up the camp. Derek would be pleased and so am I. Charlie's sandal lies discarded by his bed. I dislike the sight of small single shoes, and stow it quickly in the locker between two beds, then lean on the balcony rail to gaze at this serene world. The day is fresh but already warming; there is no sound but the bleating of lambs and ewes searching for each other, and an occasional burst of yelping from the dogs.

A well-worn track leads up the gentle rise behind the house, past the garage and stables to the single men's whares and the shearing quarters. The woolshed and the sheep yards, the holding paddocks, the killing shed and the long-legged meat safes lie on the flats beyond the plantation. Bob Jackson's trim little cottage, its garden heavy with dahlias and gladioli and vegetables, lies within easy reach of the hen house, the pig sties and the dogs. It has been well planned, Rongomaha, as carefully designed as a Victorian child's sampler inscribed *Peace and Plenty* in cross-stitch.

An old man in a wideawake hat ambles across the courtyard carrying the ex-kerosene-tin pig-bucket from the kitchen. Claude perhaps? He doesn't glance upwards, which is just as well as I am still in my nightgown. Bob Jackson's wife hoves in sight. She stops Claude, gesticulates widely, is obviously telling him to stop doing what he is doing and go and do something more important which she wishes to be done immediately. The old man stands still throughout, spits forcibly and continues on his way. Mrs Jackson is not pleased. She makes that emphatic downward humph of her folded arms, that exasperated movement which goes with 'Really!' She heads for the wash house.

I am late. Of course I'm late. This is a working farm.

Breakfast is almost over. Angus, who is having a final cup of coffee, leaps to his feet to greet me, then dashes out the back door. Bella lifts a hand and continues packing lunches in a cardboard box. She stows paper bags bulging with sandwiches, enamel mugs and thermoses. She counts, recounts, winks at me as she carries it out the back door. 'He might have waited for this little lot,' she mutters.

She tells me on her return that her mother has elected to have a tray in her room.

'Who took it in?'

'Me, of course.'

'How was she?'

'Huffy but calm. Not much chat.'

'And Jeannie?'

'Fine.' Bel's self-deprecating grin appears as she concentrates on her smoke. 'Tam for the body snatcher was a bit of a fizzer, wasn't it?'

'I thought she seemed a bit upset.'

'Jean? Yes, I think she was. So was Hare. So was Angus. And as for poor old Mum. Upsets all round.' Bella stubs out her virtually unsmoked cigarette. 'If things go on like this I'll get upset.'

'They won't even notice.'

Bella heads for the sink, hands me a tea towel. 'Oh yes. They'll notice all right.'

'So what's the plot for today?' I say.

This is a question Derek asks me quite often. He likes to know what his staff will be doing at any given time, Miss Murphy with the wonderful head for figures who makes a good cup of tea, Mr Ferguson whose wife has gastric upsets of unknown origin, the new lad who seems to be shaping up quite well, all of them he can visualise hour by hour, and he likes to be able to do the same with his wife and children. It is not intrusive, this concern; he merely takes an interest, as I do, in other people's lives.

Today, Bel tells me, will be an extremely busy day. So busy, in fact, that James has suggested I stay back at Rongomaha with the children this afternoon as well as this morning. Speed, apparently, is of the essence, as James and his team propose to roam widely. They plan to shoot Jean's abduction by Indians at Devil's Canyon this morning, and this afternoon he hopes to do some preliminary work on her rescue; plan the moves, camera positions, etc. The place he has in mind is up country a bit and he thinks they'd be more mobile with packhorses than the truck. The Ropatas have already set off, and Bella will leave when we've dealt with today's food.

'Go now, why not?'

'No. You've done your share already.'

The same thought has occurred to me. However, compared with Bel I am sloth incarnate. 'Maybe I'll take the children up to the glow-worm cave.'

Bel shakes her head. 'It's a bit overgrown at the moment. Wait a day or two. Tam's offered to give me a hand clearing it tomorrow. It's a free day, remember?'

'Decent of him.'

'Yes, he is decent.' Her candid eyes meet mine. 'Mum doesn't know yet. I must tell her.'

I nod thoughtfully, soberly, the nod of a person who has considered alternatives and found them wanting. My face cracks. 'I'll bet she sends Angus hot-footing after you.'

I haven't seen Bel blush since the presentation of the silver cups. It's rather attractive, a pink overlay on her brown cheeks, not the usual deep shaming stain.

'Don't be ridiculous.'

'I wish you'd stop telling me to stop being ridiculous about your having two attractive men panting hotly after you.'

She swings around, her eyes bright, her dish mop at the ready. 'Do you think he's attractive too?'

'Bella, Bella, I said "two".'

She gives a quick dismissive squeeze of the cotton dish mop and bongs it against the sink to let the air in. Angus is a dead duck on the floor of the Bird Room. 'I mean Tam,' she says.

Gently now. This is cool-head country.

'Yes, of course he's attractive,' I say carefully. 'Most young Maori men of his age are. Strong, beautiful bodies, friendly grins, unless of course they're hopelessly shy. You never know where you are with those ones, male or female.'

'Oh don't give me that "won't-look-you-in-the-eye" business.'

'The eyes,' I tell her, 'are the windows of the soul. Your mother says so.'

Bella's face is serious, angry. 'Please,' she says.

We sit on the kitchen table, our feet on stools, our smokes nearby. There are things more important than the making of Lemon Delicious pudding, and the scones won't take me long.

'Tam and Joe don't seem to be crippled with shyness,' I tell the Westinghouse refrigerator. 'You know where you are with those two.'

Bel sits staring at the coiled compressor on its top as though there is something puzzling about it.

'Yes,' she says. 'He is different.'

'You've done it again, Bella! Hopeless. Hopeless!'

Her glance is still puzzled. 'Do you think so?'

This is almost too good to be true. But not so funny. Scarcely funny at all. I would like to help Bella, this admirable woman who saved the lives of two of my children. I move the Dewar's Whisky ashtray towards her.

'Do you want to talk about it?'

She gives a wry smile. 'There's not much to tell.'

But what there is is interesting.

Bella is in love with Tamati. The sight of him, the sound of him, the smell of him reduce her to pulp. She tells me so. She is not joking. She can feel it in her knees, heart. It feels – she can't tell me how it feels. His voice, his laughter, the way he makes her laugh. All Bella wants is to be with him, beside him, alongside Tamati Ropata for the rest of her natural life.

'Yes,' I say. 'I know what you mean.'

She looks at me, her expression faintly surprised for a moment before she corrects it.

'Tell me,' she says.

I tell her about the hotel in Waipawa, the Fruits in Season and the sign which welcomes Commercials. I tell her how it ended. How I was determined to have his child. I tell her about Duncan, about how I made use of Derek because of cowardice. I tell her everything.

She puts her arms around me, her smoky breath meets mine, her hair is in my eyes. She thinks it is a terrible story, terrible. How can I be so funny, so generous. How can I give so much, be such a wonderful mother . . .

'Have you gone mad or something? I knew what I was doing. Derek is a good man.'

'Oh yes,' she says quickly. 'He is. A dear.'

'The reason I told you was that I had some mad idea it might help. That if you knew that I . . . understand how you feel, then perhaps it might help.' I sit up straight. 'Sorry, "I know how you feel" must be the most infuriating cliché known to man. What are you going to do?'

'Do?'

'Do, woman, do.' I realise I sound like Mrs Clements, and giggle feebly. 'How does Tam feel?'

'He says he loves me, but I can't believe that.'

'*Will* you stop being so impossible. Why in the name of heaven would the man say he loves you if he didn't?'

The Westinghouse shudders into life.

'I suppose he wants to sleep with me for some reason,' she mutters. 'Some sort of trophy perhaps. A pakeha sheila.'

'And you say you love him!'

'I have to make some attempt to preserve my sanity,' she cries. 'Why else would the son of a chief, a beautiful young man who, if you can stand the expression, can have his pick of any wahine in the district, want to go to bed with a pakeha woman years older than he is?'

Irritation casts out cynicism. 'Because he loves you,' I cry.

She glances at her forefingers. 'Nicotine. I must get a bit of pumice from the beach.'

144

'If you won't accept the fact that you're an attractive woman, look at Angus. Why's he so keen? I heard enough yesterday . . .'

'Angus,' says Bel, 'is "in want of a wife". A practical no-nonsense country girl.'

'A colonial?'

'"Some English gels don't settle",' she murmurs. 'And he plans to live here and his parents are dead. Grandfather George's horses and dray can sleep easy.'

Few things are more maddening in a woman than mock modesty, but Bel is a clear-sighted woman. It is just that in her case a natural modesty, combined with Mrs Clements' endless emphasis on her lack of charms, has blinkered her. The non-stop beating on the drum of plainness has deafened her reason.

'Oh for goodness sake. *Everyone has sex appeal for someone, Or many of us wouldn't be here,*' I croon. 'It's one of life's great truths. Besides, what's wrong with Angus?'

'I should've thought it was obvious. I love someone else.'

Something tightens near my heart. 'What exactly does Tam say?'

'I told you. That he loves me. That he's never met a woman like me, let alone a pakeha. That he could talk to me for ever. That I delight him. That he carries me in his heart.' She looks at me, hating herself, her distrust and disbelief. 'How about that? That his father will be furious. Nevertheless he is determined to marry me. "The usual thing", as Mum would say. Or else she'll say that he's after my money or that a curse will be laid on us, or probably all three.' Bella snatches another cigarette, taps the end. 'There's one thing she's left out of the equation. I want his child. Isn't that meant to be one of the signs of devotion? A beautiful well-cooked baby, not a wrinkled red prune. The "warm browns", we used to call them in the Children's Ward, remember?'

'Yes.'

She glances at the mahogany-framed clock on the wall, leaps up. 'Heavens. Look at the time.'

*

I have chivvied Bella out of the kitchen and on her way up the hill to film; have checked that the children are indeed feeding the pigs with Claude; have knocked up the first batch of the day's scones; and am feeling rather pleased with my orderly competence, or would be if I could stop thinking about my friend Bella. At least I had the sense not to cry, 'Go to him! Learn from me. If you love the man, nothing else matters.' Too easy. Far far too easy. Bella is a strong woman, as I keep saying, and I think she could withstand her mother's rage and the world's contempt. But how would Tam's people react? Would Bella 'settle'? Would she be allowed to, let alone be made welcome? Downcast eyes, through shyness or not, reveal nothing. I remember the occasional cessation of laughter as I entered a hospital ward. One of the first Maori phrases I learned while nursing was, Kati tena, kei rongo mai te pakeha. Not in front of the pakeha.

I am thinking on these things as Mrs Jackson makes her usual buoyant entry. 'Ah,' she booms from the doorway. 'Nothing like hot scones. I'll make a cuppa.'

Mrs Jackson is displeased with Claude. If ever there was a no-hoper, a real layabout, it's that Claude Earnshaw. And stubborn! She had asked him this morning polite as anything to give her a hand with the mangle and would he, would he hell.

'I don't mind of course,' she continues with a careless laugh, 'but I had to smile when I think of all those filthy duds of his I've washed and ironed over the years. Still, that's men all over, isn't it? You never know which way they're going to jump. All over you like a rash one minute, then kiss m'foot when you need them.'

She stares into the middle distance, chewing reflectively.

'But that Mr Rowan now. He's a different thing again. Lovely manners, lovely. But full of pep, know what I mean? He reminds me of that song. You know.'

The Black Watch are tall and the Seaforths are braw
But the cocky wee Gordons the pride of them all.

'He's not a Gordon,' I mutter.

'I didn't say he was a Gordon. I said he reminded me of a Gordon. There's a difference. Yes,' she sighs, 'a real goer like I said. I wouldn't mind his boots under my bed.'

I head for the door. 'I must get some lemons from the store room.'

'It's not locked,' she calls.

I lurch down the coarse drugget strip to the store room. I shut the door carefully, prop myself against the wide shelf and stare at the glass jars on the shelf opposite: Golden Queen peaches, apricots, plums and fat red tomatoes. All the bountiful colours are here, golds, reds and purples stored away by Bella who is a good provider. Deep wooden bins of sugar and flour and dry goods unknown line one wall, emergency supplies of corned beef, sheep's tongues and Maconachies Herrings in Tomato Sauce are stored beside a tin box labelled *First Aid*. The spices are neatly stacked, the air is pungent with their fragrance. Nutmeg predominates. From now on its fragrance will bring shame. Who am I to smile at Hilda's hocks, her trim white ankle socks and little black trotters, her wide florals and her wider behind?

What is so sweet about me? It is only the words which are different. I did not love James Clements any more than Hilda loves Angus. She likes the cut of his jib. He appeals to her. She wouldn't mind his boots under her bed.

And what about Duncan's father. What about the great love of my life. Why should that be sanctified because I did in fact love the man? His poor little wife out at the coast was just that to me. And he killed himself, remember. My gentle lover killed himself. Certainly he was shell-shocked, but that must have been only part of his torment. What James would call the mess and muddle of his life. I had been no help to him; quite the reverse. I had been bad medicine.

I crawl to my feet eventually, seize the lemons, throw water at my face in the nearby bathroom and walk stiffly back to the kitchen.

Mrs Jackson is now beating hell out of egg yolks and sugar. She looks up, smiling. 'Got them? I thought seeing I was here I might as well get started on your Lemon Delicious.'

'Thank you, Mrs Jackson. That's very kind of you.'

'Mum,' says Charlie as he straps on his ski pole after the icy swim, 'would you be sad if Claude took us to the glow-worms tomorrow instead of you?'

'But Bella said the track's overgrown.'

'But that's just it, see. Claude can piggy-back me if the track's rough. The packhorses have nothing on him when it comes to humping swags, he says. He's strong as an ox, he says. I should've seen him in his mustering days. And he'll tell us all about the cave and birds and everything. Glow-worms spin stuff out their bottoms, he says, that's why they glow, so insects'll bump into the strings and get eaten. And the hungrier they get the more they glow. Stuff like that. And it has to be tomorrow so Joe can come.' He puts a small cool hand on mine. 'You can come as well, if you like.

'And boy, does he make up beauty games. And he makes up adventures as well and shows you how to put your finger into the lamb's mouth so it gets the hang of sucking. Pigs are clean animals really, he says.'

The rest of the children have heard it all before. Miriama sits on the round stones, dreamily stroking the glistening blueish white ball of a fresh thigh bone Claude has given her for Patch. Ann and Duncan, equally dreamy, sit throwing stones at the waterfall. Bright drops of water splash their brown legs.

'You nearly hit a fantail!' cries Ann, suddenly alert.

'Garn. Couldn't if I tried. But I'll have a go now.'

Ann, as usual, leaps to the bait. The fantails, unperturbed, dip and flicker above the spill of water.

We walk back to the kitchen for a drink of Fifty Fifty. It's later than I thought. Almost five. I should be doing something. The children depart to find Claude while I get the potatoes. When in doubt, peel.

The back door swings open, Bella storms in, slamming as she comes.

She flings her crop and gloves on the kitchen table with all the verve and force of Greta Garbo playing Queen Christina. Never have I seen her so angry. Her eyes flash, she swings around the kitchen as though looking for something to kick.

'That man,' she storms. 'That unspeakable twit!'

My peeling knife pauses in mid-air. 'Who?'

'Angus, of course, Angus. Do you know what he said! The temerity of the creature!'

She flops onto a kitchen chair, flings her jodhpur-covered legs out in front of her. 'It was bad enough yesterday, but at least Charlie was there to put him off. But today when we were riding home alone he started again. Wouldn't you think he'd have caught on by now? I told him. I said. But today he came up with a new slant. He said not only did he find my modesty endearing, but perhaps I didn't realise that to an Englishman of his class looks are not always a major consideration when a man seeks a wife.'

'Bel, I can't believe that. The man's not an idiot. Anything but. Decent, even chivalrous, I would have thought.'

'Oh, not those words exactly, but I know that's what he meant. As for "class", I didn't make that up.' She sits on the scrubbed pine table, stares at her hands. 'He also said that he knew he could make me happy.'

'There you are. Exactly. He didn't say that he knew you could make him happy.'

Bel's anger has not diminished. 'What's the difference?'

The whole world, Bella, the whole world. I know this, I know it well. If you don't realise this, Bella, I am surprised. But then how could you?

'Where was Tam while this gross insult was taking place?'

'He had been riding with me. Rewi was skittering about a bit when Angus appeared, and he spurred him on. He turned to wave, laughing.' Her lips twitch. 'Laughing his head off,' she says.

'You'll see him tomorrow.'

She stands straight and tall. Smiles.

'Yes,' she says. 'I will.' She lays one hand on the table, looks at it thoughtfully. 'Can you think of anything worse than a marriage of convenience?'

'Bella, I don't think you're being fair.'

'Fair,' she storms. 'Why should I be fair?'

Mrs Jackson appears at the back door, carrying eggs. 'The girls have gone on strike,' she says. 'Only three today. Lemon Delicious OK? Ooh, what's up?'

Bella blows her nose on a large khaki handkerchief. 'Nothing,' she snarls. 'Nothing.'

'Ooh,' says Mrs Jackson.

Ann

It's good at Rongomaha, though the Beach is still best for swimming. The river pool's freezing but the Bachelors' Balcony is the best place I've ever slept in. It's cool even with a blanket, cooler than home or the Beach or anywhere, and if you wake up there are stars.

Charlie didn't see the stars at first. He got ratty with me in the morning for not waking him, so I did and he got rattier than ever. Next he wants to see a sheep killed.

Miri and me talk in the dark. She tells me she is so happy now Dad is a proper Maori. That she can't wait to get back to school and tell all the other kids.

'What about Eve Porter?' I say.

'Especially Eve Porter,' she giggles, and I see Mrs Henare's furious face above Miri's head as she hugs her and tells her she's not a dumb Maori and how much she and her father love her.

Miri stretches her arms up high, then drops them quick and snuggles beneath the blanket. She gives a huge sigh and tells me that she thinks Miriama Henare is the most beautiful name she's ever heard in her whole life, and don't I wish I could have such a beautiful one. 'Miriama Henare,' she says, whispering it long and soft, then 'Ann Hopkins,' boom, like that.

'I like Ann Hopkins.'

'Better than Miriama Henare?'

'Yes.'

'I don't. You know something?' She giggles. 'I asked Joe how I would get all the kids at school to say Miriama Henare instead of Laing and he said I was to say that if they didn't he'd come and bop them one, and he'll be fourteen soon and they'd better watch out.'

Fourteen. Hang. Duncan's only twelve.

Miri's still going on. 'They're going to have a ceremony on the marae to welcome Dad back. Joe told me it hasn't been worked out yet, but it'll be the full works, he says. The challenge, and the bit with the warrior and his spear dancing and putting down the leaf and Dad picking it up to show he comes in friendship. Mum and me'll be there, of course. And there'll be Maori songs and speeches and hangis. Everything.'

'What Maori songs?'

'I can't remember,' says Miri, and goes to sleep straight off.

I lie looking at the stars and thinking about Heaven and things dying. Where do they go, dead things? Our cat Betty died last year. No one did anything. It just happened. She'd been sick and then she died and we had a funeral and Dad dug the hole.

Mrs Samson next door said I was not to cry because Betty had gone to be with Jesus up in Heaven. But when I asked Mum how did Mrs Samson know, and where was Heaven, Mum hugged me and said, 'Annie, I have to tell you something. Neither you nor I nor the Pope of Rome know where Betty is now. I don't think even Dad knows, but ask him if you like. He is a good man and he knows a lot.'

Then she brushed back my fringe and said it was time we had a visit to Mr Marton the barber, who had once been the flyweight boxing champion for the whole of the Bay and has photographs of himself on his wall, young and fierce and punching away at nothing.

'But there's something I do know,' said Mum.

'What?'

'Wherever Betty is now, she will be having a nice time.'

'How do you know?'

'Because,' Mum said, 'she is at peace. Gone but not forgotten.

Happy.'

But this doesn't work either. If we don't know where she's gone, how can we know she's happy? She has nowhere to be happy in. Or with.

Once I was making drop castles by the river and Colonel Holdaway who lives along the beach came along with his shooting stick which has a spike with a ring around it to stop it going too far into the sand. The top opens into a little bit for sitting so he can prop his bottom onto it and have a rest if he gets puffed. He stuck it into the bank and sat down, old but friendly.

Dad had told us that there were many tragedies in the Earthquake, but heroism as well, and that we owed a great debt of thanks to Colonel Holdaway who did so well he got a medal from the King afterwards. Colonel Holdaway had organised everything and set up Relief Camps and Tent Hospitals and Essential Services. Dad said Colonel Holdaway's experience at being a leader of men in the War had stood him in good stead, although there were many others. Colonel Holdaway's War service had been vital to him because he knew how to take charge and someone had to.

Drop castles are easy as long as there's water handy. Rivers are best. You get a handful of wet sand from the river, then drizzle it through your fingers onto the hard sand. You have to get the sand just right. If it's too wet it melts to nothing and if it's too dry it crumbles, but after a while you get the hang of it. The drops fall and stiffen like cooked pikelets, miles of tiny pikelets dripping down one on top of the other, and after a while you have sand towers going up and up to where the last drop has stuck. They look like the towers of ogres' castles in books, tall and wobbly and different each time. Colonel Holdaway said they reminded him of castles on the Rhine when he went back after the last shindig. 'A *schloss* on the Rhine, Ann. *Schlosses.*' A bit of the sand cliff caved into the river with a splash as he said it. It didn't mess up the castle or his stick or anything. It just fell.

'That reminds me,' he said, 'of an incident during the '31 Quake.

You wouldn't remember, Ann, but the shocks were so strong in Napier that the cliffs above Port Ahuriri crashed down hundreds of feet, doing untold damage.'

'No,' I said, thinking of my Earthquake which was different, and wiping away bits of hair so I could see him talking.

Colonel Holdaway was now laughing so hard he had to stop and puff for a bit before he went on. 'I was under canvas in my makeshift office the next day and as you can imagine things were a bit rumpty, when one of my aides, Underwood, I think it was, yes, Underwood, came in and said, "I'm sorry, Colonel, but there's a man outside who insists on seeing you. He won't see anyone else, says he's got an urgent problem."

'One thing I've learnt, Ann, is that it's often best to deal with these idiotic interruptions immediately, if possible, otherwise they just keep coming back and back, so I said, "Show him in, Underwood," and in came this huge man – a giant of a fellow, back-country shepherd I shouldn't wonder, and he said, "Are you the Boss of the Earthquake?"

'Underwood said, "Yes, he is," and the man said, "Well, the Ahuriri cliffs fallen on my false teeth and what're you going to do about it?"'

I'd been squatting too close to the river and my pants had got wet. 'Then what?' I said.

But now Colonel Holdaway was laughing and puffing too hard to answer, and then I saw through my strands of wet hair all clinging that he was crying. Crying and crying with shoulders heaving like Charlie's when he was little and other kids wouldn't wait.

'Hundreds,' sobbed Colonel Holdaway. 'People of all types, ages, babies, children your age . . .'

I got out of the river and took his hand. 'Don't cry, Colonel Holdaway,' I said and couldn't think of anything else to say.

Colonel Holdaway took out a big white handkerchief and mopped his face and then wiped his hand which was all sandy because of mine, and he said, 'I'm sorry, my dear, I can't think what came over me. To a child too. I am deeply sorry, Ann. Please forgive me.'

'I don't mind,' I said, and I didn't, not really. I'd like to have found out about the teeth but knew I couldn't, or not then, and I hated about the infants, but I knew things like that had happened all the time in the Earthquake. Everybody did. Annette Ferris's mother was killed when the garage fell down on her and the baby as well. We all knew.

Colonel Holdaway and I walked home together, my pants wet and sandy and beginning to itch. We got to Laing's Point and I said, 'I go up here, Colonel Holdaway. Goodbye.'

He took my hand. 'Bless you, Ann.'

I never know what to say when people say that, so I just stood.

'May I ask one more thing of you, Ann?'

'Yes.'

'Would you be kind enough not to Tell On Me?'

I knew he was saying it sort of in capitals so I'd know it was a joke, but also that he meant it. 'The tears, I mean,' he said. 'Would you mind?'

'Of course I won't. Not ever.'

'Thank you,' he said, and I belted up the track. All I could think of was of Colonel Holdaway being Boss of the Earthquake and so good and kind and old, and soon he would be dead like Betty and the smelly sheep and Uncle Norman in the flu epidemic and no one knowing where they'd gone. And all the people sadly dead in the Earthquake. What about them? Where did they go?

Mum came round the corner of the bach carrying the washing.

'What on earth . . . ?'

I told her about Colonel Holdaway and how he was so kind and brave and would soon be dead and wasn't it sad, sad, sad.

Mum put down the clothes basket and squatted beside me, drying my face with a tea towel and saying, 'Oh Annie. Annie, my love. What are we going to do with you, child?'

I was glad she didn't laugh. I still know what I meant but I've got used to it now.

*

I wake up so early the sun isn't up. The air is misty and cool but you can tell it's going to be a humdinger of a day, like Claude says. Everything looks grey but different colours of grey. The trees are dark and their trunks are half-buried in a grey sea of mist. The main thing is the birds: tuis and bellbirds and grey warblers and the rest of them are all singing singing singing as the sky gets lighter and lighter and the sun comes up.

I go to the lavatory. I don't need to but I want to get *Seven Little Australians.* I want to read it again, especially the bit where Judy dies in the bush and all her brothers and sisters sing 'Abide with me' and the lady writing the story says up to now her pen has had only happy writing to do but now it gets sad.

Mum is still asleep with her mouth hanging open and her hair all messed up. I'd like to hop in beside her but she doesn't like being woken, not even at the Beach, so I run on to the lavatory which has shiny dark wood each side of the lid for putting books on.

The reason we came to Rongomaha was for Mr Clements' film, so that he could find a good place for the Indians to capture Mrs Henare and a flatter bit for Mr Henare the Sheriff's Deputy to rescue her back again. But there are lots of other good bits as well.

The horses and the riding at the Maori Race Meeting were good, but nothing like the Indians at Devil's Canyon. Tam Ropata is the best rider I've seen, one arm high up at the back like rodeo riders on the steepest bits, then both his hands on the reins and spurs going. And Joe! Straight down the steep hill which is almost a cliff, and all of them looking like *The Man from Snowy River*, especially Tam, who looked fiercest as well.

Everything about being there while the film is happening is good. Horses and dogs and picnics and real people, people we know, making pictures better than those at the Cosy, or will be. Occasionally Mr Clements shouts at us if we get too near, but mainly no one takes any notice and we can muck about in the dull bits. Miri keeps practising Maori stick games and so does Charlie. Joe stays with the Indians and so does Duncan, until something's going to happen and he has to clear off.

But the best part of all at Rongomaha is Claude. Claude does the rubbish and the wood and animals like the pigs and stray lambs, and puppies when they have them. He used to do the hens as well but Mrs Jackson pinched them so she can get the egg money, he says. Claude says some people don't like hens but he's always had a liking, especially bantams. Give him a fierce little cock bantam like Billy rather than a Leghorn pullet any day. Take on the world, would Billy, he says.

Billy reminds me a bit of Claude. His reddy-gold feathers are the same colour as Claude's hair, or what's left, and he struts about sort of chatting to himself and his black eyes going this way and that, quick and cross like Claude's.

The main thing about Claude is he's best ever at making up. Mum's good and Bel's not bad, but I've never met anyone as good as Claude. Some-times it's the trenches in the War with machine guns and Huns and Going Over the Top. We have a tot of rum, crouching because of snipers, then Claude counts, seven, six, five, four, three, two, *charge*. 'Come on, men,' he yells, leaping out of the trench, shooting 'Ratter tat tat, ratter tat tat, BOOM.' Charlie gets so excited he muddles it up with *Crime Does Not Pay* and the G-Men, and yells, 'They got me, Chief,' and rolls over on the paddock, clutching his front. He likes getting shot so much he does it too early, Claude says. How's Claude going to get his platoon anywhere near the enemy machine-gun nest if Charlie keeps keeling over on him the minute he's out of the bloody trench? So Charlie says, 'Sorry Sarge,' and we start again and even Duncan likes it, especially when it's G-Men with their Colt 45s and suspects being grilled and shootouts with gangsters called Puss Pacino and Eddy the Moose.

Claude calls Charlie 'Betcha', because he says Charlie's a One-Wheeled Wonder and game as a singing cowboy's horse. Betcha Barnes of course can do anything, but Charlie likes it best when it's murders with detectives crawling around the body with magnifying glasses looking for the vital clues. Bloodstains are best. Charlie's mad about bloodstains. Shaking all over, he'll point at a thistle, 'Look, Chief, bloodstains!' and Claude drops on his knees and peers at the thistle, then bangs Charlie on the back and says 'Betcha, this clue may be our breakthrough!' And Charlie looks as though he's going to burst he's so happy.

'Do it again. Let's do it again, Claude,' he yells, flinging himself at Claude's knees, but Claude would be on to the next make-up he was so quick.

I like circuses best. I was a trapeze lady who fell off and was saved by Nellie the elephant catching me in mid-air with her trunk.

Miri doesn't care much who she is so she usually lands up being the one who is dead.

Charlie says Claude's stories are better than Mr Clements' flick any day. He can't hear enough of his stories; he can scarcely bother to have a swim he is so busy with Claude. He just wants to be Claude's side-kick; to be stacking wood, doing scraps, anything, as long as he's Betcha and can be with Claude. Claude says, 'Come on, Betcha, you're the boss,' and hands the pig-bucket over to Charlie, and Rudolph and Rodney, the pigs, snuffling and honking and squealing as he tips the scraps in. Pigs are more fun to feed even than the lambs. With lambs it's just their tails that show they like it. With pigs it's all over. Charlie says he'll come and see them often. Claude says that'd be nice, that Rudy and Rod don't get much social life. Duncan says, 'Don't they pong enough already?' so Charlie biffs him but laughs anyway.

We have good times with Claude.

But that night everything goes wrong. Miriama and Mr and Mrs Henare have gone back to the Beach after the day's shooting, so there's just me and Charlie and Duncan having our supper in the kitchen. Bel and Mum are cooking and making their dinner while we eat cold meat and baby potatoes and lettuce leaves with a pinch of sugar.

Mum comes and sits with us at the table. She takes a cigarette, gives one to Bel and leans forward to Charlie. 'Has anyone told you you're a messy eater?'

'Try Muck Up, the Magic Cleanser,' yells Duncan. 'Sold in four-ounce jars, six-ounce jars and four-gallon drums for messy eaters.'

'Ha ha,' says Charlie, not laughing.

Duncan doesn't like no one laughing. 'I got a new one. Listen. One day Bel opened the fridge and there was a possum curled up asleep. Bel poked him and said, "What are you doing in there?" and the possum opened his eyes and said, "This is a Westinghouse, isn't it?" and Bel said "Yes," and the possum said, "Well I'm westing."'

Everyone laughs, especially Charlie. He keeps saying 'Westinghouse' and 'I'm westing' and laughing to himself.

'Did you make that up, Duncan?' says Bel, and Duncan says 'Yes,' and Mum blows smoke through her nose.

'So – everything all organised?' she says. 'What time's Claude coming over tomorrow?'

'Claude?' says Bel. 'What about him?'

We all start telling her at once. How it's all organised about going to the glow-worm cave. How Claude's taking a billy because it won't be too dry for a fire in the bush and Claude's not having any G-Men in his squad who can't make a decent mug of billy tea. How all we've got to take is just our sandwiches and maybe a cold drink if we like. How Claude knows the names of everything and how he'll piggy-back Charlie if the going gets tough, though he'd be prepared to bet a bob each way on Betcha pulling through. All this we tell Bel and she sits there smoking. She stubs her butt out and says, 'I'm sorry, fellas, but tomorrow's not on for the track, Claude or no Claude.'

So then we all start. 'Why not?' 'How?' 'Why?' Charlie looks as though he might cry it's so awful. Mum tells us to be quiet and listen to Bella for heaven's sake.

Bella tells us all about it being a free day tomorrow except for James and Angus and Hare and Jean (plus of course Miriama) who hope to film Jean's rescue. That Tam is coming up in the truck to help Bella clean the track to the caves. It's not possible for Charlie at the moment. Far too rough.

'But Claude'll carry me if it is.'

'And Joe's coming with us,' says Duncan. 'That's why it's got to be tomorrow.'

'Why can't you go the next day?' says Bel.

'Because of the free day. It's Joe's only chance.'

Bel turns from the oven door she's just shut. She leans her hands on the table and looks at us. 'Now listen, soapsuds. You've had a pretty good innings lately. There'll be another time. Grow up,' she says.

'Run up and ask Claude about the following day,' says Mum.

Duncan opens his mouth. 'But Joe . . .'

'You heard,' says Mum.

Claude is sitting on the steps of the verandah in front of his whare, puffing his pipe. It's so still the smoke goes straight upwards. You can hear the sheep dogs barking and their chains rattling as we stand in a row and tell him all about it, and can he make it the next day?

He tells us he can't. That it's tomorrow or nothing. That it's time he went into town on a private business matter. Some urgent business he has to sign, that they require his personal signature and it's a matter of some urgency. His lawyer left a message down at the house yesterday. In fact, says Claude, if he hadn't given us his word about tomorrow he would've scarpered before this. He's never been one to hang about when there's professional business to be attended to, but on the other hand he's given us his word and he'll stick to it. It's tomorrow or nothing, Claude says. Simple as that and he will take a slasher.

'I'm coming with you,' says Duncan.

'Me too,' says Charlie, jumping up and down.

'You needn't come,' says Duncan to me.

'Of course I'm coming!'

'Over to you,' says Claude.

Duncan stands glaring at me with his legs apart. 'Well, don't tell Mum after.'

'I don't tell!'

Claude just keeps puffing. 'So that's settled then. You come up here tomorrow when you're ready. Not early. We'll have to do the chores first, won't we, Betcha?'

Charlie puts his hand on the knee of Claude's moleskins. 'Who'll make our sandwiches?'

'Normally,' says Claude, 'I would myself, but I've been running down a bit preparatory to going into town. I have some bangers that need eating. You lot nab a loaf or two from the store room. Apples. All there waiting.'

'You can get it, Ann,' says Duncan.

My legs are wide apart like his. 'No,' I say.

'Mackerel Charley, you're a sook.'

'I won't,' I shout. 'You know what happened last time.'

When the Earthquake happened Duncan was seven and I was four and Charlie was a baby asleep by the tank stand. I can't remember much of it, just bits. Duncan and I were in Mrs Clements' house and we were pinching Mrs Clements' Queen Anne chocolates. The white box with the red picture of Queen Anne in the corner lived in the top drawer of a chest in her bedroom. We knew that, because she sometimes gave us one. Duncan and I were mucking about on the verandah, talking to Bel, and Mrs Clements was away somewhere in the Pontiac they had then. Then Bel went back to the kitchen, and Duncan was suddenly whispering, 'Queen Annes, quick,' and me thinking what a good idea. We ran into the bedroom and Duncan was taking the lid off the box when the Earthquake happened. I can remember sliding about and crying, and Duncan falling about as well. Then suddenly he yelled, 'Earthquake!' and ran to the door and banged into Bel who was running in, and she picked me up and grabbed Duncan and ran outside. Chimneys were falling and people screaming and Mum was hunting everywhere for us. I can't remember much after that. Just sleeping on the grass at Rongomaha and how good it was. I don't know what happened to the Queen Annes.

Duncan squeezes his eyes shut for a moment. 'OK,' he says. 'We'll get it together. Tomorrow morning.'

'Not Charlie,' I say.

'No.'

'OK.'

Claude winks at me. 'Got that all sorted out?' He knocks out his pipe and rubs his boot on the burnt tobacco because of sparks.

'Yes,' I say.

'Solemn little codger, aren't you?' he says.

We walk back from Claude's whare. No one says anything, not even Charlie, until Mum asks if we had any luck. Duncan picks his knee scab and tells her no, Claude can't make it the next day. Mum flicks his hand away and tells us she's sorry but there'll be lots of other times, like they always do, and that the Bachelors will be waiting for us upstairs. Tom, Dick and Harry and Willy, she calls them, and makes up things about them. Tom has the biggest moustache, Dick's boots squeak, Willy's best at tennis. Things like that, but we're sick of them tonight.

'Tennis is Tom,' says Charlie.

'I thought it was Willy.'

'Naa, Tom. You said yesterday. Anyhow Willy's gone back to the beach with his bone.'

The stars are not much good when Duncan wakes me. Charlie's still asleep as we creep past Mum and down to the store room in the dark which is blacker than any I've ever been in. We can't turn on any lights until we get to the store room and it takes us hours getting downstairs and along to it. The clock in the front hall strikes two but it makes a sort of whirring first so it's not much of a fright. We get to the store room and turn on the light.

We can't find the bread at first but then we do, and biscuits and a few apples, and hide them in Charlie's school bag he keeps things in. We leave still creeping on our toes. We can get the Fifty Fifty tomorrow.

When we're back upstairs Duncan grins and says, 'No earthquake this time eh, Sarge?'

After breakfast we tell Mum we're going to help Claude and we'll probably be with him a lot of the day. She says what about lunch? Duncan says Claude wants to show us how to cook bangers and make billy tea and maybe we could take a loaf from the store room. I want to say why didn't you ask first, dopey, but I don't.

Mum says she can't ask Bella because she and Tam have already gone up the track, but she'll leave her a note. She kisses us and says, 'Have fun, hon buns. And thank Claude from me.'

Charlie goes over and puts his hand on her knee. 'Mum?'

She looks up, smiling. 'Yes, Betcha?'

'Come on, Chas,' shouts Duncan from the door. 'Beat you to find that Joe man.'

'Bye,' yells Charlie. 'Bye.'

Joe is yarning with Claude behind the woolshed which is our rendezvous, Claude says. Claude is wearing his big hat and carrying a slasher and a little pack. He stands to attention and salutes Charlie. 'All present and correct, Sir.'

'What about the bangers?' snaps Charlie.

Claude slaps his pack. 'All present and correct, Sir. Farmers' Best Pork.'

Charlie is so excited he can hardly speak. 'Good man,' he stutters.

'Permission to speak, Sir?' snaps Claude.

Charlie nods.

'I will now give you a report on the situation. A briefing to you rookies,' says Claude, who is suddenly the boss. 'Prop your bums on this rail. Jump to it.'

So we do. Joe looks as if he's thinking the whole thing is kids' stuff and he's too old, and I want to tell him that's what Duncan thought at first but not now. But when I look I see Duncan's looking a bit funny and I think he's remembering he's too old as well.

Claude takes his pipe out of his mouth. 'Well, men, as you know from your previous briefing this operation must, of necessity, be a clandestine one. B Coy has in a sense, been scuppered, bewildered and bebuggered by the enemies' assault on Vimy Ridge yonder. The main route to the redoubt is now in the hands of the Redcoats, under the command of Generals Clements and Ropata. The main route's a goner. However,' he says, pointing at himself, 'Long Paw here has discovered an alternative route up the back side. A track used by the Big Feet since time immemorial which has lain secret for many years.'

'If it has lain secret for that long we'll all need slashers,' grins Joe.

'Get a haircut, you Maori boy,' says Claude. 'Follow me, men.'

It's hot, even in the bush. The Big Feet track is fun at first and pretty – all dark greens and bright little bushes – but after a while it gets harder. Not the steepness but the overgrown bits. At first Charlie insists on walking but he's so slow where it's tangly that Duncan gets mad at him. Then Claude and Joe take turns piggy-backing him and Duncan gets the pip because he wants to as well, but Claude says he's not big enough. We take turns with the slasher.

Then Claude won't let Charlie use it, which makes *him* mad. Claude tells him you need excellent balance to use a slasher and he doesn't think balance is Charlie's best point, no insult intended. Also it's razor sharp, Claude tells us. There's no point in a slasher that's not. Duncan tells Claude that I'm so clumsy I'll cut my foot off. Claude says will you? and I say no, and I don't.

It gets heavier, though, but after a while we stop for smoko and things get better.

Claude explains that our smoke would be a dead give-away to the Redcoats, and he tests for wind with a licked finger. There isn't any, so that's all right. Then he puts us on dry bracken detail so he can start the fire and tells us to find a green stick each. Dry sticks are useless for cooking bangers. They burn and your banger falls into the fire. Claude has brought a bit of tin to put on top of the fire because in his experience bangers-on-sticks are one of those things which sound better than they are. They often turn out either pink yuck or black as your hat.

We try them anyhow, but even my green stick burns, and my sausage bursts and Claude says it's beyond redemption. So then we cook them on the hot tin and eat them between hunks of bread. Bangers-in-blankets they're called, and boy are they good. Then we stoke the fire up a bit for the billy and when it's got a 'deep rolling boil', like Claude says, he throws in some tea leaves, takes it off the fire and bangs the billy with a stick to make the leaves go to the bottom, and some of them do. The tea's good too, if you like it smoky.

Claude puts out the fire and scrapes the embers and covers them with dirt. Then he lies down and pulls his hat over his eyes and says, 'Stand easy, men. Twenty minutes.'

It is very still in the bush – no birds that I can hear except a grey warbler and a fantail flitting around. The sun comes through the leaves in stripes of green and yellow. Charlie curls up and goes to sleep, and so do I though I don't mean to.

Now Claude's scraping over the ashes again and hoisting Charlie on his back and giving us our marching orders.

The next part of the track isn't so bad and not as steep either. Charlie insists on walking again, or trying to, though he slows us down like mad. Joe says to give him a chance. Claude says nothing, he just keeps walking.

Claude is different after lunch. Before he was showing us things all the time, like ferns that have been going since dinosaurs were around and are living fossils, he says. He knows all the Maori names for the trees and bush and that, and where to find bush orchids. Everything. And all the time he was using different voices, one minute being Long Paw and then the boss of Company B or Sarge. And by now Joe likes the making up as much as we do. He's Bare Foot of the Big Feet in moccasins, and Duncan's Captain of U-Boat 101. Charlie changes all the time like Claude.

But after lunch Claude forgets about games and showing us things. He's walking too fast and clicking his fingers and talking to himself. Even when I show him a tiny little bush orchid I found he just nods and goes on muttering.

Charlie says, 'Are we nearly there?'

Claude looks at him and says, 'What?'

'The glow-worms.'

'Yuh, yuh,' says Claude, sort of hopping about as though he can't help it.

It's all getting too hard for Charlie.

We keep on, slashing a bit, not much, and scrambling up the rocky bits, and Claude keeps on talking to himself.

I say, 'Look, Claude, filmy fern all dead from drought, like you said,' and Claude says 'Yuh' again, then goes quiet. Completely quiet. So quiet he's not moving at all. He stands still, as though he's listening for something.

Where we're standing now the track is wide, room for us all to stand looking at Claude. His face is red, his eyes staring as if he doesn't know us.

'What a fool! Hell's fangs. What a fool. You wouldn't read about it!' He keeps glancing at his wrist as though there was a watch there, slapping himself and muttering, 'Gotta go. Gotta go.' Then he calms down all of a sudden, puts on his army voice. 'You take charge, Bare Foot.'

Now he's moving again, dancing about on his toes. 'Hang on,' he says, though no one's going anywhere.

We don't say anything, just keep staring.

Claude snaps his fingers, keeps on snapping. 'Damn and blast and bloody hell,' he yells. 'I got to go. Got to get back. Get into town immediately.'

We don't say anything.

'You said you were going in tomorrow,' says Duncan after a while.

'I was, I was. You're right. I was, I admit it. But something's just come to mind. What's the date today?'

Nobody knows. Nobody says.

'Strewth,' says Claude, jumping about and slapping himself. 'It's in town. I've got to sign it today. It's today. Not tomorrow, today.' And then he starts moving again, jumping about, all excited, dancing about on his toes. He snaps his fingers, crack, crack. 'It's only five minutes to the cave. Just round that old man rock there,' he says. 'You'll be sweet. Take this, boy,' and he flings his pack at Joe and charges down the track, muttering, 'Gotta go, gotta go.'

We stand looking at each other, listening to Claude leaping and bashing down the track so quick he's gone in a flash. We stand until there's no noise at all. Nothing. Not even a warbler.

Joe picks up the pack. 'Porangi.'

'What's that?'

'Mad. Crazy.'

'Claude's not mad,' says Charlie, but he doesn't sound too sure.

'OK,' says Joe. 'What're we standing around here for? Want to see the caves, don't we? Glow-worms? Pick up there behind. March.'

Ann

So off we go, still not saying anything but wondering, or I am, and I bet Duncan and Joe are too. We climb around the big overhanging rock and Charlie trips over a root, he's so tired. Suddenly I get furious. Drat Claude, I think. Duncan picks Charlie up. 'OK?' he says. Charlie says, 'Fine, fine,' like Angus and wipes his nose on his hand and grins. Charlie is a born mimic, everyone says so, but he looks a mess to me.

'Give us him,' says Joe. He hands Duncan the pack and swings Charlie up onto his back. 'Wait till you see the strings coming out their bums, eh?' he says, and Charlie ducks his face into Joe's neck and giggles.

Claude was right about one thing. Once we crawl round the big rock all covered with lichen and hanging over the track, the path widens and it's smooth and easy and no overgrowth; no scrub, branches or bush-lawyer tangles or mossy dead logs with ferns, anything. You can see where the main track joins our back one and where Bella and Tam and their slashers have been. All the rubbish has been hacked off and cleared and the track looks like something in a park in town labelled *Bush Walk*, all tidy and green and yellow sun filtering, not the face-slapping mess of Claude's track. Charlie and me'll go back the main way whatever happens. Blow mouldy old Claude.

The track widens onto one of those flat green bits you sometimes get in the bush. The grass is different from lawn grass, softer and greener and quite long, and the whole place looks like one of those bowers in stories where the Princess lies down to have a rest though the track to the cave goes straight through the middle of this one.

The entrance to the cave is wide and dark, but not black dark. We creep across the soft grass, Joe still carrying Charlie, and me close to Duncan. 'C'mon,' he whispers, and we go into the cave but not very far.

It is dark in the inside of the cave, no glow-worms or anything, just dark and still and smelling of dryness.

After a minute or so our eyes get used to the dark and we can see that the narrow part of the cave turns into another one and we go on holding our breath, or I am. We turn the corner still creeping and then, Wham, it happens! There's a sort of scuffling in the dark, then a worse, miles worse noise getting louder, grunting and heaving like a monster moaning, and we yell and turn and run fast as we can, all of us, tripping and scrambling with Charlie still on Joe's back.

Then suddenly Bel, it must be Bel, I know it's Bel, gives a sort of yelp and starts moaning worse than ever, and I can just make out the shape of her on the ground and Tam on top of her.

I yell and run to her, but Charlie's already off Joe's back and charging forward, hitting Tam and shouting, 'Let her go! Let her go!'

Then out of the dark comes Joe, and he yanks Charlie off Tam and he's shouting at him, 'They're rooting, y'daft twit. Give over.'

Charlie swings round on him in a rage and overbalances and falls and cracks his head on the floor of the cave and lies still.

It is all so quick, so sudden, everyone yelling and screaming, and Tam tripping over his pants it looks like, and Bel scrambling up and falling on her knees beside Charlie and holding him saying, 'Charlie, Charlie, Charlie,' and the cave sings back, 'Charee, Charee,' and we stand around shouting at Charlie to wake him up and he doesn't move.

Then Tam picks him up and carries him outside. Duncan is mad at him, we all are. 'Give him to me,' he yells, trying to snatch him. Tam doesn't even look at him. He lies Charlie down on the soft grass and Bel checks his pulse and breathing and things and says, 'His pulse is OK.'

Tam just nods and Charlie lies there with his eyes closed, and I think of 'Abide with Me' and them all singing.

'It's all right, Annie,' says Duncan.

'Is he going to die?'

'Of course he's not going to die, you daft tart. Unconscious isn't dead.'

Tam picks Charlie up. 'Come on,' he says. 'We'll get straight down.'

'Give me his ski pole,' says Bel.

'Why?'

'Just give it,' she says, and Tam unstraps it from Charlie and gives it to her, and we set off down the main track. No one says anything. No one looks at anyone except Bel and Tam at each other. Joe doesn't look at Tam, Duncan doesn't look at Joe, we just head down the track quick as we can. I can't remember whether it was sunny or not, whether there were birds. One of Charlie's arms bounces against Tam as he moves. Everyone looks at the track and still no one says anything and the noise is only our feet on the track. I say *Gentle Jesus* for a bit because it's the only one I know, then stop.

After a while Tam whispers to Bel, 'What are we going to say?'

Bel shakes her head. 'Hurry, darling. Hurry.'

I stare at the heels of Joe's bare feet padding down the track in front of me and think about darling. I think darling is for when you really like someone. Dad calls Mum darling but Mum doesn't do it back. Sometimes she calls us darling, but not often. Mrs Clements calls James darling, but not Bella. The Henares say it all the time, they call each other darling and Miri too. Sometimes Mr Henare calls Mrs Henare darling when he's crabby, like, 'Isn't lunch ready yet, darling?' They never say dear. Ladies say dear when they're being kind. 'Let me help you, dear,' or 'How's your back, dear?' Mum doesn't say dear either.

'Duncan?' I whisper.

'Yeah?'

'What's rooting?'

'I'll tell you later.'

I bet he won't. But Dad will.

'Bella?' I say.

'Yes?'

'Why don't Duncan and Joe and me run ahead so Mum can get Dad?'

Bella stops. 'And Dr Appleby from the Beach. Good idea.'

'We'll be there in a minute,' says Tam. 'Keep going.'

So we go on with me not knowing anything and no one talking or looking at each other and Charlie's arm still bonging against Tam.

A bush pigeon takes off with that clatter like they do, and everyone looks up then hurries on down the track faster than ever, almost running.

We didn't see any glow-worms, not one.

'How long will he be unconscious?' I say.

'Not long,' says Bel, and turns to take my hand but I won't.

What were they doing in the spooky dark? Why were they moaning, yelping even? Why did she call him darling after that and Charlie just lying there?

I hate them. I hate Bella and Tam and Claude. I want us to go home. I want to go home to my new blue dog bedspread and my Dolphin Cards and Mrs Samson next door's new kittens. I don't want to be here, not even at the Beach.

And then, quick as a fish I'm off, jumping, leaping, charging past everyone to get to Mum.

'Stop,' yells Bel, but I don't and never will, and then there's Duncan catching up. 'Hang on,' he yells, but I go faster and faster to see Mum and Dad, though Dad won't be there yet.

And now Duncan changes his tune. 'Keep going, Annie, quick, quick,' he yells, and we slide and slither and jump down the track, with the rest of them miles behind because of having to be careful with Charlie.

At the bottom the real bush track fizzles out in a little valley where Mrs Clements has her rhododendrons and the tallest lily in the world, but we don't look we're running so hard. Then Duncan grabs my arm and says, 'Stop!' and we stand staring at each other as though we're going to have a fight.

Another fat bush pigeon clatters off a branch, its front shiny blue and purple like the inside of a paua shell.

'Stop gawking and listen,' says Duncan. 'Don't you go screaming up to Mum yelling your head off. OK?'

'You're not the boss of me. Charlie's unconscious. You said. And it's their fault and I hate them.'

'Listen, Annie. Just listen.' He tries to mop my face with his shirt but I kick him off. 'Of course we'll tell about Charlie. Get Dad, get the doctor, all that. Get him better in no time.'

'Will he wake up?'

'Holy mackerel! Of course he'll wake up, I keep telling you. It's the other I mean.'

'What other?'

'Bella and Tam.'

'What's rooting?'

Duncan stands in front of me, his elbows sticking out and his face crabby. 'All that ballyhoo. Don't worry about it. Forget it.'

'Why didn't she mind?'

'I said, didn't I? I'll tell you later.'

'Why did she call him darling?'

'Mackerel Charlie, give us a break.'

I'm just going to say, 'Tell me now,' but I don't. All I know is I hate them. 'I'm going to find Mum.'

He grabs my arm. 'OK. But don't tell her about all that. Or Dad. Just about Charlie. God's honour, Annie. Please.'

Duncan's never said please before, not to me. We stand staring at each other.

'OK,' I say, and start running.

The shingle on the drive crunches, bits spurting up round our sandals as we race to the front verandah. Mum and Mrs Clements are sitting having cups of tea. The minute Mum sees us she jumps up and comes running. 'Charlie?' she says.

'He's unconscious,' I yell, 'but he's still breathing.'

'He's only concussed,' snaps Duncan. 'Bel thinks he's OK.'

'Where, where?'

'Tam's bringing him down from the cave.'

'How did he . . . ?' says Mum and brushes past us as she runs to the track.

Mrs Clements heaves herself up. 'I'll ring the Store. Get a message to Dr What-not.'

'And Dad,' I say.

'Later,' she says and hobbles off.

Duncan and I sit on cane chairs. There is a hole in the arm of one to put a glass in when you have a drink. Duncan takes two pikelets and sticks them together and eats them as Mum disappears down the track. We don't say anything. Just sit.

Duncan wipes his hands on his shorts. 'There's the sea down there.'

'Where?'

'In the gap of those two hills.'

It is too. It is just there. No Island, no ship sailing, nothing but a vee-shaped bit of sea miles and miles away and us up here staring.

'Want a pikelet?' says Duncan.

'Yes.'

'Bella's good at pikelets. We had them at the Earthquake.'

'What's rooting?' I say.

'It's when a man sticks his willy into a lady.'

'What!'

'Like I said.'

'But why?'

'I don't know. He just does.'

'Why does the lady let him?'

'Because she wants a baby.'

'What if she wants another baby?'

173

'He has to do it again.'

'Yuck. So Mum and Dad . . . ?'

'Yeah. Three times. Want another pikelet?' he says.

I take two and we're still chewing and me thinking like mad when Bel and Joe appear from the track and then Mum and Tam carrying Charlie. Tam is holding him differently – Charlie's head now hangs over his shoulder like a swag.

We jump up to start running. I grab his arm.

'Duncan?'

'Yeah.'

'What're we going to say?'

'Nothing. I told you.'

'But Claude. All that. Being where we said we wouldn't.'

'It's so bad now that won't matter. Not at first. Come on.'

Mrs Clements appears as we reach the steps. She clamps her hand on my shoulder, then Duncan's. 'Wait,' she says. 'This is an anxious time for your mother. You'll only be in the way. Stay here, both of you.'

She clamps harder than ever, but Duncan gets away and so do I in the end. She shouts, 'Children children,' and shakes her stick, but we keep running.

Mum is walking behind Tam, watching Charlie. 'Don't worry, chaps,' she says, grinning like mad. 'He'll be all right. Go and ring Dad, Duncan. And Dr Appleby at the beach.'

'Mrs Clements's done him.'

Mum nods. 'Dad then.' And Duncan takes off like a rocket.

Mrs Clements stands at the top of the verandah steps and tells everyone that Charlie will be all right and that James was concussed once when he fell off a ladder and he was perfectly all right. She pats Charlie's shoulder and tells him he is a little warrior.

'Take him upstairs, Tamati,' she says to Tam. 'Show him the way, Lorna. Simple concussion is nothing. Come with me, children. You too, Joseph, and we'll see if we can find a Queen Anne chocolate.'

And suddenly I am bawling my head off. Bel tries to give me a hug but I push her off and run upstairs in front of Tam and Mum and Charlie and don't stop until I've grabbed my book from the Bachelors' Balcony. They'll be here in a minute, and I hide in the lavatory and I lock the door and I sit on the hole with the dark shiny wood all around. I stop bucketing, Duncan calls it, but I stay there till I hear them going past, Tam's feet going thump thump and Mum's sandals. Then I take my book and get out quick, and hop out the open window in the hall and onto the wooden fire escape ladder which we're not allowed to play on but do anyway. There's a big drop down from the last rung onto the courtyard where the garages and all the sheds are and I'm looking for a good place to read because Mrs Clements doesn't like children reading during the day and I'll stay there till Charlie wakes up and Dad comes and we go home.

And there, just when I'm getting up from the big drop from the last rung, backing out of one of the sheds and swinging round comes Mr Jackson's car which is black. Mr Jackson is driving, and sitting up beside him in his town clothes and wearing a brown hat is Claude, getting a lift with Mr Jackson who goes into town sometimes after work to have tea with his mother who is poorly.

I start yelling at Claude through the open window. 'Charlie's concussed and it's all your fault,' I shout. 'Why did you leave us, you pig?'

And Claude smiles at me and lifts his brown hat.

'See you later, Princess,' he calls. 'Urgent business. Urgent.'

He smiles again and the car disappears round the corner.

Pig.

Lorna

We don't speak as we climb the stairs, Tamati and I. He stops beside my bed, Charlie still dead to the world in his arms.

Tamati gives a quick chuck of his head. 'This one?'

'Yes. I'll bring another one in later from out there.'

'I'll bring it.'

'Don't bother. They wheel.'

'I'll still bring it.'

'No,' I snap. 'Put him down.'

He lays him down on the bed. As he takes his arms away, Charlie moves slightly, groans.

'That's a good sign. Any sound, any movement, that's good.'

'He groaned a bit coming down.'

'You didn't tell me.'

'You didn't ask.'

We stare at each other with cold formality. Our faces, even our movements, stiffen.

'What were they doing in the cave? The children? Where was Claude? What happened?'

Tamati straightens, relaxes visibly. This is not the question he has been expecting. I am sure of this.

'I don't know.'

'Why were you there? You and Bel?'

He looks at me.

'Tell me what happened!'

'Why all the questions? Later, woman, later.' He nods towards the unconscious child. 'He's yours. He's home. Look after him.'

He is right. Even in rage I realise this. This stupid passion, this longing to know. Why now? Later will do, when Charlie wakes up. Not now. Not at the moment.

'Yes.'

I sit on the edge of the bed, adjust the sheets with quick flicking hands like a competent charge nurse awaiting the return to consciousness of a patient with simple concussion. Charlie looks very peaceful. We stare at him.

Our uneasy silence is broken by the quick clatter of Bella's sandals on the landing, the brush of her hand across the flax cloak as she enters.

Tamati puts his hand onto Charlie's forehead, murmurs something in Maori and straightens to greet her. They are glad to see each other. Ten minutes apart has been too long for these two. Their eyes slip past Charlie and me in momentary exclusion. They don't mean to ignore us, not for a moment. They are worried sick, both of them. Finally Bel turns to me. 'It's our fault, Lorna,' she says.

'It's no one's bloody fault,' says Tamati.

'How can it be your fault, your stupid piddling fault? And what does it matter? The child has simple concussion! Simple,' I cry. 'In the name of all that's merciful just stop talking.'

Bel's mouth drops. Tamati grins, a wide grin, but tough. 'Like I said, Mrs Hopkins.'

Bel gives me a quick hug and runs after him as he leaves.

I sit silent, dismiss all irrelevant thoughts, as suggested by Tamati Ropata.

Charlie's hand is as cool and soft as ever but, naturally enough, no longer confiding. His wits are on hold and you need to have them about you if you're going to respond to someone else's grasp. Charlie is too young to know this. I must tell him when he wakes up. I have told the others.

I must see Claude, if and when he returns. Demand explanations, though I feel I am unlikely to get any. Neither Mrs Jackson nor Bella has stressed the man's sense of responsibility. Bel told me he took off once in the middle of shearing and didn't come back for six weeks.

I watch Charlie, hypnotised by his regular breathing, the infinitesimal rise and fall of his chest, his 'good colour'. I watch the curve of his eyelashes, the blue pallor of his eyelids. 'Juno's violets,' some poet called such eyelids. Or was it Venus's? No. Too many esses would be a mistake, and again, who cares.

Another thought, less happy and one to be dismissed immediately. Charlie's face reminds me of a portrait I saw once of a sleeping child, the same blond hair, the dark eyelashes below closed lids. The difference being that the painter's son had just died.

Also he did not have a large bump on his forehead.

Stop this nonsense. Charlie has simple concussion. You know about simple concussion. What is non-simple concussion? Why does the appellation 'woman' sound faintly insulting, whereas 'man' sounds comradely?

Charlie looks better in bed. He no longer flops, he is steadied by support and his colour is better as I have just said. Why doesn't the doctor come? Now. Immediately. I leap to my feet. Sit down again. Down, woman, down.

Derek cannot be here for at least an hour.

I can't remember the precise treatment for simple concussion. Rest, obviously. Cold compress? There must be something else.

This deep sleep is uncharacteristic of Charlie. He has always been an indifferent sleeper. One of those infuriating children who appears an hour after being bedded down to tell you that he has had his sleep. Has done with the whole dreary business and what will we do now. Last week I went to check them two hours after bedtime. Duncan and Ann

178

were sound asleep. Charlie stared up at me from the lower bunk. 'I'm still here,' he said accusingly. 'It's too hot.'

Duncan appears. 'Dad's coming straight out.'

'Good. Good.'

Duncan pokes his brother in the chest. 'Has he done anything? Woken up or anything?'

'No.'

He makes a fist, takes a mock punch at my arm. 'He will soon.'

'Come and help me move a bed,' I say. 'Quietly as you can.'

'Why? You want him to wake up, don't you? More row the better.'

I wish everyone would stop being so sensible. We rattle and clang the bed in from the balcony. Duncan lies full length on the elderly mattress and closes his eyes.

'Where's Annie?' I say after some time.

'Don't know.'

'Do go and find her. She'll be such a mess.'

'OK. After the doctor's been. Remember when I had that fish hook?' Duncan gives me a long look and begins his rambling story. How it happened. Where it happened. Which finger it was embedded in. How Dr Appleby came in his togs straight from a swim. Navy blue with a white belt and a gold buckle they were. How he asked questions all the time. Where Duncan had been fishing (Bully Pond). What had he caught (nothing). How you have to snip the end of the hook because the barb's designed to not come out of the unfortunate fish, and how Duncan was just thinking about fish being unfortunate and wondering if they were when, strike a light, the hook was out.

'Just like that and his togs still dripping. He'd done it on purpose, all that talking, to distract me, see.'

'Like you.'

He rolls over on the lumpy mattress. 'How d'y' mean?'

'Trying to distract me.'

He grins his father's grin. 'Naa.'

I take Charlie's pulse yet again. 'At least his breathing's regular.'

Duncan kicks his bare feet, rolls back over in disgust. 'Cor, Mum, you sound like Annie.'

'Tell me what happened.'

'I said I would, but the doctor will arrive in the middle if I start now.'

'You haven't said you'd tell me anything.'

'Annie, then. It must have been to her.'

Charlie mumbles something.

'Listen!' I yelp.

'I told you so,' says Duncan.

Gravel crunches below as a car sweeps up the drive. There are footsteps, welcoming voices. 'Do go and find her. Please!'

'Not now. Not when he's just coming to,' he says.

Nevertheless he goes.

Dr Appleby, escorted by Bel, wears khaki drill trousers and a white shirt. His nose is grossly sunburned and peeling, but his bedside manner is unimpaired. One enormous hand grips his high-domed bag, the other shakes mine as Bel departs.

I thank Dr Appleby who is kind and has come. I tell him how kind he is. How grateful I am.

'Not at all,' he says, still shaking my hand.

Preliminaries over, he begins his examination. I watch his blunt fingers as he checks blood pressure, pulse, the Vital Signs, they call them. The hairs between his knuckles are pale ginger. I suppose that is why he burns easily.

'So far so good,' he murmurs.

Charlie opens his eyes.

'Look!'

'Even better.' he says. 'And he's been concussed for half an hour, I gather.'

'About that.'

'Mmm.'

'Is that too long?'

He looks up, distracted. 'Too long for what?'

'Simple concussion.'

'No. No. Not really. No.'

Yes or no, man. Yes or no.

Dr Appleby continues his gentle probing without further inter-ruption. The news is good. No bones are broken. Simple concussion, nothing untoward. Charlie, is that his name, Charlie must stay in bed for at least twenty-four hours and be watched for some time after that. Probably about ten days or so. Kept fairly quiet, that sort of thing. May tire easily, possibly be slightly muddled. But there will be no permanent damage. The professional diagnosis and treatment roll on; words of comfort drift towards me on the faint breeze from the balcony. He lifts Charlie's wrist.

Charlie's eyes snap open. 'Who are you?'

Dr Appleby smiles. 'About time you woke up, isn't it, sonny? Don't want to worry Mummy, do we?'

Charlie closes his eyes.

The top of Dr Appleby's bent head is peeled and flaky, his voice benign. 'Your prayers have been answered, Mrs Hopkins. The Lord is merciful.'

I had forgotten that Dr Appleby is a devout man. Not only is he a true believer, but is known to be so. He drives into town every Sunday of his well-deserved holiday to preach at the prayer meeting of his non-conformist church.

He moves to the balcony and gazes down at the scene below him. 'Truly a Peaceable Kingdom,' he murmurs.

I dislike having my favourite clichés churned back at me. 'There's nothing else I can do?' I ask. 'Nothing you can think of?'

'Watch and pray, Mrs Hopkins. Watch and pray.'

'I'm so grateful to you for coming, Dr Appleby.'

It is his pleasure. He is a good man and I am indeed more grateful than I can say. Nevertheless his goodness does not interest me, there is no mystery in it.

He moves to the bed for a final pat.

Charlie's eyes snap open. 'Who are you?'

'That's exactly the type of confusion I mean, do you see? You mustn't be concerned. This is to be expected for a day or two after such a knock. I'm surprised the contusion is not worse.' He peers at the egg-shaped swelling on Charlie's forehead. 'Skin not broken, however.'

'Mum,' says Charlie.

'Oh, Charlie, Charlie, Charlie.'

'And another thing,' says Dr Appleby, still smiling. 'He probably won't remember anything about what happened for some time both before and after the event. The Lord is merciful indeed.'

Bella and Duncan appear. We clutch each other, grin like apes, give thanks. That must be one of the joys for Dr Appleby, having someone definite to thank.

'G'day, Chas,' says Duncan, poking his brother once more. He tells him he has been out cold. That he could have conked out completely. Passed away.

The corners of Charlie's mouth lift. He looks dazed but happy.

'Where's Annie?' I ask.

'Disappeared,' says Duncan.

'What?'

'Well, I can't find her.'

Bel takes over. Charlie's eyes close as we leave.

'She won't be inside,' says Duncan. 'She'll be hiding somewhere dumb outside.'

We work systematically through the Backquarters, peering behind wheelbarrows, under boxes. We call her name as we hunt through garage, washhouse, sheds, all of which Duncan has searched before. 'Annie,' 'Annie,' 'Annie.' Where is the child? This has gone on too long.

I stop suddenly, swing around. 'I know. She may be hiding in Claude's whare even if he isn't there. He wouldn't lock it. No one does.'

Duncan stands still. Hot, sweaty and sticky with cobwebs, he is convinced. 'No, she won't be there.'

We set off past the kennels, the pig sties and the hen house. Hens hang around the open door, moving from one foot to the other, glumping and clucking like disgruntled residents awaiting a meal at an Old People's Home.

'We've forgotten the Bird Room!' I cry, already running.

'The what?' says Duncan. He does not know the whitewashed brick cell with its single bench, stray feathers and the smell of bird. He would never dream of hiding in such a place. He would have enclosed spaces, places with doors which lock and windows which seal.

Not so me, not so Ann. We like to have our escape routes visible – as she has today in the small doorless cell. She sits crouched on the wooden bench with a book in her hands, looks up blankly. Her eyes are wet with tears.

'Hullo,' she says.

We tell her the good news, our words spilling over each other's.

'Awake and all. Talking,' shouts Duncan.

Annie jumps up, flings her hands together in her usual gesture for enthusiasm. 'I knew he would be.'

'Then why're you bawling y'head off, dopey?'

'It's so sad, so sad when Judy dies,' she says, snatching *Seven Little Australians* from beneath his feet. 'I'll go and see him, eh!'

She runs off, knock kneed and scrambling, one finger keeping her place in the bit where Judy dies.

Half-way across the yard she swings round to Duncan. 'When're you going to tell her?'

'Now.'

Annie nods slowly. 'Good,' she says, and runs on.

I sit down on the wooden bench. 'Tell me.'

'Here?'

'We won't be interrupted.'

'I'll bet we won't. What a dump.'

He stands before me in his don't-touch-me stance, arms akimbo, legs apart, face stern. He tells me all. He tells me about their lies, how they pinched food from the store room in the middle of the night. How they thought they'd get away with it easy, and it was the only day Joe could come and what was the harm. Claude said it would be all right up the back track to the cave and it was at first but later it got too tough for Charlie so Claude carried him like he said he would. How they had smoko, sausages with green sticks, billy tea, everything.

'And then Claude went funny.'

My mouth is dry. 'Funny how?'

'"Porangi," Joe said. Nuts. Weird. He stopped showing us things on the track, stopped looking at anything we showed him, even Annie's little orchid thing, he didn't care. And . . .' His voice trails off, his eyes stare across me to the framed blue sky beyond the glassless window. 'He stopped the games, making things up, us all being different people and that. And then . . . then he started talking to himself, quick and fussy. You know how he does.'

'I don't. Tell me.'

'I'm trying to, aren't I? Sort of mumbling on and on about how he had to get into town. Urgent. Couldn't wait. Something about signing something. Lawyers, papers, all muddled up. We couldn't hear half of it, him going on and on, jumping about all over the place and sort of patting himself. I tell you. He was bonkers.' He pauses, kicks his sandal at the dirty floor.

'And then he just dumped Charlie and ran.'

I put out my hand. He ignores it.

'And then?'

The rest of his story comes out in a rush. How they went on up round a big rock, and there was the cave like Claude said. How it was black as your hat but it got lighter when you were in. How it was a bit spooky for the little kids but they went on, and then there was a weird sort of moaning noise. Duncan looks at me hesitantly, then ducks his head.

'Bel and Tam it was. Bel moaning and groaning, and him on top.'

184

'Oh.'

'Yeah. Rooting.'

'Duncan . . .'

'Well, what d'y' call it?'

I shake my head. His belated truthfulness demands answers but I have no quick one to this question. 'Making love, I suppose.'

'Huh,' he grunts, more morose than ever. He stares out the window for a moment, then swings back angrily.

'Yeah,' he says, dragging one hand down his face like a defeated old man. 'Then Charlie hopped off Joe's back and went belting forward to stop Tam hurting Bel, he thought, and I don't blame him.'

He strokes the wooden bench, gives it his whole attention.

'Mum?' he says.

'Yes?'

'Does it hurt?'

'No.'

'Then why was she yelping, moaning?'

'Because she was . . . excited.'

'Didn't sound like it.'

'You'll understand when you're older.'

His hand brushes the front of his grey shorts. 'Sticking his thing inside. Does the man like that?'

'Yes.'

'Why?'

'Because they love each other,' I mutter. 'Babies,' I gabble.

His expression changes to deep scorn. 'I know that.'

He sits, staring at the dirty whitewashed bricks around us, the dingy concrete floor. The smell is dry, slightly acrid, not unpleasant.

'And if she wants another baby he has to do it again?'

'Yes.'

'On and on?'

'Yes.'

'The poor bloke.'

He sits in silence for a moment then continues. 'Then it all went mad. Charlie ran forward like I said, and tripped and fell and lay still. Like that dog my first day at school. Remember?'

'Yes.'

I do remember. It was before Charlie was born. Ann in her pushchair and I were escorting Duncan on his first day at primary school. He walked close to me, alternating between swaggering bravado and concern as to where he would eat his raisin sandwiches. Ann pointed a stiff finger at the sky. 'Moon,' she said. 'Moon.'

'Why's it there now?' said Duncan.

'It's a day moon.'

'Watch the dog!' I screamed at the passing driver as hurtling out from nowhere, leaping and prancing across the road, came a fox terrier. I was too late. There was a squeal of brakes and the dog lay dead. That total stillness after bounding action stays with you.

'Then what?'

'Nothing. Tam carried him down.'

'Tell me about it.'

'There's nothing to tell, I said.'

The late afternoon heat blazes down. The square of colour in the window frame has faded to milky blue. The sun lies in the open doorway like a slab of gold.

'It must have happened before, darling,' says Derek. 'It can't be the first time.'

'Oh yes. Of course. It's not that exactly.'

He puts his arm around me as we sit on my bed. I lean my head on his shoulder, am filled with the most extraordinary feeling of comfort. Of, if you can stand it, belonging. Charlie will be all right. How could he not be?

'It's so good to see you,' I mumble. 'To talk things over. Will it have some dire effect on Ann? And if so what? And what should we do? Duncan seems all right but how do we know? Charlie won't remember anything for some time before or afterwards, according to Dr Appleby. You've met him?'

'Mmm.'

'A good man.'

'Very.'

We smile at each other in the amiable collusion of those who don't have to decode signals. This has not always been so between us. We are aware of this slight shift and are shyly pleased.

'I've nothing against goodness,' I say. 'I find goodness, disinterested goodness, mysterious, glamorous even. You, for example. Bella. How do you do it?'

'Me? Probably because I'm dull.'

'No. True goodness is never dull.'

Never have I been more convinced, more insistent, that anyone should understand something as elementary as goodness and truth. I am transfigured by knowledge and longing to share.

'It's because you are both utterly unselfish. Selfless. I find that mysterious, inexplicable, a source of wonder.'

I turn to him, anxious for assent and enthusiasm, to find his face is not happy. Anything but.

He strokes the crease of his trousers. His voice is precise, matter of fact. 'No wonder I'm boring.'

'Oh, don't be ridiculous,' I snap.

He smiles. 'Are you really concerned about Annie?'

'I don't know. I hope not. I'd love a cigarette.'

'No.'

'No,' I agree, adjusting my head. 'I've always felt that children should not be lumbered with adults' assumptions as to how they should react. Children are different. They are not small adults and should not be treated as such. They exist. They learn. There they are, putting one foot in front of the other, getting on with the business of growing up like any other young animal. Bear cubs watch their adults suss out the best route up the honey tree, small beavers watch which logs the big ones choose for the dam. Where's the difference? Love them, teach them and leave them alone.'

'Bugger beavers. We're talking about a shy, self-conscious child.'

'Of course, but even so I think, hope, her reaction will be nothing more than distaste.'

'You're probably right. And the way to find out is to talk to her.'

I poke him amiably. 'You talk to them too much.'

'And you too little.'

I am interested in this comment, and am about to pursue it when Charlie opens his eyes and smiles.

'Look, Charlie,' I say, leaping up. 'Look who's here.'

Charlie puts out a hand. 'Daddy,' he says.

The stars snap and glitter as we lie side by side on Derek's bed on the Bachelors' Balcony. Derek tells me their names once more. They are good names and I like hearing them, and Derek is happy to repeat them. There is no compulsion for me to remember Betelgeuse and Bellatrix, Alpha crusis and Beta crusis. I will one day.

'When I say I don't think we should fuss, that doesn't mean not being aware.'

'True,' he says, dreamily stroking my throat which I find pleasant.

'But what about the rest of it?'

'Oh, darling. The rest of what?'

'What will happen to the film?'

He yawns. 'Does it matter?'

'To James it does.'

'Then it will happen.'

'What do you think of James?'

'James?' Derek, as always, thinks before he speaks. 'I think he is well educated, privileged and unusual.'

'In what way?'

'To be well educated and privileged in the Bay at this time is unusual enough, isn't it?'

'But more than that?'

'I think he is a "cat who walks by himself".'

'It's no use quoting. That just lets you out of thinking.'

'Exactly.'

'So?'

'Unusual will do.'

'Nnn. I'll tell you what I think. I think Mrs Clements will explode. There will be the most monumental row and Bella will leave and we will all be sent packing and thank goodness for that.'

'Perhaps she's waiting until Charlie's completely OK,' he says.

OK. Derek never says OK. Straws. Straws in the wind and I'm glad to hear them. 'Possibly. She's a kind woman.'

His hand moves.

'Wait a minute, would we hear him if he woke up?'

'Of course,' says Derek.

Charlie is up and running well before Derek goes back to town on Sunday night. Claude has not reappeared, nor the Henares. There is no sign of the Ropatas or Angus. The atmosphere at Rongomaha is edgy and the heat unremitting. Bella clicks around attending to her duties with silent competence, but I feel she has gone somewhere else and I have not been invited to join her. This saddens me. I had not thought I might lose Bella. But she would confide in me if she wanted to and obviously has decided against it.

Rongomaha seems to be peopled by those either fuming in corners or attempting to keep out of their way.

James has retreated into sulks of the darker sort. By now they are two days old and festering. His displeasure hangs over Rongomaha like a pall. So much so that I am nervous lest Duncan might be infected by such gloom. Ann also has retreated into her own world. Bella's childhood books, *Miss Bobbie* and *Not Like Other Girls,* engross her. They demand her full attention as she hides from Mrs Clements and keeps her head down in the Bird Room.

I discuss the situation with Bella as we prepare food for the depleted household. I tell her our still being here is ridiculous. That we must go back to the Beach. That we are no help here, in fact quite the reverse. I say Mrs Clements has been very kind insisting that we wait till Charlie is quite well, but he is now and we must go. Perhaps James would be kind enough to drive us down later in the day? Or Bob Jackson?

Bella swings from the sink, her knuckles white about the small knife. Its small blade sticks from her hand, crimson juice drips on the bench.

'I have never explained what happened. How Charlie was hurt.'

'Don't. Not now.'

'I'm not apologising.'

'No. No. I . . .'

'As you please,' says Bel, her voice crisp and dismissive. 'Mum is in her room if you want to see her.' Her mouth twitches. 'Attending to her correspondence.'

I knock on Mrs Clements' door, am invited into the large room where she sits at a pretty little desk which is too small for her. The tall windows beyond frame climbing roses and cloud. The curtains at the windows are faded lemon silk, slit with long rents from age and decay. The double bedspread beneath the mahogany headrest is an ancient patchwork pattern with one of those cheerful busy names like 'Calling the Cows' or 'Up and Under'. Its colours also have faded to the subtle shades of old rose petals seen by lamplight: pale pinks, apricot, buff and creamy whites. Mrs Clements has had the good sense not to change anything since Harold died. She and her furnishings will fall apart gracefully and together. She likes old things. It is new things which alarm her.

She looks at me, her face as stern as Bella's or James's. She waves a hand at a small chair covered with more faded roses. These ones twine with green leaves but have no thorns. 'Sit down, Lorna. I have a bone to pick with you.'

If there is a more unpleasant greeting than this I do not know it. I would have expected better of Mrs Clements. The phrase is not only a euphemism, but a simpering one, the type usually accompanied by a coy smile. Though not this time.

I sit up straight in my rosy doll's chair and stare back, my eyes wide and unblinking. 'Oh,' I say.

Mrs Clements also straightens. Her bosom, which is of the all-in-one style favoured by Queen Mary, lifts.

'Why did you not tell me that Isabel was having this disgusting liaison?'

'Mrs Clements, I came to tell you that I think the children and I should go back to the Beach as soon as possible. To thank you very much and say I would be grateful if . . .'

'Please will you answer my question?'

'I am explaining why I came to see you.'

'If you hadn't I would have sent for you.'

My reaction must show in my face. Hers flushes slightly. 'I have every right to ask you the question.'

'I beg to differ.' This is a useful Edwardian phrase of my father's, who shunned attack as assiduously as a retreating pipi.

The force of Mrs Clements' irritation almost rocks her desk on its small feet as she stands to confront me.

'How dare you speak to me like that in my own house. Your father would have been appalled. He was always such a courteous man.'

He was too. 'I'm sorry, Mrs Clements, but I'm just trying to explain. Bella is my friend. Her private aff . . . life is no concern of mine. Besides I know she intended to tell you of her friendship with Tamati.'

'Friendship! Affair will do. Did you see the back of her frock that day?'

'No.'

'Blood.'

There is something both prurient and archaic in her delivery of this evidence. We are back with blood-stained sheets displayed from balconies to waiting crowds, with terrified peasant girls being examined for the web-footed stigmata of witches. I sink down into my chair.

Mrs Clements also sits. Her eyes are full of tears.

'Have you spoken to Bella?' I say.

'Yes.'

'And?'

'I have lost her,' she says, and turns aside to weep. 'My darling darling Bella.' She straightens, gives a sort of gasping sniff. 'You realise she could have had Angus? He was hers for the taking. He had already spoken, he told me when he left. Spoken!'

'Angus has left Rongomaha?'

'Yes, last night. Some nonsense about getting back to give Garth a hand with something. Dagging, I think he said. I'd like to know when anyone last dagged a ewe in January. I wasn't fooled. I understood exactly. He had to get away as soon as he could, poor man. And to think he'd asked her. Proposed! And she sent him packing for a Maori shearer. Oh, oh, oh,' wails Mrs Clements, rocking backwards and forwards with the intensity of her grief and rage.

I sit speechless, my mind racing. Pull yourself together, woman. It's 1936. He's a fine young man. They love each other. His father's a chief. Cliché follows cliché and all remain unspoken.

I put my hand on her arm. 'It's her life, Mrs Clements,' I say, and mean it with all my heart.

She wipes her eyes with a lace-trimmed handkerchief. Women of independent means possess beautiful handkerchiefs. It is one of the signs. She raises her faded blue eyes to mine. 'What on earth has that got to do with it?' she snaps.

I have few illusions left about Mrs Clements. Why then do I feel so sad, not only for Bella who is faced with such intransigence, but for poor foolish old Phoebe who has been kind to me and mine.

A breeze from a verandah window drifts across to one opposite. A cross-draught is a help in the heat, as her pioneer forebears would have known.

I can't leave her like this.

But Mrs Clements has pulled herself together, has bucked up. She has mopped and sniffed, sniffed and patted. Her face is strong once more. 'Well,' she says, 'if that man thinks he's going to get a penny of my money he has another think coming.'

She heaves herself up from her desk and heads for a large chest of drawers, the polished surface of which is covered with family photographs in silver frames. Harold smiles beneath a panama. He wears a large rosette labelled Official Judge 1929. There are baby and toddler photographs of James and Isabel, their different physiognomies already defined, though I realise I have the benefit of hindsight. In a larger photograph Harold and Phoebe stand beaming beside Panache the day he won the Cup.

Mrs Clements returns, holds out a box of Queen Anne chocolates and offers me the chart to help me choose: Vanilla Cream, Caramel, Chocolate Rough. 'I need some glucose,' she says. 'And you?'

I must get out of here. 'No, no. Thank you,' I mutter. 'Excuse me,' I say, once more leaping to my feet. 'Charlie, I must find Charlie.'

'Take one for him,' she says, smiling. 'Poor little one-legged sparrow. And the others.'

I snatch three chocolates of unknown flavour. 'Thank you,' I say, and run for it. For some reason Ann flatly refuses to eat Queen Anne chocolates, but this is not the moment for irrelevant chat.

Charlie and Ann sit on the back porch bickering over the ownership of a two-inch-long orange sports car. I sit on the step for a smoke, hand Charlie a chocolate, find myself shaking. I am not going back, ever, or not at the moment.

'Has Claude come back?' I inquire eventually.

Ann looks up, shakes her head.

'Dunno,' says Charlie, triumphantly snatching the orange car from beneath her nose. 'When are we going back to the Beach?'

'Soon. Where's Duncan?'

'Dunno.'

'Have you seen Bella?'

More head-shaking.

'Mr Clements?'

'He'll be with his orchids,' offers Ann.

But he is not. He is searching for me, Bella, anyone. 'Where is everyone? Has Ma got the sulks? Angus? Where's Angus?'

'He's gone back to the Rowans.'

'He can't have. What about the film?'

The film. Ah yes. The film.

'Won't it be abandoned?'

'Why on earth should it be abandoned? Derek's gone back to town, has he?'

'Yes, two days ago. When Charlie was well again.'

'Ah yes. Wretched business. All right now though, isn't he? Come into my office.'

'Thank you.'

James's office is like other farmers' offices I have seen but bigger. It is dark, the wallpaper stained with nicotine, the walls lined with bright red, blue and gold show ribbons plus Champion of Champions dating back to Grandfather George's day. There is the same proud photograph of Panache and his beaming owners, the jockey's face has faded to a light smudge. There are more recent photographs of amateur theatricals, *Hay Fever* with James as lead, *Journey's End* with James as the gallant doomed hero, Captain Stanhope. A signed photograph of Noel Coward, the one with him biting the end of his thumb and smiling knowingly, sits on top of the desk.

There is a swivel chair and a roll-top desk and another chair for stock agents, bull breeders and other stud owners – employees and men on business bent. The desk is exquisitely tidy. There is a place for everything, including a beautifully made mahogany container for envelopes of different sizes. The pen is in the penholder, the ink in the pot, the blotter in the blotter pad and God knows wot.

Despite being on his home ground, James is agitated. Never have I seen him so disturbed. His grace, his strength, his beautiful profile are all as obvious as ever, but his serenity has gone. He keeps leaping up, sitting down, leaping up again. He lights another Craven A and swings to me on his revolving chair, the curved barrel shape of which is pleasing to the eye.

'What are we going to do, Lorna?'

'Do?'

'Yes. Do. Do. I'm not going to abandon *Lust in the Dust* at this stage.'

'But hasn't there been the most appalling row?'

'Yes, yes, of course. That's the point. What in the name of heaven Bel thinks she's doing I cannot imagine. The whole thing is sordid in the extreme. She might at least have had the decency to wait till L.I.D. was in the can.'

Once again the man has silenced me, but not for long. I laugh and laugh and laugh. Tears, unexpurgated, glorious tears, slide down my face.

'Oh dear, oh dear, oh dear,' I gasp.

James, not unnaturally, is not pleased. He tells me I have always had a very peculiar sense of humour. Quite vindictive in some ways, he has sometimes thought. He murmurs Derek's name.

Which brings me to my senses. It is always a surprise to discover that people judge you with the same lack of charity you bestow on them. 'I'm sorry. Please believe me. I didn't mean . . .'

He lets me swing. Why should he not? 'I would have thought that if I wanted to discuss possible solutions to a problem which is very real to me, you might have had the courtesy to take me seriously.'

'Yes,' I say. Hapless and contrite, I appeal once more for absolution. 'I'm sorry.'

'We'll leave it at that then,' he says graciously. 'The point is, as I said before, what are we going to do?'

I swallow air. 'I can see what you mean, James, but . . .' I resist saying I sympathise. I do not sympathise. The man's self-absorption is undoubtedly extreme. 'But honestly, with all the good will in the world, I can't see what anyone can do. I would like to finish the film too,' I say.

195

'Angus, lots of people, would, but that surely is because we're not involved emotionally. But how can Mrs Clements, Bel, the Ropatas, probably the Henares, how can they all go on pretending that there has not been a serious rift? A flaming row between your family and the Ropatas?' I look at him. He won't get it, I fear, but I say it anyway. 'Your sister is being torn apart, you mother is heart-broken.'

'Oh, you know Ma,' he mutters.

'The Ropatas, I imagine, feel the same. What makes you think otherwise? Mr Ropata does not want a pakeha wife for his only son.'

'I thought,' says James, swinging his chair to me once more, 'that I might consult Colonel Holdaway.'

'Colonel Holdaway?'

'Very astute man, the Colonel. He's done wonders liaising with the Maoris. For years, long before the Quake. And after. That's why he's always at the Pa. Highly regarded by the lot of them. Foot in both camps as it were.'

'James.' My hands move helplessly, have nowhere to go. 'What on earth can he do? This is a family matter. The situation is explosive, seen as an insult by both families. Colonel Holdaway is a dear man, but I can't imagine what he could do.'

'There's more there than you think. A wily old bird. Very. I'm going to see him now.' He stands. Our meeting is at an end and I have not done well.

I long to ask him if he could give us a lift to our bach, but must farewell Mrs Clements and Bella. Besides, I am not sure that he would be pleased.

He turns as I leave the dark nicotine-scented room. His expression is detached, amiable.

'By the way, what were you laughing about, Lorna?'

Lorna

Bella is not in the kitchen – a bad sign. She should be and she isn't and the place is a mess. There are unwashed dishes, fly-ridden jam pots and butter on the melt. I take over: quite simple really, any fool could do it.

Outside the back door Charlie's brrm-brrmming with his cars continues, punctuated by Ann's quick chirps. No one has suggested they should go anywhere or do anything else, and they are unaware that the ship is foundering, the Captain has retired hurt and the First Mate is nowhere to be seen.

I tell Annie where I'm going and head upstairs to Bella's bedroom. Once again I am knocking tentatively, requesting an interview. Bel comes to the door tugging the drawstrings of a tartan sponge bag. She smiles her slow beautiful smile. 'Come to help me pack?' she says.

And so she is. Bella Clements is leaving. Despite everything, my previous knowledge of her commitment to Tam, my belief in the strength and courage of her convictions, I am taken aback. The scene, the whole scenario, has changed. This is no longer a lovers' drama at a distance, a glimpse of stolen meetings and secret delights. This is Bella, my calm well-conducted friend Bella, sorting underwear, folding woollies and rolling stockings into neat balls. She is taking only the essentials, she tells me. 'Sensible, don't you agree? Goodness knows where we'll land up.' She smiles. 'Mr Ropata is just as enraged as Mum.' She pauses. 'Have you seen her?'

'Yes.'

'Pitiful, isn't it?'

I keep my eyes down, nod. 'What an enormous suitcase,' I say.

She strokes the leather surface. 'Magnificent, isn't it? Good timing too. It was Mum's Christmas present.'

'Oh.'

'I know. Heaven knows where she thought I'd be going, other than down to the aunts occasionally.'

'Bel,' I say, clutching her arm. 'I have to say it.'

'No, you don't.'

'Your mind is made up?'

'Completely,' she says, slapping a jersey into shape with quick no-nonsense movements.

'Have you thought it through? The whole thing. It's too soon, too sudden, all that. I mean it, Bel.'

She lifts her head. 'Oh do be quiet.'

'But you won't let me discuss things rationally. I have to jolly you along. Behave like a halfwit.'

She stops, suddenly contrite. 'What did you want to be rational about?' she asks, picking up a shrunken cable-stitch and gazing at it doubtfully.

This is no Hollywood movie scene where the act of Leaving Home is conducted at lightning speed, where the heroine snatches six garments from a wardrobe, flings them into an empty suitcase and storms out on teetering heels. That is not Bella's style. She goes about the job with her usual calm competence, as though it is a part of her everyday routine.

'Money,' I say.

'You know better,' she says, her grin mocking me, 'than to talk about anything as indelicate as money.'

'Such niceties are for those who have it.'

'True. And we won't. And truly, I know you . . .'

'. . . Mean well,' I snap.

'Oh Lorna. More than that. Much much more than that,' she says and hugs me. 'Oh dear,' she sniffs. 'You don't by any chance want a dun-coloured cardigan with horn buttons, do you?'

'No thank you. That suitcase worries me.'

'In what way?'

'How are you going to ride off into the sunset with a thing that size?'

The hug re-forms.

'Lunch,' she says suddenly. 'Silverside all right?'

The children are hanging around the kitchen door. James sits at the table dragging aggressively at his Craven A.

'Where on earth have you been? It's nearly one.'

'Packing my suitcase.'

'Very funny. Though I must say I consider the remark in poor taste.'

We are a denuded group around the left-over corned beef. No Mrs Clements. No Angus, the mystery of whose departure continues although there is no way of solving it at the moment. No Henares. James is still edgy and morose. Bella carves meat, hands chutneys and tomatoes, slices bread with her usual briskness, but it is obvious her thoughts are not with us. She has forgotten the mustard, leaps up to remedy this omission. Duncan, Ann and Charlie munch on in silence. Like all children when unease is present they are aware, cautious. Ann's eyes never leave Bella's face, which seems indicative of something, though I am not sure what.

Duncan's reaction to the scene in the cave I know, and find, I think, healthy. Ann's I sense but I don't know and must find out. A mixture of confusion and distaste, I imagine. Children are wary of unexpected behaviour by adults, as well they might be. Derek and I stopped kissing in front of Ann and, by extension, the other two, years ago. Ridiculous, I know, but when she was little she flew into tantrums at the sight of our embrace, would totter between us and attempt to push us apart, dimpled fists pummelling, face scarlet, size oo feet drumming the boards. It was Derek who suggested we should be more discreet. I thought he might have been mildly irritated by his daughter's territorial reaction, but he is a generous father.

The sooner I talk to Ann the better, but it might not be as easy as talking with Duncan. Her shyness, plus embarrassment, could make frank explanations difficult. It is important to get this right. Communication is all.

And yet, at a surprisingly early age, parents become visitors to the inner lives of their children. They become, like Damon Runyon's narrator, guys who are just around. Necessary individuals, who may be dearly loved and are welcomed occasionally to the real world within their offspring's heads, but who, until they themselves become adults, are best treated with the detached and amiable tolerance they extend to travellers from another country.

I smile at Annie. She dips her rolled lettuce leaf in sugar and smiles back.

'Am I spirited, Mum?'

'Spirited?'

'In Bella's books she lent me, in all the best ones, the main girl is spirited. It keeps saying.'

I open my mouth, am saved by Bella. 'I'll tell you something good, Annie,' she says. 'You don't have to start off spirited. You can get spirited later on, if you want to.'

The relief on the round brown face is palpable. Ann munches harder. 'Good,' she says.

James pushes back his chair. 'Does anyone want to come to the beach with me? I've made an appointment to speak to Colonel Holdaway at three o'clock.'

Bella reaches for a cigarette from his open packet. 'What on earth for?'

'You'd like a swim wouldn't you, fellas.' I say quickly. 'See Miriama. You can have a rest there, Charlie.'

They would like a swim and say so. There is a barefooted scuffle of departure from the kitchen. A hunt for togs, a 'wait for me' from Charlie.

'And hats,' I cry.

'Now, James,' says Bella. 'It's time we had a talk.'

'I agree.' He turns to her, a startling flick of rage in his eyes, glimpsed for a moment then gone. 'It probably hasn't occurred to you, Bella, but this debacle you've perpetuated . . .'

'Can you perpetuate a debacle?' I ask.

'Please,' he says without a glance. 'As I was saying, your extraordinary exhibition has left the filming of *Lust in the Dust* at a complete standstill.'

'It wasn't intended to be an exhibition,' says Bella.

'I must go,' I say.

Impatient hands flap. I sit.

'Not, I suppose, that you have given L.I.D. a moment's thought?' continues James.

'Not a moment.'

He springs upwards. 'My God, you make me seethe. What about Ma? Me? The film! What do you think you're doing, you and this layabout! How will you live? What will you do?'

Bella leans her chin on one hand, gazes at him thoughtfully. 'I don't know,' she says. 'But he's a good shearer and I can cook.'

'You may not have noticed, but shearing is a seasonal occupation.'

'I am aware of that,' says Bella gently. 'When necessary we'll live like any other itinerant workers. Go where the work is.'

'Itinerant workers!' hoots James. 'Oh, I like it. Swaggers, you mean.'

I don't think I have ever seen anyone actually shake with rage before. For a second I wonder whether he might hit her, but James masters himself with effort. Breathing deeply, he draws himself upright and gives his verdict.

'You two women, you're both the same. A pair of half-educated smart alec trivial-minded females without a thought in your heads for anyone, anything, in the whole world except your own pleasure. Females!'

It is the last word he hates most. He spits it out. Loathsome, slimy as toads, it skids across the kitchen. 'And,' he storms, 'I wouldn't be surprised if you weren't both oversexed as well.'

I am shaken. I admit it. Bella is not. If anything she is faintly amused, but enough, she indicates, is enough.

'More coarsely expressed than Mum, but the sentiments are the same. It will make it easier for me to leave.' She makes a small sound, something between a gulp and a gasp. 'Much easier,' she says, and runs from the room.

I turn to follow her, my face burning with rage, scorn and a touch of shame. I particularly disliked 'half-educated smart alec'.

James stows his cigarettes and matches, glances at me. 'If you round up the children, Lorna, I'll get the papers I need and we'll go down straight away.'

'If you think for one moment that I am going anywhere with someone who has insulted me as you have, has spoken to me as I have never been spoken to in my life, then . . .' I gasp, practically stamp my foot. 'You have another think coming,' I say, realising too late that once more I sound like his mother. 'I'm going. Now.'

He puts out his hand as I flounce past, pats my arm. 'The truth is sometimes painful, even between friends,' he says gently.

I lose all dignity. 'Pig,' I snap like Charlie in a bad moment, and storm past.

Or attempt to. His hand tightens on my arm. 'Of course you must come, Lorna,' he says. 'How will the children get their swim otherwise? It's not their fault.'

On cue the children appear. Tentative and strangely quiet, they line up at the door; hatted, sandalled, with togs and towels at the ready. Their eyes are anxious.

'You said you'd take us, Mum,' says Charlie.

Derek had an aunt whose husband was unfaithful to her. She must leave the man immediately, cried her two unmarried sisters. Where was her dignity? Her pride? Aunt Bessy declined to do so, saying firmly that she would stay on as Jack's housekeeper for the sake of the two little girls. Whereupon, to no one's surprise, she had three more children and her husband continued his dalliance as before. She should have made a stand, raged her sisters.

I will make a stand. A small, an infinitesimal stand, but I will make it.

I open my mouth to say I am not coming.

Charlie slips his hand in mine. 'Mum?' he says.

'All right,' I say. 'I'll come.'

'Besides,' says James, shepherding us towards his car. 'I may need a witness – one never knows.' He opens the door for me.

Charlie grins at Ann.

James has our expedition worked out. He will leave the children with Jeannie who will take them for a swim. She will be delighted to see them and so will Miriama. Duncan, disgusted at the absence of his friend Mike from the Store, asks why can't he go and see Joe at the Pa. James says certainly not and drives on undeterred, in fact totally oblivious to the smouldering unrest in the back seat.

He stops for ice creams at the Store.

I explain that I am unable to accompany him to see Colonel Holdaway. That Charlie, although quite well, is my responsibility and I will not leave him.

James replies that we shall see.

Charlie asks when Claude's coming home.

During this discussion Angus Rowan comes out of the Store with an ice cream held well away from his dilapidated jodhpurs. He stops short, hands his cone to a surprised and delighted child, and marches over.

'Why on earth did you leave in such a rush?' says James, shaking his hand through the window. 'I need you to finish the film.'

'Not with me,' says Angus, glancing at the children licking at the back. 'I have explained my reasons to your mother.'

'She didn't tell me. It's no use telling Ma anything at the moment. She seems to have gone into some sort of decline.'

'Also,' says Angus, 'I felt it was time I gave Garth and Midge a hand.'

'What on earth do they need a hand with at this time of year? Even Garth can remember to put the rams out. Or Midge, more likely.'

'James,' I say, attempting a backwards chuck of the head towards the back seat where the licking has stopped and the faces are still.

'What?'

I renew my efforts.

'Oh. Well, come on, Angus, come down to the beach anyway. You can't let me down at this stage.'

'I see no reason why not.'

James laughs. 'No, no more desertions. We'll all have to double up as it is.'

'Who else has deserted?' says Angus, his voice steeped in uninterest.

'Mum,' says Ann, 'Charlie's ice cream's melted all down his front.'

By the time I have cleaned up with a wet rag borrowed from Mrs Girlingstone, James has revealed his plan. He and I will go to see Colonel Holdaway. Angus can have a gallop on the beach, give the chestnut a dip in the Pacific, take tea with Jean and Harry after the children's swim, and await our arrival.

Angus taps the canvas bag on his shoulder. 'I have the Rowans' bread.'

'Well bring it, man, bring it.'

'I'd like to see Jeannie. Yes,' he says, drawling the word like us rather than snipping it off as usual.

He swings onto the skittery chestnut and canters down the dusty road.

'I'll talk him round,' says James. 'You'll see. Poor man's bored stiff, I suppose. Odd way to help, collecting the bread on a good horse like that. Take minutes in the truck.'

Colonel and Mrs Holdaway's house is different from the other baches, both at Laing's Point and along the rest of the beach. It is small and rather dark, with mullioned cottage-type windows. It has not been built for unlimited light and air and ease. It has been designed, rather, to keep safe, to enclose Colonel and Mrs Holdaway and the girls when they can get up, and, of course, the young. Colonel and Mrs Holdaway are known as the olds and the arrangement appears to suit everyone. There is much that suits Colonel and Mrs Holdaway, the most interesting of which is the pleasure they take in each other's company.

The Colonel told me once that during his time in the trenches one of the things he longed for most was something which was not designed entirely for practical reasons. 'I missed Florence horribly,' he said. 'She has such a flair for comfort.'

And thus they sit, in their hot little house, surrounded and cushioned by things knitted, things constructed, sewn, woven or crafted with loving care and happy patience by Mrs Holdaway.

I know her patience is happy because it shows on her face. Mrs Holdaway is uneasy only if she has nothing on the go, her knitting needles are empty or she has run out of thread. Her colours, however, do not meld. A crimson velvet cushion behind her husband's head lies alongside one made from orange tweed with tufts. A patchwork toucan lies beneath a ginger bear and a moon-faced gollywog with green hair. In the next chair a long-legged doll with the white face and coal-black eyes of a Pierrette wears an unexpected pink tutu. She was designed, I am told, to disguise the unsightly intrusion of a telephone. None of the holiday houses have a telephone, as we know, but the Pierrette was fun to make, and Brenda and Bobby love tying her legs in knots.

'The whole cottage,' says the Colonel serenely, 'could be described as a Riotous Assembly.'

Mrs Holdaway chuckles and continues two plain two purl. She agrees with me that it is hot work in this heat but Dinah's pregnant again and the first-size baby singlets have shrunk.

'Have you ever had to read the Riot Act, Sir?' asks James.

Colonel Holdaway tells us he has not and inquires whether we would like to tell him the purpose of our visit. I attempt to dissociate myself from the whole business, which is difficult as my presence denies this. We decline tea.

James takes over. As before, when he was telling us about *Lust in the*

Dust, outlining the plot and revealing his plans, he is articulate and concise, his voice as sonorous as ever.

'I presume, Mrs Holdaway, that my mother has confided her concern to you as regards my sister.'

Mrs Holdaway can knit without looking. Her head cocks to one side, her needles fly. 'Phoebe spoke to me in confidence.' She smiles.

'She needn't have bothered. It'll be all over the district. Bella says she's going to marry the man.'

'Oh.'

'Precisely.'

Colonel Holdaway takes a quick sideways munch of moustache. 'What is Wiremu Ropata's reaction?'

'Bad, I gather,' says James, glancing at me for the first time since we entered the house.

I bear witness. 'Yes.'

'But with respect, James, what has this sad affair to do with me?' says Colonel Holdaway. 'Us?'

Mrs Holdaway smiles.

'There are several points,' says James. 'The slur on the family to start with . . .'

'And the Ropatas, according to their lights,' murmurs Mrs Holdaway.

'And, of course, Ma's reaction. She's quite done up, isn't she, Lorna?'

'Yes.'

Mrs Holdaway makes a small mew of concern.

'Then there's the matter of the film.'

'What film?'

James drops the Sir. '*Lust in the Dust*. What else?'

'Oh that.' The Colonel fills his pipe, tamps it down with a tobacco-stained forefinger, lights three matches in quick succession and sucks hard. 'So?'

'Apparently the Ropatas have disappeared back into the woodwork. I tried to make contact yesterday. Drove down to the Pa. Total failure. Refused entrance. Literally.'

The Colonel's words come through drifts of pipe smoke. 'But that is understandable, is it not?'

'Understandable! I find it intolerable. All I want them to do is to let me finish the film and they can do what they bloody well like. Excuse me, Mrs Holdaway.'

Mrs Holdaway looks through him. There is silence, the embarrassed silence of onlookers who witness a man accidentally displace his wig, reveal his stays.

'How well,' says Colonel Holdaway finally, 'do you know the Maori?'

'Very little, and it will be less than that from now on, believe me.'

'But your father, your grandfather . . .' The Colonel interrupts himself, starts again. 'The problem as I see it is this. Early travellers to this country, and the missionaries, often mention the generosity of the Maori, the good will. "Manly and Mild," Captain Cook called them, "showing all ways a readiness to oblige us." But to a man those early reporters all stress how sensitive to insult they are. Overly sensitive. Proud but touchy.'

'So?'

'So how can you possibly expect men of the Ropatas' calibre to continue in your amateur theatricals after this business simply because you would like them to?'

This is a difficult question for James. It is obvious from his stance, his irritated gestures, that he regards the fact that he wishes the Ropatas to be present as adequate reason for them to be so. Another irritant may be that Colonel Holdaway has seriously diminished the artistic value of James's enterprise, has tossed it aside, figuratively speaking, into some dusty cupboard with the disused magic lantern, the crystal set and the doll with no head.

He keeps his dignity. 'I can see there is no point in discussing the matter with you any more, Colonel. I had hoped that your long friendship with my poor mother might have perhaps . . . But no, I can see that we are arguing from completely different premises.'

'Are we arguing?' asks Mrs Holdaway dreamily.

'Differing, my dear,' chuckles the Colonel. 'We are differing from different premises while sitting in one.'

Mrs Holdaway giggles back. The knitting needles are suspended. Such shared pleasure from such a modest outlay is beautiful to see. It is even better when the participants are old.

We leave, me over-effusive with thanks, James less so.

Colonel Holdaway shakes hands at the gate. 'How is my friend Ann?'

'Well, thank you. Did you hear about Charlie?'

'I did, I did indeed. Quite better, I trust,' says the Colonel, holding open the picket gate through the taupata hedge. None of the other baches have hedges, and few have adequate fences. Wooden posts lean and wires hang slack. The glossy green thickness suits my romanticised image of the Holdaways' lives, their containment and their virtue.

The Colonel puts out his hand once more to James. 'I'm sorry I couldn't be more help.'

'Not at all. Not at all,' grunts James.

The Colonel makes a vague gesture, a small wave which goes nowhere. '. . . If you would still like me to go and see Wiremu Ropata on your behalf . . . ?'

James looks him in the eye. 'Thank you, that was what I had hoped you would do.'

'Oh,' says the old man. 'But . . . ? Well, certainly, if you think there's any point. When?'

'As soon as possible.'

'Very well.'

James, driven perhaps by reciprocal generosity, asks Colonel Holdaway whether he would like to come along to the Henares. Hear what Harry has to say.

Colonel Holdaway declines. 'What do you intend to do now, if I may ask?'

'Go and see Harry first. To be quite frank, I had hoped to avoid it but . . . needs must.'

The Colonel lifts a hand. 'Ah. Please give them our greetings.'

Jean Henare, true to her word as always, has insisted on Charlie having a rest after his swim. As I have mentioned, Charlie is usually bad rest-material, but now he lies sound asleep surrounded by old comics on a bed at the back of the verandah.

Duncan lies torpid on the couch grass, reading about Lord Emsworth and his prize pig. The old bloke is just as mad about pigs as Claude, he says. He looks up, flushes slightly, mutters and returns to Wodehouse.

'Where are the girls?' I ask.

'Mucking around out the back.'

I would like to muck about also. I would like to lie on a sofa and go to sleep, or go down to the beach once more and fall into the sea. It looks inviting, this peaceful expanse of ocean shimmering in the heat. Good breakers, too.

How did I get into this unenviable situation? Playing backstop for James, a position whose duties are ill defined but should by their very nature be supportive, is not what I had in mind. I dislike the man. I wouldn't, shall we say, touch him with a barge pole. So why am I here as cheerleader, supporter and possible witness? Surprise at being asked, perhaps, and the fact that we normally treat people like James and Mrs Clements as they expect to be treated. Why we do this is another question.

James, I am sure, asked me in the certain knowledge that I would come. Certainly my wish for the children to have their swim in the sea was part of my acceptance. However, if I am honest, and there is no reason for not being, my main reason was to see what James planned to do. James's behaviour over the last few days has struck me as highly unusual. His desire to get *Lust in the Dust* laid to rest seems to have lost all sense of proportion. His behaviour, I feel, has been bordering on the paranoid. I wish in a purely anthropological sense to see what he will do next.

So far, in respect of his behaviour at Colonel and Mrs Holdaway's cottage, I have not been disappointed. Nor, I think, was Mrs Holdaway.

I cannot speak for the Colonel.

James's voice cuts across my reverie, or rather my scrambled thoughts. Reverie is not a word for the way I think.

'So when will Harry be back, Jeannie?'

'Hare, long "a",' says Jean automatically. 'Any moment soon. More tea, Lorna?'

'No, thank you.'

I think of Colonel and Mrs Holdaway. Of Derek. The three of them share the mystique, the glamour, of disinterested goodness. I stare at the sea. Derek deserves better from me, and in future he will get it.

I feel quite heady for a moment at the thought of this transfiguration, as though I were a new creation already. I can understand why people look forward to changing their lives, are prepared to work hard at it. The very thought of improvement is an uplifting experience.

'What are you smiling about, Lorna?' laughs Jeannie.

'Change,' I say.

'Oh,' says Jeannie.

When James and I came up from the beach Angus and Jean were sitting at the back of the verandah, their chairs close together beside Charlie's bed. Angus was leaning forward, serious, intent, obviously confiding to this sympathetic and understanding woman. She also leaned forward, nodded occasionally but said nothing. She is a good listener, Jeannie.

They sprang apart when we appeared. This is a slight exaggeration, but only slight. Angus, particularly, looked discomfited. Jeannie put her hand on his bare arm as they stood, murmured something as she came forward to greet us.

We hear the distinctive sound of the Henares' funny little Morris as it buckets up the track from the gateway.

Hare comes in smiling with Miri on his arm and Ann trailing behind. 'Ah,' he says, glancing at James. 'Are we having a hui?'

'If you mean an organised meeting,' says James, 'no, we are not. Nevertheless I would like a word with you, Harry.'

'Long "a".'

'Hare then.'

'Do sit down,' says Hare. 'Lorna? Angus? How are we?'

Neither Angus nor I leap to answer. We are not quite sure either how we are or what we're meant to be doing. Our smiles are tentative.

Jeannie flicks through a magazine.

James, however, is businesslike. He sits with his legs crossed at their usual sharp angle, opens his folder, and turns to address us.

'There is currently a problem with some members of the cast of *Lust in the Dust*. Defections. I have a strong suspicion that the Ropatas have reneged on the whole thing. I tried to have the thing out, man to man, with Ropata himself yesterday. Hopeless. Wouldn't let me past the gate.' His hands spread in puzzlement. 'I've organised Colonel Holdaway to go down to the Pa,' he says, 'to see if he can get any sense out of anyone.'

'Poor old Hubert,' says Hare. 'Why on earth?'

'Well, at least he'll get past the gate. I would have asked you, but I knew you'd probably go all Maori on me and refuse to intervene. "Align", as Ma would say.'

Hare stands slowly. 'What do you mean by "go"? I am. Also, I am already aligned.'

'Yes, yes, so you keep saying, and good luck to you and yours. But can't you see how difficult it's making things for *Lust in the Dust*?'

'Tell me,' says Hare, leaning forward in his chair with an expression of mild interest, 'what exactly do you mean by *it's*?'

'*It's*. What *it's*?' says James.

'You said "*it's* making things difficult" for your film.'

'I mean,' he says, 'the whole wretched business. If I'd known how prophetic the working title was going to be I'd have picked something else. And worse than that. You know Bel says she's going to marry the man?'

A chair scrapes. James looks up. 'Where are you going, Angus?'

'I must get back with the bread.'

'Wait a minute. This won't take long and you're essential.'

Angus sits.

'When's Bella's birthday?' asks Jean. 'Aries, isn't it?'

'April the fourth,' snaps James. 'So you won't help with Ropata, Hare.'

'We'll help them both in any way we can. Won't we, darling?'

'Oh yes,' says Jeannie. 'But listen to this. *Aries: You will entice members of the opposite sex with your passion for life and your quick wit. True love was never easy but YOU know best. Health good.* Her smile is beatific. 'Isn't that wonderful! Oh, I do long to see her.'

Angus, who has lost his would-be confidante as well, looks more miserable than ever. Jeannie smiles radiantly at him, inviting him to share her pleasure. He stares at his boots.

'For God's sake,' says James. 'Will you listen to me?'

We do. Our reactions differ but we all listen. Jeannie, anxious to help as always but lost in a fuzz of romantic empathy, smiles happily. Hare, who may be feeling the man has had enough, sighs.

'What did you wish to say?'

James has, he tells us, faced up to the fact that there seems little likelihood that the following cast members will return to finish the filming of *Lust in the Dust*. He reads the names of the casualties with the slow solemnity of a tolling bell.

'Indians: Wiremu Ropata, Tamati Ropata, Joe Ropata. Cameraman: Isabel Clements.' Obviously, he explains, this leaves him seriously short of Indians. The only one left is Hare, who he presumes is still a starter.

Hare, his smile serene, nods his head. 'Why not?'

Working on that assumption – and James must say at once that he is very grateful to Hare – working on that assumption, all is not lost. 'Let us,' he says, 'examine where we have got to and how to proceed. Angus, I assume you're still on?'

'If I can ride bareback. Otherwise no.'

'Excellent. Excellent. Just what I hoped. As I say, it's Indians we need. With you and Hare it should be quite easy for me to punt up a stockman or two from Rongomaha or from Garth. They'll be masked like bandits anyway. It's the bareback riding that's the main problem. The other one is the cameraman. This also may not be impossible. You and I can alternate doing the camerawork, Angus. Let's flick through and see if there's any time when we have to be on together. I've made a few rough notes. But first let's see what we've achieved so far.'

We have in fact achieved a lot. The location shots are in the can, also plenty of gambling den/saloon ones. Personalities and locale have been established and Jeannie safely abducted.

'We'll need a cameraman to shoot the scene when I rescue her. Won't need anyone else though, other than Harry and Jeannie. So you could fill in there for me, Angus. That should be quite straightforward. We blocked it out the other day, as you know, when the others had their free day.'

'Are you going to snatch her back from Hare's horse?' I ask.

'Of course. Then all that remains is my capture, imprisonment and near drowning by the Indians, and my rescue by you, Lorna, and that child, dammit. His part will have to be rewritten, possibly deleted. It's a great pity of course. There is always more dramatic tension, or maybe pathos might be a better word, when the hero is being rescued by a woman and child. The weak rescuing the strong etc. Plucky woman saving her man. *The curfew shall not toll tonight.* That sort of thing.' He sighs. 'But I doubt if I'll be able to conjure up another Indian child who can ride like the wretched Joe.'

I am thinking. Duncan can't ride like Joe, but he would love to try. I am about to say so but remember. I will discuss it with Derek first.

Charlie wakes up. The other children appear on their way to the beach. Duncan will mind them and make sure Charlie doesn't take his hat off or charge around like a nutcase. Of course they'll be back in three-quarters of an hour, says Duncan, glancing at his watch as they depart.

'I can be more frank now, I suppose,' says James, 'as to what my true feelings on the whole business are, but . . .'

Hare, his face solemn, interrupts. 'But as an officer and a gentleman you will restrain yourself. I'm sure you'd agree, Angus?'

Angus leaps to his feet with clenched fists. 'Oh for Christ's sake, shut up, you sarcastic bastard. Bugger the lot of you! The whole idiotic, narrow-minded, block-headed lot of you. Snivellers, mealy-mouthed snivellers to a man: white, brown and coffee-coloured!' He swings to Hare. 'And that includes you.'

He moves to Jeannie, takes her hand, holds it for a minute while they stare at each other, then dips his head. His lips touch her hand. 'I'm sorry,' he says, and runs.

'What about the film?' shouts James.

Angus swings around. For a moment he looks as though he will tell James about the film in some detail, then he stiffens, stands straight against the sky for a moment, cries 'Sod the film!' and disappears around the corner.

James's head is in his hands. 'Bugger, bugger, bugger, bugger.'

We sit silent. Jeannie, obviously upset, moves to Hare. He touches her arm briefly.

'Well,' he says, 'I think we could all use a beer. Any objections?' He turns at the entrance to the kitchen. 'Oh, by the way,' he says, 'the reason I didn't take Miriama to the Pa with me was that I was discussing with Wiremu Ropata what he thought the legal position would be as regards Laing's Point. He didn't mention the film.'

Ann

We're building ordinary sand castles down on the beach to try and stop Charlie tearing about. We've brought a bucket and two spades, the big one for digging the moat and the ditch down to the sea. We don't usually bring the big spade. It's a bit sissy having a big one, but Duncan says we've got to keep Charlie quiet somehow or Mum'll get the pip.

Duncan starts digging with the big spade and Charlie makes the towers with the bucket and the little spade. Then Duncan gets on with the ditch down to the sea for the water to come up. The tide is low so he has to dig a long way, but it looks as though it's going to work all right. After he's done that he shoves off with the big spade and starts digging further along the beach. We're not supposed to look because it's a surprise, but who cares anyway.

I go looking for good shells to put round the windows and the door bit, and then smaller ones to show where the garden is, and bits of black seaweed for the flowers. I get longer bits to stick up for trees, but I can't put any of it in yet because Charlie keeps adding more towers and won't stop.

A black and white oyster-catcher is pottering around and some terns are diving for fish. They fly low over the sea then, wham, in they go. I've never seen one catch anything. Sometimes there's fish when we swim. They whizz sideways along the waves before they break. Quite big they are sometimes but mostly little.

'Hey,' yells Duncan. 'Come and look at mine.'

His isn't a castle. He's made a lady and she's big, or big for making with sand. She's lying there on her back, this lady, and she has nothing on. Her arms are going out sideways and her legs are going down, and on her front between her head and her middle he's built busts sticking out like the front page of the lady in *Your Body – Female*. He has bits of seaweed for her mouth and nose and a few bits for hair but not many, plus two seaweed pods, one for each eye, and little ones for fingernails and toes as well. And right in the middle of each bust he's put a seaweed pod.

'Duncan,' I say, meaning those ones.

'Why there?' says Charlie, pointing.

'Nipples,' says Duncan.

Then lo, right at that moment, charging down the beach at us so fast they're there before Charlie has time to say anything, come Bella and Tam and Joe Ropata on three Maori horses. They're all shouting and yelling and so are we, especially Charlie.

Duncan snatches the nipple pods and shoves them in the pocket of his shorts and I stand wondering what to do. Last time I saw Tam and Joe was at the caves and I was hating them. So I don't rush up, not straight off, but then I do.

'That's not your proper horse, Bella,' says Charlie, as she jumps off the pony and hugs him. 'Where's Thompson?'

Bella shakes her head. 'At Rongomaha,' she says.

'Nice lady, Duncan,' says Tam, grinning, and Duncan goes all red and kicks the lady to bits, bust first.

'Where's Miri?' says Joe.

'She didn't want to come. She's sick of castles. But we had to come because of Charlie,' I say.

Charlie sticks his tongue out at me and says he's all better now and why don't I shut up? Then Bella hugs me and says I didn't mean it did I, and I say yes I did and Tam laughs. Bella stands there with her hair blowing all over her face grinning back at him.

216

'Why don't you fellas take my horse,' she says, 'and give Duncan a gallop down to the rocks?'

Joe says he's going up to the Henares to see Miri and Tam tells him he's not and Charlie's grizzling because he wants a ride too and why can't he. But Duncan's up and away, and Duncan and Tam and Joe are off whooping and shouting and having fun and I feel like Charlie.

Bella sits down beside the lady who's all messed up now. The only bit that's still the same is her toenails and fingernails and some of them are busted as well.

Bel digs in the pocket of her pants and hands us some wine gums. Mine's raspberry.

'Annie,' she says.

'Yes?'

'There's something I'd like to tell you and Charlie.'

'Mmn.'

'Tam and I,' she says, 'are going to go away together.'

'Why?' says Charlie, sneaking a look at his sucked wine gum which is green but brighter.

'That's what I want to tell you. So you'll know. You can tell Duncan for me.'

'OK.'

She doesn't say anything for a bit. Just sits there poking a stick at the sand. Then she says, 'Tam and I love each other, and we are going to get married.'

'Like Mr and Mrs Henare?' I say.

'Yes. Everyone. Your Mum and Dad.'

'Why do you have to go away?' I say. 'Mr and Mrs Henare didn't go away, nor did Mum and Dad.'

'That's because the men's jobs were here. Tam and I will have to find work.'

'Oh.'

'Who'll look after Joe?' says Charlie.

'We're not sure yet.'

'Why not?'

'He has to decide. He and Mr Ropata.'

'If you're going away, I hope he stays here,' says Charlie.

'Let's rebuild the lady,' says Bel, and we do.

Miri and Patch have gone to the Store by the time we get back. There's just Mr Clements and Mum with Mr and Mrs Henare. No one's doing anything or saying anything. Just sitting.

'Ah,' says Mr Clements, 'at last,' though we're not late because of Duncan being bossy with his watch.

'I had a beaut ride, Mum,' says Duncan.

'Who with?'

'Tam and Joe. On Bella's horse. Not Thompson, her Maori one. Right down to the rocks and back. Whoosh,' he says, doing it with his arms.

'It's all awful, Mum,' says Charlie. 'Joe might be leaving with Tam and Bella.' He tugs her skirt, makes her look at him. 'He's my friend, Mum, and I've just got him. He can't go away now.'

'They're going to get married, Mum,' I say. 'Because they love each other.'

Mr Clements picks up his felt hat and bangs it on his head. 'Time we were off. Into the car, children. Pronto.'

We whizz past the Store not stopping. Mr Clements is going on and on about how he will not be beaten. 'I refuse, absolutely refuse!' he says. 'I'll get straight onto Trevor Warwick at the Cosy in town. He's the most likely man to know someone who can take over the camerawork, paid or unpaid. And I'll start checking around the local stockmen for an Indian tomorrow morning. I'm sure there'll be some starters. We're past fussing about colour. As I said, they'll be masked, or heavily made up. The bareback races at the Race Meeting: there were white faces there, weren't there?'

'Yes,' says Mum.

'Tam won,' says Charlie.

'If you think what I've achieved,' says Mr Clements, then goes on about why it's so astonishing. Two shoots at the most is what he's done, and on the evidence of the stuff he's edited it's nothing short of miraculous.

'Yes,' says Mum.

'So,' says Mr Clements, giving a fancy tooty-toot on his horn at the corner. '"On with the Show." At least we know where we are.' He laughs. 'I have to say, the adrenalin is pumping.'

'Good,' says Mum.

Mr Clements drives on. It seems to take longer than usual. Charlie goes to sleep against me. Duncan stares out the window. No one in front says anything.

As we drive over the cattle stop, Charlie wakes up. He sits up and says, 'Mum, why can't Joe come and live with us?'

'Because Tam and Bella want him, love. And so does Mr Ropata.'

All those people.

'But he'd like to come to us, wouldn't he, Dunc?'

'No,' says Duncan, 'he wouldn't, and don't be daft.'

Mrs Clements is waiting on the verandah. She waves and waves and Mr Clements stops the car. We all get out and Mrs Clements is crying.

'Where've you been, James? Oh dear God, where've you been?' she says.

'Trying to get some sense out of Henare,' says James.

'Henare, what's Henare got to do with anything? She's gone, James. Gone. Packed her suitcase, the brand new one I gave her for Christmas, and disappeared. I don't know where she is. She wouldn't tell me. She came to kiss me goodbye. She was going to leave a letter but she couldn't, she said. A letter, a letter! Oh James, James, do something.'

'Such as what?' says Mr Clements, taking off his hat.

'Bring her back. Make her see sense. She can't do this to me. My darling Bella. When I think, oh dear God, when I think what her life will be. You must make her see reason. Talk to her. She loves you, James, she's always loved you. And what will we do, you and I? What will we do without her?'

'I've been thinking about that,' says Mr Clements, pouring himself a cup of tea. He takes one drink and puts it down. 'Cold,' he says. 'I'm sure Mrs Jackson would be prepared to help out. In fact she'd probably be happy to take on the position of housekeeper permanently. She's a damn good cook as you know, as well as a very pleasant woman. Very loyal to Rongomaha, just like Bob.'

'Can I have a pikelet?' says Charlie.

'Yes, yes,' says Mrs Clements all sniffy and wet.

So then we all have one too. 'Bella made these, I'll bet,' says Duncan. 'Like at the Earthquake.'

Mrs Clements goes 'Waah' and sits down crying more than ever. Mum takes her arm and says wouldn't she like to go to her room and Mrs Clements says she has no intention of going to her room, there are things to be dealt with and the sooner the better, and obviously she is the only one who has any intention of doing anything.

'Where is she?' she says, crying. 'I don't even know where the poor child is.'

Charlie takes another pikelet. 'On the beach with Tam and Joe and Maori ponies,' he says.

'Tam and her are going to get married,' I say. 'Because they love each other. Bella said.'

Mrs Clements goes 'Waah' worse than ever.

'And Joe's got no one to look after him,' says Charlie.

Duncan tells him to belt up and stop telling lies.

Charlie sits chewing.

I take another pikelet.

Mr Clements stands up and stretches and yawns. 'I'm exhausted,' he says. 'By the way, Ma, Henare told me he'd been discussing the legal aspects of Laing's Point with Ropata senior.'

Mrs Clements goes quiet. 'Laing's Point,' she whispers. 'Oh dear Lord, not Laing's Point.'

'Yes,' says Mr Clements. 'I suppose I'd better get on to the lawyer. What's the new man's name? Peacock? Partridge?'

'Nightingale,' whispers Mrs Clements.

'Ah yes, Nightingale. I knew it was one of the weird ones.' He yawns again. 'God, what a balls-up the whole thing is.'

Mrs Clements doesn't say anything.

Lorna

Our departure from Rongomaha is strangely muted. Normally Mrs Clements' farewells are conducted with the same enthusiasm and expertise as her welcomes. This time is different.

Early this morning I popped in with Mrs Clements' breakfast tray. Popped is a word much used by Mrs Clements. The rest of us, particularly Bella, are often invited to pop in, out, up or over on some mission for her while we are on our feet. This is understandable as our feet, including Charlie's, are a great deal more able to pop than Mrs Clements'. However it is the phrase I like. So quick, so simple and rather fun, to pop upstairs for the book she can't find, over to the sheds with the men's smoko, down to the cattle stop for the mail. Hop, skip and a pop and it's done.

James does not pop.

Mrs Clements was waiting for me, propped by pillows and ready with her thanks. Too kind. Too kind. As she looked at me, however, her smile faltered and so did mine. We were conscious, so conscious of the fact that I was the wrong cup-bearer and probably the first of many inadequate substitutes. Bella had gone for ever.

I tried to persuade her mother not to get up early to farewell us. I could bring the children in to say goodbye, I said. There was no point. Please. Why not? She dismissed this idiotic notion and now stands, leaning on her stick before the front door with chocolates at the ready.

There is nothing wrong with the chocolates, quite the reverse, but

Ann's refusal to touch them always involves a bit of to-ing and fro-ing. Why doesn't she just take one and give it to me, mutters Charlie. Ann refuses.

Mrs Clements seems to have shrunk, to have changed shape like a rag doll whose stuffing has been misplaced.

James and his car appear around the corner. The children thank their hostess for a nice time and clamber into the back seat with faintly indecent speed, not because they dislike her but because their hearts are no longer here. They are down at the beach, the Bully Pond and the sea. They fidget impatiently.

At the last moment Mrs Clements realises to her horror that we have no farm meat, nothing. We cannot leave Rongomaha empty-handed. She insists.

She disappears to the kitchen and comes back distraught. There isn't any, not a skerrick of meat in the place. Surely Bella would have told one of the men to kill before she, before she . . .

James stops drumming his fingers on the steering wheel. 'Oh yes,' he says. 'I forgot. She asked me to tell Bob to get one of the men on to it.'

A shining cuckoo calls, *Ta ta ta ta, tiddely pom*.

'There you are,' whispers his mother. 'There you are.' She sees the children's startled faces turn to her. 'Off you go, dears,' she cries. 'Off you go, and come again soon.'

She waves a pathetic sketch of her usual sweeping gesture and totters up the steps, pauses in an attempt to brush a leaf or two from the steps with her stick, fails, and disappears through the open doorway.

'She didn't give us a chocolate,' says Charlie.

James, he tells me as we set off, has not been idle. He rang Trevor Warwick at his home last night about a possible cameraman. He had been quite helpful, seemed to think he would have no trouble teeing someone up.

'I explained that the man didn't have to be an expert. That Angus and Bella had caught on quite quickly, and the whole thing, as I've said, is mostly common sense.'

'Why are we going away?' says Charlie suddenly.

'Because Bella's gone and there's no one to cook the dinners,' says Ann.

'Oh.'

'Mr Clements is talking, children.'

James gives me a brief nod of acknowledgement. 'But on the other hand, as I also explained, I won't accept sloppiness. He'll have to be pretty quick on the uptake.'

'Yes,' I say, watching Mrs Clements' Rhododendron Dell at the end of the track glide by. In the spring her rhodos are a joy to behold.

We clatter over the cattle stop, feel it in our bums.

'Also,' he continues, 'I spoke to Bob Jackson last night. He's going to check, but he thinks one or two of the men have done quite a bit of rodeo riding. Different, of course, but if they can stay on those beasts it sounds hopeful. Oh, and Garth Rowan's going to check with his men. Angus answered the phone. He sounded quite peculiar. Couldn't get off the line quickly enough.'

'Oh.'

'When I've dropped you off I'll go along and see Colonel Holdaway. See how he got on with Ropata.'

'But he won't have seen him yet, surely.'

'Why not?'

'He won't have had time.'

'He said he'd go and see the man, didn't he?'

'Yes but . . .'

'I'll call in on my way back. Let you know how I get on.'

'Thank you.'

'Not at all.'

He does so. Colonel Holdaway has not yet seen the man. James can't understand it. He could have gone up yesterday after we left. He departs, his back view disconsolate but resolute.

The rhythm of our Beach life picks up again, plenty of sea, sun and sand, and less food. The thought of hot meat no longer appeals to me, nor, thankfully, the children. They muck about, lost in their private worlds once more after the alarms and excursions of Rongomaha. Duncan meets up with Mike Girlingstone, they work on their canoe which they plan to relaunch at the weekend with Derek.

Dr Appleby examines Charlie and tells me that he has never seen a healthier five-year-old. In his experience, he adds, the more active a child the quicker it recovers from trauma of any kind and that Charlie is a little warrior. 'Aren't you, Sonny Jim?' he says. Charlie disappears out the door.

Nevertheless, nevertheless, there is tension in the air. At the Store Mrs Girlingstone, or the lady who is a friend of Mr Girlingstone's, is full of chat. Had I heard, she asks, that Laing's Point is going to be all cut up for Maori housing and isn't it sad? Her usually defeated-looking face is aglow with excitement, but it could be the heat. Mrs Girlingstone, I suspect, does not have much fun.

'Won't it be awful for you?' she insists. 'Especially as the best sections along the beach front have all gone now. So sad.'

The children ask about Tam and Bella and more especially Joe. Even Miriama does not know where he is. She hasn't been to the Pa lately, she tells us, but she's seen most of the things there anyhow by now. What she is looking forward to is the official ceremony to welcome her parents and herself back to the Pa, and the hangi after. Has she ever told Ann and Charlie how delicious the food was when they took all the top stuff off at the Race Meeting and opened up the oven? The pork, she tells them, melted in her mouth. Yum.

Yes. She has.

Mr Ropata's canary-yellow truck is often seen outside the Henares' house. Once the old man arrived while I was sitting on the verandah catching up with Jeannie. We have things to discuss. She and Hare will begin rehearsing the rescue of Jeannie any moment now, and would I be able to look after Miriama and Patch during that time? I am delighted and so is Annie, yummy pork notwithstanding.

Jeannie is not sure how she feels about going back for the filming at Rongomaha. She will obviously meet Mrs Clements, and although she does feel sorry for her she is quite unable to understand her attitude. 'How in the world,' begs Jeannie, her bright eyes searching mine, 'can she be so archaic, so hopelessly misguided?'

It is not for me to point out to Jeannie that not only did Hare inherit money from his stepfather, but also that he had received an education not available to many of his race.

She tells me that Bella and Tam seem to have disappeared completely. Apparently no one at the Pa knows where they are. Apart from my children's meeting with them on the beach the other day, no one has seen them for days.

'And what about Joe?' I ask. 'Where is Joe?'

'That's the other thing,' she says.

Mr Ropata and his stick appear around the corner of the bach. I leap to my feet like a guilty child. I am cross with myself for asking after Joe within earshot of Mr Ropata. He comes towards us slowly, anger and grief stamped on his face. Mr Ropata is an old man.

'Please don't let me disturb you, ladies,' he says, dipping his duck-feathered hat. 'I have an appointment with Hare.'

'Yes, yes of course. I'll take you to him,' says Jeannie.

'No, no. I know the way.' He heaves himself up step by step and heads inside.

'Don't go, Lorna,' says Jeannie.

But I do. Quickly.

Charlie tells me as we trail single file along the stamped track to the Store that he is looking forward to seeing his *Rainbow*. And Dad. So am I. This new feeling I have for Derek pleases me. I have always respected Derek: how could I not, a man so decent and so kind. This feeling is more than respect, and certainly not gratitude. Much more. I feel I must hold this new thing carefully as a brimming cup. I do not want to lose a drop. It is most extraordinary, this feeling. Not love surely.

Nevertheless it is one to be cherished, and I will do so.

They go on, don't they, about love. From passion to casual warmth, love is all. We are told on the highest authority: Jesus, Mohammed, Buddha, all are in agreement. Without it, they say, life is not worth a fish's wink. They thunder, they roar, they pity those who are without this sovereign remedy. Better a dish of herbs where love is, says Solomon, son of David, than a stalled ox withal.

To love and be loved is a fine thing. Without it we are lost.

But how do you get it, how do you give it, this ooze of comfort and joy, unless it has been there from the beginning. From conception, you might say. What if the salt has not so much lost its savour as lacked it from the start?

Can it sneak up on you, this fine good thing, this salty tang? Unlikely, surely, after thirteen years.

James calls at the bach to tell me that Colonel Holdaway has failed in his mission as a mediator with Mr Ropata. 'Quite hopeless apparently, the whole thing. Not only the Ropatas themselves, but not one of the tribe will be involved in any way whatsoever with *Lust in the Dust*. Typical of course. Look at Rua, clearing off just when she's wanted. What on earth Bella thinks she's doing putting herself into the hands of that little lot, God knows. However, I refuse to have anything further to do with the whole grisly business. Bella has made her own bed and she can, er . . .'

We both see Bella lying on the bed of her own making. Our images are different, no doubt, but vivid.

'However,' continues James quickly, 'I'm happy to tell you that the shooting of the recapture of Jeannie from the Indians went like a dream. One of Garth Rowan's men, Stan, that's right, Stan, is a good horseman, and Trevor Warwick's cameraman, Roger something, is excellent. Knows nearly as much as I do. Streaks ahead of Bella and Angus. Streaks.'

James stretches, scratches his back against one of the verandah pillars. It is only three weeks since the same animal-like gesture filled me with longing. Astonishing, quite astonishing.

'So,' he says, 'we'll knock off my imprisonment scenes next. That's really what I came to talk to you about, Lorna. I've been thinking of Duncan for the Indian lad, with a handkerchief over his face when it's feasible, otherwise a ton of Five and Nine should disguise things all right. His riding would be good enough. The tricky riding scenes, thank God, are already in the can. And it's only a bit part.'

'But surely it will have to be well acted to be emotionally sound? An Indian youth, changing his deepest allegiance to his own tribe. Why on earth does he do it?'

'I told you. Hero worship.'

'Ah.'

'Don't worry. I'll coach him. Tell him exactly how to play it. Have you by any chance got a beer to speed me on my way?'

'Yes, yes, of course.'

Warm beer is even worse in the middle of the day. I take a sip and put it aside. We sit in silence for a moment, our eyes on the endless blue, the flouncing frills of white as seen from Laing's Point.

'James,' I say.

'Yes.'

'I think you should know that the children, particularly Duncan and Charlie, are very concerned about Joe.'

'Why on earth?'

'Because he's their friend. Who is he with? Where has he gone? Even Mr Ropata doesn't seem to know, Hare told me. I haven't mentioned it to the children, of course, but presumably he's with Bella and Tamati somewhere. Where?'

'I haven't the slightest idea.'

'But it's important. A child that age.'

'In the good old bad days Maori boys of his age were full-grown warriors. And frankly, I'm not in the slightest interested. I'm afraid I'm beginning to think poor old Ma might be right. The whole lot of them seem to be getting decidedly uppity.'

'I think,' I say carefully, 'that Duncan may feel that taking over Joe's role might be disloyal to his friend.'

James is on his feet, his beer slopping. 'God Almighty, Lorna, have you gone mad too? And since we're on the topic may I say, in all seriousness, that I can't imagine why you let your children play with our brown brothers in the first place. It's certainly never happened before with any child from Laing's Point.'

I do not say that I didn't so much let my children play with Joe as discover later that they had, and that this news disconcerted neither me nor my husband Derek in the slightest. We are liberal-minded people. Liberal in every way. Friendly. Tolerant. Woolly-minded in some ways, no doubt, possibly a touch smug, but better than nothing. Whereas you, James, are a reactionary, and how this fundamental change in your family's outlook (with the exception of Bella) has come about within one or two generations puzzles me.

'Nor presumably,' I murmur, 'with any young woman from Laing's Point.'

I have been smart. Possibly even smart alec. I smile. Friendly vivacious misguided Lorna. I am not pleased with myself. Nor, understandably, is James. He makes an appointment to audition Duncan and drives off. Fast.

His departure is followed closely by the arrival of Colonel Holdaway, who meets and greets me with his usual courtesy. He trusts I am quite well and is delighted to hear that this is so. And the children? Good. Good. And yes, he will sit down for a moment or two if that suits me. But have we had lunch? He could easily come back at a more suitable time?

Such concern for others' convenience is endearing, especially in an elderly Leader of Men. It takes me some time to convince Colonel Holdaway that I am at leisure and pleased to see him. I mention that I have not seen either him or Mrs Holdaway during the last day or two.

The Colonel lowers himself carefully into a chair that is higher than the rest. He clutches its wooden arms tightly and drops the last few inches with a thud. He smiles in faint apology at such excess. 'Hip,' he says. 'Thank you, yes, we've been into town for a few days. Florence drove. Loves it, you know. Loves it. Never happier than when she's behind the wheel.'

'Like Mrs Clements?' I smile.

His gaze drops. 'Perhaps,' he says. He takes off his spectacles, huffs on each lens, and polishes them slowly with a large white handkerchief. Equipped once more, he gives a small regrouping movement and looks me in the eye.

'I have a message for you, Lorna.'

'From Derek?'

'No. From Isabel Clements. That in fact was why Florence and I went into town.' He lifts a speckled hand. 'I had better begin at the beginning. I had a message from the Store to ring a town number. I must say it was a little awkward. I sometimes wonder if Mrs Girlingstone takes rather an excessive interest in the telephone calls. Understandable, of course, poor woman, not much of a life. Yes, well, I hope I was discreet.

'It was Tam, you see, Tam and Isabel asking Florence and me to be witnesses at their wedding at the Registry Office on Tuesday. They particularly wanted us to be there. They said we were neutral ground so to speak and something about trusting us – friendly neutrals perhaps.'

The old man draws a deep breath. 'The whole thing was very, yes, it was very moving. Sad. Glad. Something. The two of them standing there happy as larks in front of dyspeptic old Ewan Brewster droning away. There was nobody else there except a shearing mate of Tam's and his wife, the Burtons. Tam and Bella had been staying with them. Nice pair: they asked us round afterwards, but we excused ourselves. We felt, both of us, that we must get back with all speed to tell Phoebe and Wiremu on our way home. Tam and Isabel both wanted that, you see, that was another reason for our being there. Isabel begged Florence to break it gently to Phoebe, though I'm afraid we were unable to do that.

'It was distressing. Naturally enough. Very. Finally I left Florence with Phoebe and went down to the Pa, which I think was even worse. Bad business, the reactions. Sad. Very.' He shakes his head. His face creases slowly into a smile. 'But if you'd seen the two of them standing there, if you'd seen them . . . ,' he beams.

'I wish I had.'

'Yes, yes. And Isabel particularly asked me to send you her love. She says she will write when,' he snorts happily, '"when the dust settles", was how she put it. Now I must be off. Florence is with Jean Henare on a similar mission.'

'But what about Joe? What's happened to Joe?'

'Oh, Joe was there. Didn't I mention him? Oh, goodness me, yes. That's part of the tragedy for Wiremu.'

'But wasn't he asked what he wants to do? What happened?'

'I don't know, my dear. And I didn't ask.' Colonel Holdaway chews his moustache reflectively and stares out to the Island where there is no life at all. 'This film, this *Lust in the Dust* thing has been a disruptive influence. Very. Ah, there's Florence.'

Mrs Holdaway continues her stately progress across the rough grass from the Henares. The Colonel holds the slack wire of the fence up for her. She climbs through and they depart.

James seems to have forgiven my recent sharpness. 'Duncan,' he tells me, his face bright with excitement, 'is a born actor. I suppose he gets it from you. He has that natural ease of movement which is so essential, good timing and a highly developed sense of the dramatic. He's coming along splendidly. Much better than Joe.'

'So he didn't mind taking his part?'

'Lord no. He's lapping it up.'

So much for my priggish comment about loyalty in children. I say they are a different species, and believe it, yet am surprised when they behave as such.

'By the way, James,' I say, 'you realise that we will have to go to town at the end of next week?'

'That might be a bit soon,' says James thoughtfully. 'Garth might have to let you stay on for a bit. There's quite a lot to do still.'

He sits beside me at the table as I slice beans, declines tea, smokes furiously as he explains.

'There'll have to be a large number of shots of the tide coming up the river. That will require a lot of good camerawork and skilful editing if we're going to catch the drama, the almost unbearable tension as the water rises and I struggle against my bonds.'

'Yes. How is your mother?'

'Ma? Oh she's fine. Mrs Jackson is turning out to be an absolute treasure.'

'But when she heard Bella was married. Wasn't she . . . ?'

James stares at his beautiful hands, lights another cigarette.

'Colonel Holdaway indicated she was very upset,' I say. 'I wondered if she'd like me to go and see her.'

'Well, I can ask, I suppose. Tell me, does Derek have any rope at home? It'll be important to get the right strength. Tow rope's too thick, and I'm not sure that washing line is what we're after. I'll have to find old stills of captives in some of the books. He has? Oh good. Ask him to bring it out on Friday and I'll have a look at it.'

After breakfast each morning Hare and Duncan leave for Rongomaha to film the original capture of James by the Indians and the development of Duncan's adulation for his erstwhile enemy, the white man.

Mrs Clements sends a message by Duncan, asking me to ring her. Yes, she says, she will be pleased to see both Jean and me, and do bring the children. Mrs Clements will send one of the men in the Pontiac. But is she quite sure? I ask, anxious not to intrude on her grief and relaxed at the possibility of not having to do so. No, no, it will be no trouble, she says. Henry is a good driver and we can bring back the bread. He will meet us at the Store at 3 p.m. tomorrow.

Mr Ropata, Jean whispers as we wait for Henry on the stamped grass outside the Store, is not pleased with Hare's continued participation in *Lust in the Dust*. No, no, not seriously, but he and Mr Ropata have agreed that it would be better to defer the welcome ceremony for the Henares until the pakeha have gone home.

'So you'll no longer be one of us?' I smile.

She looks at me, her eyes puzzled. 'It's odd, but no, I don't feel I am. No longer wholly white, not proper Maori. Just . . . at ease.'

Bully for you, mate, I think. I wonder how Angus is. Bella? Tamati? Joe? And poor foolish fond old Mrs Clements herself.

'Who will make the pikelets?' asks Ann as we drive over the cattle stop and are welcomed by stillness.

'Mrs Jackson,' I say, 'and stop sucking your thumb, for goodness sake.'

'I'm sucking the wart, not the *thumb*.'

'Well stop.'

Henry halts the Pontiac at the front door for us to decamp. Charlie insists on accompanying Henry and the Pontiac to the car shed. Henry, who is tall and lugubrious and has not uttered a word since we boarded, says nothing.

Poor old Mrs Clements comes to meet us. It is several days since last I saw her and I am astonished at the change in her appearance. Phoebe has certainly pulled herself together. Gone are the tears, the depleted air, the sad lessening. She seems to be firm in wind and limb and glowing with health. Almost, one could say, reborn.

She stands at the top of the steps with her arms wide to greet us. 'Where's Charlie?' she cries.

'He's gone to help Henry put the car away,' says Ann with an eye on the laden tea table.

'Oh, Henry will send him round,' says Mrs Clements cheerfully. 'He hates children. Now. Where would you like to sit. Jean? Lorna? So much to tell you! But I must begin by saying how wonderful Mrs Jackson has been and is. She's a superb cook, absolutely superb, wait till you taste her sponge drops. And her pastry! How she manages it in this weather I'll never know. And so obliging! I've always known that she was a pleasant woman and an excellent laundress but when I think of all those years . . . Have one, have a sponge drop, both of you, and you'll see what I mean.

'And she's such fun to be with, you know how some people are? Entertaining, you know what I mean? Knows everyone and everything that's going on in the district. I can't tell you the laughs we have. Sometimes I have to say, "Oh Mrs Jackson. Please, please, you're killing me." Have a sponge drop, Ann?'

Ann looks doubtful. 'Where are the pikelets?'

'Pikelets? Who'd want pikelets when there's sponge drops. Ah, here's Charlie. Henry sent you packing, did he, lamb? Never mind. Have a sponge drop.' She smiles at us all, happy and in charge once more. 'I thought we'd have a quick cup of tea and then walk up to the woolshed where James is tied up, poor dear. In one of the holding pens, I believe.

'Yes. I've just had a wonderful idea. We'll take them the rest of the sponge drops. Mrs Jackson took up their smoko earlier, but they'd love a treat. Ann, pop into the kitchen and ask Mrs Jackson for plates. And tea towels for the flies. Now, how are your cups? Lorna? Jean?'

'C'n I have a drink of Fifty Fifty?' says Charlie.

'Yes, yes, into the kitchen. Mrs Jackson adores children.' Her voice lowers. 'A great grief to her that she and Bob . . . never, yes, well, never mind. Off you go, children.'

We walk up the gentle slope to the shed, Mrs Clements with her stick and Jean and I bearing covered plates. Mrs Jackson had begged to take them for us; she'd love to get a look in at that little lot. It was not to be. Mrs Clements murmured that if the Spanish Cream was not made immediately it might not set in time. Mrs Jackson nodded, stacked her tray with the remains of our feast and headed back to the kitchen with her usual good humour.

I like woolsheds. Never having done a full day's work in one at shearing time I can afford to be sentimental about them. Hare likes them too. He showed me a poem by a young German.

Of all the works of man I like best
Those which have been used.

. . .

Half ruined buildings once again take on
The look of buildings wanting to be finished
Generously planned: their fine proportions
Can already be guessed at . . .
                    . . . All this
Delights me.

We agreed it sounded like a shearing shed, one of the old ones where the oil from countless fleeces has stained the floor of the stands mahogany and the surface of the wool sorters' table is polished teak. The smell, to anyone who has ever helped in a busy shed as a child, is childhood revisited. That pungent blend of grease, wool and ancient droppings beneath the slated floor is the breath of life to sheep men.

The sponge drops are received with enthusiasm by James, Hare and Duncan, and Stan the ring-in Indian whose services have been lent for a week (but no more) by Garth Rowan. We are introduced to this solemn young man and to the bright-eyed new cameraman from town who sports the biggest cowlick I have ever seen. The front of his black hair shoots up into a large quiff. The back is left to chance.

Things are going superbly, James tells us as he brushes icing sugar dust from fingers and shirt. We have arrived at exactly the right moment, just before his and Duncan's big scene, the hero's attempted escape. He tells us he has just broken from his bonds in that pen over there.

We look at the empty pen in silence.

'I was trussed up, you remember, and Stan here was on guard with his rifle at the ready but he was completely worn out, you see. Exhausted. Went to sleep, didn't you, Stan?' Stan stares at his boots and nods. 'So after a long struggle, which I think went quite well, don't you, Roger?' The cameraman grins in agreement. 'Roger's been having a hard time with the light in here but you think you'll be right now, don't you, Rog?'

'Spot on,' says the cameraman.

'So that's all in the can,' says James, flinging his hands apart as though distributing a shower of gold. 'As I say, you've arrived just on time, haven't they, Duncan?'

'Yes,' says Duncan, his face dark with make-up and concentration. He looks, I have to say, rather beautiful.

Charlie titters at the sight, an unfortunate sound at the best of times. James swings round at him.

'Out,' he cries. 'Once more and you're out. If you Hopkins can't be silent, and I mean silent, go outside now.'

They promise, both of them. Their eyes are huge, their mouths clamped tight. Miriama smiles.

'Very well. As I was saying . . . No, on second thoughts I suggest you just watch the action, I won't spoil it for you. You'll get a good view from that pen over there.'

A small stepladder is found for Mrs Clements to prop herself on. The rest of us, the three Henares and the still subdued Hopkins, go to the sheep pen indicated by James. The children climb the slatted sides to see the action; the adults lean on folded arms, attentive as farmers at a stock sale.

Stan the Indian now sleeps, slumped in the corner of the holding pen with his rifle across his knees. James drapes himself with broken bonds in the diagonally opposite corner. Duncan seems to have disappeared. Roger and his camera are at the ready.

'Camera,' barks James from the floor.

The camera rolls, its whirr loud in the silent shed.

James stretches, rubs his chaffed wrists, and stretches some more. He stands. Poised and silent as a giant cat, he creeps across the pen to the sleeping Stan. Instinctively I place my hand on Charlie's shoulder. He gives a quick shake of his head. Talk: of course he won't talk. Nor could anyone. We watch, breathless, as James reaches his captor. Stan stirs in his sleep. James freezes. Then, with infinite care, he reaches for the rifle. More stirring. I wonder nervously when Charlie last relieved himself.

James reaches towards the rifle, withdraws. Slowly, slowly, unbearably slowly, he extends the arm once more. He stands upright with the gun in hand. It is his. He is armed.

Assisted by our soundless sighs of relief James creeps to the swing door of the pen. It creaks. We freeze. James creeps on. I wish I could describe the beauty and strength of his movements, the lithe grace, the smooth placing of each step. He is on his way.

Roger and the camera follow his progress as he tiptoes towards the light from the open doors and nears the ungainly-looking wood and iron structure of the wool press.

Whereupon, to our gaping astonishment, Duncan, stripped to the waist and armed with a Bowie knife, leaps from behind its bulk. Our hands fling to our mouths. Never have we seen anything like this: the suspense, the agony, the joy.

The action slows. Duncan and James stand yards apart, staring at each other with weapons poised. Their faces are taut, steely. Duncan puts one moccasined foot forward, and another; James lifts his rifle, levels it. Charlie, Ann and Miriama duck their heads. Mrs Clements' eyes are shut.

And another step. And another.

There must be a close-up now. Roger must take a close-up of James's haunted, haggard face as he makes his decision whether, in self-defence or no, he can shoot this child warrior, this young brave so resolutely creeping towards him with his knife raised. He lifts his rifle once more, takes aim.

He cannot. Oh thank God, he cannot. The good, the noble loner, the conscience of humanity, groans, flings his head against his bent arm to hide his weakness as the rifle clatters at his feet.

The young brave stands still for a moment in awe, then quick as a whip leaps forward to seize the rifle. 'Ai ya!' he screams at the sleeping jailor.

The Sheriff is recaptured.

'Cut,' calls James and totters to the railing.

The whirring stops. There is no sound.

A dog barks. Sheep bleat. Mrs Clements sobs.

'Oh James, oh darling,' she cries. 'It's wonderful, wonderful. Oh James.'

Lorna

Meanwhile, back at the Beach, we progress. Yes, Garth Rowan tells us, we can stay in his bach for a little longer if James requires us. No, he won't accept any rent. The show, he says, must go on.

'That's all very well,' says Derek, 'but how do we repay him?'

'Apparently we don't. This is his gesture towards Art.'

'But we'll have to make some pathetic gesture of thanks. Whisky, I suppose.'

'That usually goes down well.'

'If I'd said that you would have groaned.'

True, but I wouldn't now. I refrain from mentioning this. It is too soon to make such a sweeping statement, too early a declaration that spots will be changed. Too risky. Nevertheless I still think I would not have made the quick deflating comment with which I have sometimes greeted Derek's attempts at wit over the last thirteen years.

Derek, you see, has no sense of humour. It is one of the tenets by which we have lived. He can do fun and comfort of all kinds, and loyalty and faithfulness and love, but not jokes. He said so himself, long ago. We have never discussed the topic since.

It is only now, this summer, especially after comments such as his reply to my feeble effort, that I have been wondering whether what latent talent Derek does have for delight in the ridiculous, for pleasure in the minor absurdities of life, might not have blossomed in a more favourable environment.

Not a happy thought.

The tendency to appreciate someone, to be pleased or amused by what they say or do, depends first on imponderables such as empathy, sympathy, attraction. You give the benefit of the doubt for small lapses from those you love. Less so from those you do not. Other attributes as well as beauty can lie in the eye of the beholder.

'By the way,' he says, 'I have decided to take a day off from the office on Friday, so I can watch the build-up for the final scenes on Saturday and Sunday.'

'Good. But who will make the pikelets?'

He sighs. 'Must it always be jokes?'

'I meant mind the office. Be there. Minding. Like Bella, always in the kitchen.'

'But she got out.'

'Yes, she did.'

She did indeed.

On Friday the entire cast, plus director and cameraman and Derek, are to assemble on the far side of the river to begin rehearsals for the final scenes.

Car access to the site, across the river from the Bully Pond, had given James some concern. Most of the land on this side, including the best track to the river, is Maori land and belongs to the Pa, which, as James said, made it no longer available to us. Mr Girlingstone, in whom James had confided while he filled his petrol tank from the Store bowser, had agreed. There was no point in giving them a chance to go crook at this stage, and had anyone seen or heard anything?

'Nothing.'

'Hang on,' cried Mr Girlingstone. 'Tell you what, I'll ask Dickie Reynolds. Good mate of mine, Dickie, decent rooster, owns a few acres on the other side with river access. I'll ask him. Give him a tinkle now if you can wait?'

'Right as rain,' he told James a few minutes later. 'Just as well, you'd have been left with your sarong hanging otherwise, wouldn't you, Mr C?'

Mr C and I agreed. Another problem had melted away.

James had consulted the tide tables long before he mentioned his plan for *Lust in the Dust* during our vodka evening at Mrs Clements'. He has studied them very carefully indeed. The time of the high tide will control the filming of the last few scenes before his and Jeannie's final ride into the sunset.

Stan and Roger join us at the river, having ambled down from the Bed and Breakfast where they, financed by James, are staying. It is run by Mrs Girlingstone in her spare time, as Mr Girlingstone puts it. It's not bad, Roger tells us. Good breakfast. He has always had a weakness for black pudding.

Mrs Clements may come down sometime over the weekend, James tells us, but she will want details of the track first. She says she's sorry but she doesn't want to wreck the suspension of the Pontiac unless she has to. Mrs Clements often prefaces sensible comments by apologies. She's sorry, she says, but she can't be doing with dirt, deceitfulness, drunkenness. There are many things which Mrs Clements can't be doing with, most of which are presented with this preliminary little flutter of apology.

We have much to rehearse today. The arrival of the Indians with their prisoner. The transferring of the already bound Sheriff to the river and retying of him to the post where he will be left to drown. There will be no need to bind the feet, James tells us, but his legs must be bound.

'Why the legs?' asks Derek. 'No one will see them either, and they obviously can't have been bound while you were on your horse.'

'Of course not, but they can't be flopping around while they carry me into the water, can they? Also the movements of my upper body would be completely different if my legs weren't tied above the knees. Much too free. There must be constraint. That's where the tension lies.

They can't be waving about all over the place. Think, man, think.'

'I am,' says Derek.

Then, continues James, some well-timed shots of the incoming tide surging up the river must be filmed. Probably better to get plenty of these in the can as soon as the tide is right today. This is the obvious way to do things, otherwise James is going to spend the whole weekend jumping in and out of the river and bugger that.

'Then of course there will be the scenes of my trying to break free from my bonds. Roger and I have decided that there will have to be quite a few close-ups to get the agony and tension in my face. Haven't we, Roger?'

'Yes.'

'But of course the whole thing will have to be most carefully rehearsed.' James laughs, takes us into his confidence. 'I'll never forget the first time I realised that the genesis of audience anticipation is, or can be, based on deceit. It never occurred to me as a child, in the few times I ever saw a film, that all those lions and fleeing ibex, all that cat and mouse stuff, can be filmed in two parts. The only place where they must collide is the final pounce. I suppose,' he says, 'you could describe that moment of perception as one of the deaths of innocence.'

'Give me strength,' murmurs Hare Henare.

'Ssh,' says Jeannie. 'It's only his way.'

'Yes. And I don't like it.'

'Why did you say you'd take part then?' sniffs Jean.

'I wish I knew.'

'Sssh.'

'So,' says James. 'We'll get plenty of the tide surging and me writhing . . .'

'. . . against your bonds,' mutters Hare.

'. . . and only need a few climactic shots of my release.'

'How does your hat drift away, Mr Clements?' asks Duncan politely. 'If the water gets right up to it you're drowned, aren't you?'

'It falls off,' says James.

'Oh,' says Duncan, 'is that all?'

Hare Henare's shoulders shake.

'And then of course,' says James, 'you, Lorna, the, ah, girl with the golden heart, assisted by Duncan here, ride to the rescue and plunge in to save me.'

Duncan and I grin at each other. We are going to enjoy this. So are the rest of the family. The Hopkins' smiles are smug and bland as butter.

'There are some things,' continues James, 'that we'll have to get right. Plunging in and untying wet knots, for example. I think we should do a few try-outs of you both in action, with rubber life belts just off camera.'

Duncan and I look at him.

'This is the sort of thing one is always coming up against in filming. It's the simplest things which can take so much working out. But I'll get on to it. Don't worry. And once I'm free I canter off and then there's just the last scene.'

'Which is that, darling?' says Mrs Clements.

'Jeannie and I ride off into the sunset, don't we, Jeannie?'

Jeannie smiles.

'What happens to your gallant rescuers?' asks Hare. 'Are they left surrounded by sundered bonds, wringing wet in the river with one horse?'

'They will know they have saved my life,' says James.

Hare nods.

Derek laughs, pats my brave noble bottom.

The Hopkins family departed for location in festive mood surrounded by thermos flasks, drinking water, bathing togs for rehearsal rescues, sunhats and Q-tol. I am glad to be acting once more. I feel my part, small though it is, is both vital and flattering. The role of the bad girl with the heart of gold appeals to me. Not all of us can ride off into the sunset with the hero, and the thought of cantering to the rescue of someone I love but who I know in my heart can never love me fills me with pride. Especially with Duncan at my side.

Participants from Rongomaha must have made an even earlier start. Bob Jackson is already installed at the river side with the horse float. We inspect Duncan's pony. An attractive animal, it is by no means identical to Jackie but roughly the same size and colour. I am to ride Bella's bay gelding, Thompson, which gives me pause. Bella would have hated leaving Thompson. Surely she could have taken him. But how?

Derek and Ann help us saddle up. Charlie, bright pink and shiny with importance, supervises the handing out of tack. They escort us, running behind as Duncan and I trot off through the rough grass and hillocks. Dick's land is poor, with few trees and little evidence of cultivation. A hundred years ago it must have been pure sand. 'Dog-tucker country,' sniffs Duncan as we canter off. There is nothing like being astride a good horse to make you feel superior.

Charlie and Ann are torn between envy and pride at our modest prowess. Derek is relaxed. We continue practising, cantering to rescues over Dick's ground. We find a suitable good straight run for our final gallop, and return at our appointed time feeling both exhilarated and pleased with ourselves.

The Indians, Hare and Stan, are also mounted. They circle at speed, charge across the flat. Any moment, I feel, Stan may make a flying leap from his horse to Hare's, catch an overhanging branch and swing skywards, or slip to the offside of his own black horse to avoid the white man's bullets. His bareback expertise is impressive.

James is now supervising the positioning of the captive's stake, a long pole which Bob Jackson has brought from Rongomaha.

He and James lean on the front bonnet of the farm truck and discuss technicalities. Bob, who came down on his day off last week and took soundings of the river with the aid of Stan and the dinghy from Laing's Point, is well informed.

'At low tide today,' he says, pointing, 'your best bet for placing the pole is right here, but she's damn heavy. Any volunteers to double check the depth for us before we shift her?'

The younger children's immediate acceptance is squashed by

Duncan's scorn. 'Your heads wouldn't even show, dummies.'

Stan retires behind the float to get into his wetwater gear. He returns shyly, his chest, upper arms and legs creamy-white against his togs, the rest of his body tanned leather. He takes to the water with flying strokes.

'She's right, Bob, just like you said,' he calls, standing with the water lapping his navel.

'Good-oh,' says Bob.

'Why is the post already in the river?' asks Hare.

'Because it's too much of a fiddle to spend time and effort filming you men put it in there. Apart from Samson and an elephant or two, there's never been much dramatic content in brute force.'

'So it's just sitting there waiting for the execution?'

'If you must, yes.'

'But I thought,' says Hare gently, 'that you would be following Indian lore.'

'Law or lore?'

'L - o - r - e. You must know that in Indian lore the bravest heroes are always honoured by their enemies with the most torturous and lingering deaths, into which category drowning by inches as the tide rises must surely fall?'

James straightens. 'Yes,' he says.

Derek turns to hide his smile. I try but fail.

'Then how can you use some sweaty old second-hand post where any felon might have been bumped off?'

'Hare!' hisses Jeannie.

'Nonsense, darling. You can't have a cowboy flick without bumping off, can you, kids?'

'No,' they shout happily.

James, on the other hand, is silent. Torn, perhaps, by concern at the thought of the second-hand death post (Hare undoubtedly has a point) versus the logistics and effort of filming the insertion of a new one worthy of a hero.

He tugs a hand through his beautiful hair. Common sense prevails.

Time is short. It cannot be done. Nevertheless, he is cross with Hare who now stands in the bulrushes talking to Derek.

'Thank you for your concern, Harry,' he snaps. 'But I wouldn't bother about it if I were you. These things can be fudged.'

Hare nods in calm consent. 'Good,' he says.

James and the Indians rehearse their arrival at the river with their bound victim – none of them are dressed for the part, but James wears his white cowboy hat. He sits upon his horse tightly bound (with the woolshed rope, I notice), the reins held between his tied hands as the three of them ride down the track. This scene, James says, should be completely straightforward; however, it is always best to check if you can. 'Remember when we're shooting,' he says, 'you Indians must express much more emotion as you manhandle me from my horse.'

'But it's all in the day's work for us,' says Hare. 'Besides, aren't Indians inscrutable? Like, who is it? Ah yes, the Chinese.'

'And Japanese,' says Jeannie.

Hare nods inscrutably. 'And Japanese.'

'I want,' says James, 'more emotion. This capture is an enormous coup for you men. It must be seen in your faces. That is essential. Get it?'

Stan and Hare nod.

'What have I missed?' murmurs Derek in my ear. 'Has it been as good as this all the time?'

'Not all, but some. I miss Bella.'

'What about Angus?'

'Nice man.'

'And Tam?'

'I don't miss him. Nor forget him.'

'No,' he says. 'No.'

'Lunch,' roars James. 'And afterwards we'll have to get the pole securely in position and the business of tying me up worked out.' He nods towards us. 'And releasing me later. Right, Lorna? Duncan?'

'Yes,' we say.

'There's a lot to do,' he says.

'There is indeed,' says Derek. 'I wouldn't have missed this for worlds.'

I think about Bella. Where is my friend Bella Ropata? And Joe?

We are conscious of the lack of trees as we eat our lunch. We huddle beneath the shade of the horse float, cheek by jowl like drought-stricken stock beneath a lone pine tree. Dickie's cattle beasts come to inspect us. They form a half circle, their limpid eyes staring as they chew. There is something slightly unnerving about the curiosity of cattle, something unremitting about their glum attention. Having done all, they stand. They know you will crack in the end.

Charlie scrambles upright, bangs his arms against his sides. 'Scram,' he shouts. 'Shove off.' Rubbery lips curl, one or two turn their heads, streams of spit swing in the air. One, less resolute than the rest, swings around and lumbers off, its hindquarters loose limbed as a cowboy's.

'Get!' roars Charlie. They stare. He lunges after them and steps through the crust of a cowpat, fortunately with his bare foot, which will be easier to clean than his ski pole. He is outraged. He jumps up and down. He makes a fuss.

'Townie,' drawls Duncan, spitting watermelon seeds.

'Townie yourself,' shouts Charlie. 'You're more a townie than what I am. You're older.'

'Come and we'll clean you up, lad,' says Derek.

My eyes close. It must be the heat.

There is nothing wrong with our riding, James tells Duncan and me, and he approves of our chosen track for the gallop. We can always tell if he's pleased, he says. When a perfectionist like himself says there's nothing wrong, it means it's good. Not just good enough. Good.

He adds that the filming of the hero's rescue is going to be more difficult than the tying up. That he can't very well drown Duncan and me, he realises that. However, fortunately he has worked things out.

'The obvious thing is for me and the river to do the work. Let's have a look.'

He flings himself on the ground beside the pole, measures it against his waist and neck height, and makes a rough guess as to how much will be needed to drive it securely into the river mud.

'It doesn't need to be immovable, the post,' he says. 'We just need the effect of the tidal change. See what I mean?'

We don't. We stare, our faces blank as cattle.

'All we need to do is adjust the bonds,' continues James, 'to enable me to crouch slightly, to bend my knees during the rescue scene. You two will crash in when the tide is at my original waist-high level, pretend to stand up when you reach me – but, and this is the point, *don't*. The release, the cutting of my bonds, can be done with us all crouching, so that the water *appears* to be lapping at my chin. You two must just look as though you're treading water.' He stares at us. 'Get it?'

'Yes,' we say firmly.

Bob shakes his head with awe. 'You wouldn't read about it,' he says.

'Where did you get such a long pole, Bob?' asks James.

'Your Dad got it in,' says Bob. 'He'd had an idea of a flagpole with the Union Jack flying for some time. Down one end of the old tennis court, he reckoned. Going up and down at night, all tiddly like they do. He was looking forward to it. But he died before he got round to it as it were. It's been up the back ever since.'

We gaze at the length of wood in reverence.

'So now all we need to do is cut it to the right length,' says James. 'Where's the saw, Bob?'

'Up the hill.'

'At Rongomaha?'

'That's right.'

'But why on earth?'

'Last I heard there was nothing about it being cut in two. Not a squeak.'

'You mean you thought I was going to be lashed to a full-length flagpole in the middle of the river?'

'Not a squeak.'

'So what do we do now?'

Bob licks the paper of his roll-your-own, puts it in the corner of his mouth and lights up, instinctively cupping his hands to keep out a non-existent wind. He makes no comment

'There's a saw behind the bath in our bach,' says Derek. 'I'll go and get it.'

'Excellent. Thanks, Derek. And we'll get on down here. Quick as you can, there's a good man, and in the meantime . . .'

Derek winks in my direction and departs.

The tide is now on the turn. To save time, which is precious, James tells us once more, he and Roger the cameraman will get some shots in the can of the tide racing up the river. We decamp and straggle down the track through the bulrushes. Ann checks in a desultory way for signs of Moses or his cradle.

During the worst of the Depression a man came to Derek's office selling, or attempting to sell, copies of *The Bible Designed to be Read as Literature.* It was an expensive book and I was not best pleased at the time, but as Derek pointed out I didn't have to say no to the unfortunate man.

The book has been a success, has coloured Ann's life ever since. Although she has no illusions that an abandoned baby will appear in the rushes near the Bully Pond, nevertheless she enjoys finding possible settings for her biblical characters. Places where they might feel at home.

The tide coming up this narrow river is always impressive. Hare told me once that the speed at which it surges in must be among the fastest in the country. He has always meant to check it, he told me with a grin, but how would he start? None of us has ever watched the sight from this side. Possibly, both from the novelty and from the emotions aroused at the thought of the hero's incipient fate, I find the sight more dramatic than ever. Nothing can stop the power, the speed with which the small unbroken waves storm up and over the placid surface of the water beneath, swallowing the stream as it disappears beneath them.

The Sheriff will face terrible odds. He will be trapped in the direst of all possible straits, victim of both the implacable forces of nature and the cruelty of man.

Roger, directed by James, moves up and down the river filming the waves. The children and I watch the incoming tide with our mouths open. I hate Derek missing this.

But he doesn't entirely. As Duncan hears the sound of the Buick he rushes to tell him to hurry hurry hurry, which he does, saw in hand.

I turn to him. 'Look, look.'

'Good, eh.' says Charlie proudly.

'Yes.' Derek grins.

After some time he whispers in my ear. 'Come over here for a minute.'

I leave the awe-inspiring sight reluctantly, but Derek's news is worth every lost moment.

'I drove up the slope from the gate,' he tells me, 'and straight on past the Clements' and the Henares' to our house. As I said I'd seen the saw propped up behind the bath, thought at the time it wasn't the best of places. All that steam. When I took it out there was a bit of rust on the blade so I had a quick look round for some oil. Nothing doing there but I remembered I'd seen a can of Three-in-One sitting on one of the dwangs of the Clements' verandah, so I left the car where it was and cut through the Henares' section. I could see you all, by the way, just stick figures, but easy enough to pick out Roger and James with the camera, and your red hat. I hopped through the fence into the Clements', and walked round the side of the house – you know how it sits a bit further forward than the other two. And there, large as life, sitting on the verandah steps, smoking and yarning away . . .'

'Bella!'

'And Tam.'

'Tell me.'

'Give me a chance. And take that grin off your face. James will think we've struck gold. They were surprised, of course, both of them, but very pleased to see me. Delighted it wasn't James. Tam offered me a smoke . . .'

'But where are they?'

'They wouldn't tell me. Camping, they said, and glad the good weather's holding. I must say they looked remarkably well and happy.'

I spare a glance at the action. No one is looking at us. The small waves roll on. 'What on earth were they doing at the bach?'

'Odd really. They had a battered tin box open at their feet, Bella's father's apparently. She'd told Tam about some old programme for a Maori Race Meeting and he wanted to see it. "So we rode down," she said calmly. "Left the horses tethered down the road and toddled along." She has a wonderful smile, Bella, hasn't she?'

'Yes.'

'They knew we were all at the river, and she didn't think James would shoot them even if he did appear. She was so friendly, so matter of fact. Even the way she smoothed the programme on her knees, folded it, touched Tamati's arm as he sat there smiling, happy as a sandboy. "We're going to take it, aren't we, love," she said. "It's too precious to leave with the rapacious and licentious soldiery. I'll let James know. He can have a copy if he wants one."

'I said I had to get back and she asked me to wait, then ran off and came back with this for you, with love. Hide when you read it. I'll join the others.'

I snatch the envelope from his hand, drop down behind the rushes, eager as lovers are.

Friday. Or is it Saturday?

My Dearest Lorna,

I was going to write from town, but can't resist the chance of a scrawl via Derek's friendly hand.

I am happy, happy, happy and so, I think, is Tam. I'll let you know our address as soon as we have one. I long to know how poor old Mum is. If you get a chance to find out please would you tell Colonel

Holdaway? Kiss the children for me. Can't wait to see you. It won't be long.

Love you,
Bella.

Bella. My good friend Bella.

I sit among the bulrushes, sniffing with happiness and the vicarious joys of true romance.

'Wipe that sentimental smirk off your face,' mutters Derek. 'Oh, by the way, I think I know where they are.'

'Where!'

'There were a few strands of new wool on the back of her trousers.'

'Rongomaha! Surely not?'

'Thank God you don't play poker. No, my bet would be Ted Clark's woolshed along the beach. Weren't we all going to have a party there after the filming? Ted's part Maori. And a good friend of Colonel Holdaway's.'

'I thought he belonged to a different tribe.'

'That's the whole point, isn't it?'

'Brilliant. I wish I could see her.'

'Not a chance. Come on. They've cut the pole and they're setting it up in the river.'

I grab his arm. 'Joe? Where was Joe?'

'Certainly not there.' He looks at my face. 'Perhaps he stayed behind with the Clarks' children. They have boys his age, don't they?'

They do, yes, they do. Nevertheless I want more. Joe is a worry.

The next few hours are hectic. Duncan and I leap on horses, canter to the imaginary rescue and pass muster. The filming of this scene will take place tomorrow but James cannot envisage any problems.

The much longer scene, where James is to be tied at waist level to the pole by Hare and the hired gun Stan, will require several rehearsals. Slip knots will be used at all times. Allowance must be made for the fact that the tide will be an hour later tomorrow. James decides that a few takes should be made of the tying to the pole now. 'At the same time tomorrow,' he says, flapping an arm across his chest, 'the water would be up to my nipples.'

Charlie and Ann giggle. Duncan glares at them.

Roger agrees with James about getting the best use of the tide. He films several shots of James bending his invisible knees at the stake so that the incoming tide appears to be creeping higher and higher up his body. As this is a take, James is dressed for the part. His Sheriff's badge is in place, his kerchief freshly ironed. He looks magnificent. He writhes. His head, plus hat, is flung backwards, his eyes roll heavenwards like an anguished St Sebastian's.

He has brought a dry shirt in case it is required

The differing length of the stake behind the Sheriff's head as he crouches can be smudged out later, Roger assures Bob Jackson.

Now it is our turn to rehearse our scene. Exhorted by James who is already bound and crouching, Duncan and I crash through the bulrushes, prepared to fling ourselves headlong into the river.

'Cut!' shouts James, the water lapping at his neck.

'There'll have to be a cut here,' he shouts to Roger, 'so that Lorna can kick off her skirt.'

'But it's a dress.'

'Oh well, just do the best you can. It's not out of your depth but your swimming must look as though it is. Everything must give the illusion of depth. The last thing we want is to be seen to be *crouching*. And remember, deep water. Good. In you come. Go!'

We fling ourselves into the water and swim vigorously towards the writhing captive.

'Stop!' he cries again. 'Not overarm.'

We stop, stand up in the river. 'What then?' we ask.

James gives the matter some thought. He suggests a sort of sideways crawl for me and heaven knows what for Duncan. Duncan suggests fast dog-paddle. 'Then I can carry the knife in my teeth.'

'Good man,' says James.

We fling ourselves in once more and do better in our approach.

'Now this is the tricky bit,' says James as we draw level with him. 'You have to stop swimming and pretend you're treading water when in fact you're crouching. Give it a try. Let's see how you go.'

James is right. It is difficult, if not impossible, to achieve the desired effect. Duncan and I try bunny hopping with both knees, a biking movement with one knee after the other, and an occasional sideways kick. James, crouching a few inches deeper in the water, stops writhing and concentrates on us.

After some time I suggest that Roger could get a shot of us treading water somewhere else and we could just crouch here.

James reluctantly and crossly agrees. He and Roger will have to fudge something.

'And now,' he says, 'the cutting of my bonds.'

Duncan removes the Bakelite Bowie knife from his mouth and sets to, grappling manfully with his arms in the water at the appropriate level. James explains that tomorrow he must gaze at him throughout with an expression of hero worship and he had better start practising now. Duncan, looking like a lovesick cow, obeys.

'Now, Lorna,' says James, 'this is your moment.'

Driven by impatience at the slowness of Duncan's efforts I am to plunge my hand down my cleavage and produce a cut-throat razor, open it, close it as soon as my hand is hidden by the water, and reach for the slip knots. Bonds, apparently, are not easy to cut under water, especially with a cut-throat razor. I am, in fact, to slip the knots. I discover this is not easy either. Duncan and I struggle, impeding each other. 'Stop, Duncan, stop,' I mutter. He does so, and to my relief the bonds come apart in my hands.

'And again,' shouts James. 'That was a bit hairy.'

'How do you feel about our big scene, Duncan?' I ask later as Derek hands me my second beer and the ocean rolls.

'Easy. What are you worrying about?' He yawns. 'How do we know there's no life at all on the Island? Who says?'

'Someone must have checked. I'm not worried about the scene but I think . . .'

I am interrupted by the clashing of Green Flash bottles in a string bag as Annie runs up the slope followed by an enraged Charlie.

'You said. You said I could tell,' he screams. 'It was me, not you.'

'Tell then,' huffs Ann, reaching across Derek for the bottle opener.

'Guess what?' says Charlie, clutching himself with the wonder of it. 'Mrs Girlingstone at the Store says she knows where Tam and Bella and Joe are.'

'Did she say Joe?' I say quickly.

Derek, his eyes down, moves his head. He takes the tops off two bottles of virulent green fizzy drink.

'No, but he will be, eh,' cries Charlie, so happy, so sure.

'Don't say eh,' I mutter, aware that I would not have been concerned about the purity of his language if I hadn't been such an idiot as to mention Joe.

'She's not Mrs Girlingstone,' mutters Duncan.

'Did she say where?' says Derek, dividing the contents of two bottles equally into three glasses.

'I don't know because she saw me and started whispering,' says Charlie. 'Be good to see him though.'

'Yeah, yeah, yeah,' they shout, flinging mock punches at each other in their usual gesture of enthusiasm.

'You choose, Charlie,' says Derek, offering Green Flash.

This takes time.

'I think,' says Derek eventually, 'there will have to be more rehearsals tomorrow for your rescue of James. It seems a bit casual to me.'

'But what about Joe?' says Charlie, scrambling for his lost audience.

'Joe'll be all right,' says Duncan. 'But we won't see him.'

'We will.'

'We won't'

'We will.'

'Garn.'

We set off at the same time on Saturday morning. We wave gratefully to our host Dickie and his wife as they sit on an ancient sofa on their verandah drinking tea. Mrs Dickie has a white Leghorn hen in her lap. She lifts a wing, waves it to us in welcome.

James has had the same reaction as Derek to our releasing scenes. 'We will rehearse them again to iron out the wrinkles.' This we proceed to do, endlessly.

Mrs Clements arrives in her Pontiac before lunch. She has brought Colonel and Mrs Holdaway to see the fun. They sit three in a row, their shooting sticks sinking into the boggy ground as they chat.

Onlookers have begun to congregate on the opposite side of the river. They stand or sit or lie around the large rock of the Bully Pond. They too have brought picnics and plenty of water. They are not going to miss this little lot.

Mr Girlingstone and his lady appear, but separately. They take their entertainment in turns: he comes, she goes, he comes again. A roster at the Store perhaps. Mike sits stolidly all day. Dr Appleby and his wife stand arm in arm. Perhaps they feel they must watch proceedings while they may. Tomorrow they will leave the Beach early, their feet squeezed into tight town shoes, their hats on straight and their hearts at peace as they drive towards their glory.

More people gather as the day goes on. There are no Maoris, or none that I can see.

Fortunately, just when both Duncan and I have given our all to speedy releases, to treading water and not treading water, to lunging in and plunging out, to dealing with occasional stabbing attacks of cramp and keeping our eye on the ball, James shouts, 'Lunch. And straight afterwards we start filming. No more rehearsals.'

Lunch is more than welcome. It is some time since I made the corned beef sandwiches, and the bread has lifted from the meat at the corners.

This slackening, this loss of union between component parts, reminds me of the sinister gaping of an uncooked mussel shell which signifies death within. Nevertheless, the sandwiches taste good washed down with water in the shade of the old horse float. We lie like logs afterwards, Duncan's moccasins two inches from my nose.

We are not left long on our backs, however. I climb into my Dutch girl outfit, Duncan pulls on his sacking trousers and throws off his shirt. We mount our respective horses and canter down the track for the first shoot of our rescue. Roger positions himself. No extravagant gestures are called for, just do it as fast as we can. One or two shoots should be plenty. Barring accidents.

We do well. James calls the team together to discuss 'the state of play'. He is very pleased with yesterday's work. So that's in the can, as well as Duncan's and my gallop to the rescue. All that remains, then, apart from a few tiddly bits with one or two individuals, are, first, his and Jeannie's ride into the sunset. Secondly, more shots of the Indians lashing him to the stake. And thirdly, Duncan and my rescuing him. And yes he has the same shirt. Mrs Jackson laundered it last night. This plan will give us more leeway for filming the rescue tomorrow, which he says may be even more fiddly. Time and tide wait for no man, and especially, in his opinion, tide.

'So,' he says as we prop ourselves against the float, the truck, the car, the shooting stick. 'These two scenes are also the most demanding parts of the whole film. Wouldn't you agree, Roger?'

Roger, his cheerful face now stern with responsibility, nods.

'Therefore my suggestion is,' continues James, 'that you Hopkins go home if you'd like to. Your big moment is tomorrow. Get some rest.' He gives a brief sigh. For a moment I think he is going to tell us that he, for his sins, cannot, but we are spared.

The Hopkins, delighted at their luck, decamp with all possible speed, taking Miriama as well.

'Let's have a swim.'

We do. Then we read books.

There is no early mist to be burned off by the sun this Sunday morning. Duncan's and my Big Day, like the first words of a school essay, dawns bright and sunny.

Duncan sidles up to me in the kitchen where I am packing lunch. 'Mum,' he mutters.

'And four hard-boiled eggs, yes?'

'Mum, listen.'

'I am listening.'

'Listen properly.'

I know what he means. I rinse my hands, pat them dry, smile at his worried face. 'What?'

'This rescuing.'

'Yes?'

'It's OK but . . . Well, I don't quite know what I'm meant to be doing.'

My stomach clenches for a second, relaxes. 'You don't have to do anything, love. I'm the one who cuts the bonds.'

'Why's it always bonds?'

'I don't know. But don't worry. You're doing splendidly.'

'Why do I have a knife then?'

'Just to wave about a bit in an Indian sort of way. And don't forget to look worshipping.'

He grins, nudges his head against my shoulder for a second. 'OK,' he says.

The morning, once again, doesn't require any Hopkins participation, which gives me too much time to think. Twelve is old enough to rescue heroes and so is thirty-six, but I wish I was more conversant, not with what I have to do, but with the best way to do it. Slipping slip knots underwater is a challenge, especially holding a cut-throat razor, albeit closed. James's suggestion that I should slip it down my front once more, when I am underwater of course, is easier said than done. I feel I may run out of hands.

The first takes today are to be the final scene with James and Jeannie. The horse float departs with cameraman, hero, heroine and horses up the hill behind Dickie and his wife's house. There is a track up this hill which cuts off several curves of the road and serves as a short cut for anyone riding from the beach to the main road.

'How are they going to ride into the sunset at this time of day?' asks Stan.

No one answers. No one knows.

Derek hands around the very last tray of Mr Morley's white freestone peaches. Colonel and Mrs Holdaway and Mrs Clements decline; they sit in the Pontiac with the windows open, fanning themselves with old newspapers and talking quietly. I sense that they are reaching saturation point with *Lust in the Dust* but do not want to leave at this stage.

The rest of us sit about in our togs, our costumes are draped carefully over the back of the truck. Stan sits eating his peach in silence; his Indian headband with pigtail attached fitting neatly over his short back and sides. He rubs his sticky peach-juice hands on the coarse grass and finishes them off on his pigtail. He reckons the lunch sandwiches will be pretty stale today. Mrs Girlingstone told him that the bread was usually pretty chronic by Sunday but she'd done her best.

Bob Jackson says that Hilda has tried everything, damping, reheating it in the oven, everything. Now she reckons toast is the only way.

Hare says he wonders where the hell the happy couple has got to. Derek and I exchange startled glances, then look away. Hare says the three of them could have climbed the hill on hands and knees by this time. 'Not a sign,' he yawns, and lies flat on his back once more.

The scene where the lovers ride off into the blazing sun is in the can, and pretty damn good it is too, James tells us. Jean, slightly pink about the edges, sits by Hare. They eat lunch. There'll be more hanging about afterwards, James warns us. He and Roger will tidy up a few bits and pieces until the tide is right for Duncan and me to plunge to the rescue. Frankly, he is exhausted, but at this stage the old adrenalin usually takes over. He had noticed this during the War.

I smile furiously at Duncan to show him what fun life is and how it will be even more fun when we're in the river surrounded by broken bonds and our task done.

The tide is on the make at last; small waves begin to surge up the river.

I smile even more furiously.

'Action,' shouts James.

We plunge in the shallow river, dog-paddling and sideways crawling towards James who is writhing with his white-hatted head flung back.

Duncan whips out his Bowie knife, slashes away, then slips it beneath the water into the pocket of his trousers and pretends he's lost it. He expresses horror, despair. I take over. Whipping the cut-throat razor from my bosom, I bend, pretending to slash beneath the waves, which are coming faster than ever. They are already level with what the audience must assume is the height of James's chin. My hands fumble at the knots binding his legs.

I am taking too long. Flustered, I glance at James in apology and am startled. Far from being irritated, James's face looks dreamy, as dreamy and beatific as Jeannie's as she watched over her sleepy child.

There is a piercing scream from the bank. Charlie.

I swing round.

At the same instant James groans and gives a long sigh. His body goes limp. His head falls forward into the water. His hat falls off.

'Hold his head up. Like this,' I cry as we scramble to our feet.

'Help,' I cry. 'Help! Help!'

Ann

And now, just when it's getting a bit boring and smelly round the bulrushes, and we're wanting to get back to the beach for a swim like yesterday, the most amazing thing happens.

'Look!' screams Charlie, loud as anything, pointing up to the hill behind the cottage. Miri and me take one look and start dancing around in the mucky rushes yelling and pointing too, it's so wonderful.

There, riding along the top of the hill, are Tam and Bel on their horses, looking like the picture in Mr Clements' Smoking Room saying *Mum and Dad 1905*. They are so dark against the sun, you can't see much but the shape of them against the sky. But the whole thing is different because riding behind Bel is Joe on Jackie, it must be.

Everyone is looking now and pointing, and Colonel and Mrs Holdaway and Mrs Clements are standing up and turning round the other way so they can see too.

And now, just when it's good and everyone's happy, except Mrs Clements, you can see, it all turns into the worst thing that's ever happened. Worse than Charlie and the cave, miles worse. Worse than anything I can remember except the Earthquake.

Mum and Duncan are screaming from the river. 'Help! Help! Help!' Dad rushes in. Colonel Holdaway shouts, 'Keep his head up. Keep his head up,' but Mum and Duncan are doing that already.

Now Dad is trying to free Mr Clements' bonds, which he does, but not quickly, and the three of them start carrying Mr Clements all limp and floppy to the bank. Dad is at his head end, and Mum and Duncan are helping at the legs and shivering, and everyone on the bank starts rushing towards them.

'Space. Give them space,' shouts Colonel Holdaway, and people move back a bit, but not enough. Mrs Clements is crying but she moves out of the way and so do the others, and Mr Jackson and Stan take over from Mum and Duncan and they carry Mr Clements through the bulrushes and up to the grass where it's dry.

'Face downwards,' says Dad and they lower Mr Clements and Dad starts doing Artificial Respiration. He kneels beside Mr Clements and moves himself back and forward, back and forward to his heels, counting, 'One and two, and one and two,' and pressing with both hands on Mr Clements' back like people do to get pretend drowned people breathing again when they're going for their Life Saver's Badge.

Then suddenly Mr Clements, still lying on his front, coughs and splutters and chokes, and tons of water, all mucky and awful, comes rushing out his mouth onto the ground.

'Sit him up,' says Colonel Holdaway, and they do, Dad and Mr Jackson and Stan propping from the back. More and more water comes out as Mr Clements still coughs and chokes, and Miri starts crying, she's so scared.

Then it stops and Mr Clements sits there gasping and shivering and all wrapped in travelling rugs which Mr Henare has got from the Pontiac. Other people find warm things and everyone who was in the river gets wrapped up, Duncan in a horse blanket, and they are all breathing OK. Mrs Clements is still crying but not so much. She nearly fell off her shooting stick before, she was rocking so hard. Mrs Holdaway is patting her and saying, 'There, there, Phoebe. He'll be all right, dear. He's all right now. Just a little turn. The pressure of his bonds perhaps. Too tight, and such a lack of sleep.'

'Mum,' I say. 'What about Joe? Where's Joe going to live?'

She pushes back my fringe, her hands still wet and cold.

'Yeah, what about Joe!' says Charlie. 'With Bel and Tam, is he?'

Duncan sits in his horse blanket, shivering, and doesn't say anything.

'I don't know, fellas,' says Mum. 'I don't know. But we'll find out.'

'Promise?' says Charlie, still tugging at her all wet.

'I promise.'

'Good,' says Charlie and turns towards the river. And suddenly he's off again, pointing and jumping up and down and yelling. 'Look!' he shouts. 'Look!'

And there, floating away up the river almost beyond the Bully Pond already, is Mr Clements' white cowboy hat which no one has noticed before but now they do.

'Better get it, eh,' yells Charlie.

Dad puts his hand on his shoulder and squeezes.

'Leave it, lad. Leave it,' he says and how could Charlie get it anyway.

'My hat!' shouts Mr Clements, still wrapped up. 'My hat!' he says, pointing at his beautiful white hat sailing along on its wide brim with the middle bit pointing up happy as Larry.

Duncan picks up a stone and throws it, but he knows it won't hit. And it doesn't, not by miles.

'Do something!' yells Mr Clements. 'Do something.'

Nobody does. Nobody except Roger who lifts the movie camera and turns it on.

We all just stand on the bank staring, all of us. Nobody says anything. We watch the hat bobbing across the Bully Pond, and we keep watching it all the time till it sails around the bend of the river towards the bridge and disappears.